FULL
COUNT

WESTLAND UNIVERSITY SERIES

FULL COUNT

WESTLAND UNIVERSITY SERIES

LYNN STEVENS

Entangled Publishing, LLC
2614 South Timberline Road
Suite 109
Fort Collins, CO 80525
Visit our website at www.entangledpublishing.com.

Embrace is an imprint of Entangled Publishing, LLC.

Edited by Heather Howland
Cover design by Liz Pelletier
Cover art from iStock

Manufactured in the United States of America

First Edition June 2017

embrace

For Mark, Dexter, and Miles
Thanks for letting me play ball with you in the front yard.

Chapter One

We'd only been playing about five minutes when I went down. The rookies kicked the soccer ball right at Chuck, who caught it against his chest. I broke down the field as he flung the ball toward me. The throw was perfect, hitting the grass in front of my feet. I deked left to fake out Rosenthal, a freshman pitcher who could clock ninety-nine on the gun. He was also tall and a bit of a klutz. He raced my buddy Seth who blocked for me. Seth was fast, but the lanky freshman's stride was too much. Rosie's long pipe cleaner of a leg caught my calf as I fell. My knee bent in a way God never intended, and I hit the dying grass with a thud.

I think I screamed. I think I cried. I know I passed out, because I woke up in the hospital.

Fluorescent lights flashed over my head as the EMT rolled me down the hallway. My eyes burned at the glare. We weren't in any hurry. The guy grunted and turned the gurney right. The room was small—no window, just a bunch of machines, a bed, and a small TV high on the wall without any sound.

"All right, Mr. Betts, let's get you on this bed," the EMT

said, blowing his coffee-scented breath over my face.

I held him off, using my own strength to get from the gurney and onto the bed. It felt like someone stuck my knee into a blazing fire and decided to stoke it with a sharp poker. My teeth ground together as I tried not to let the EMT see how much it hurt.

My father always told me, "Never let them see you flinch." It was a lot harder than it sounded.

"You okay, Mr. Betts?" he asked.

Was I okay? Fuck if I knew. Why did I play that pickup game? If Chuck hadn't insisted it was my responsibility as co-captain to haze the rookies, I wouldn't have bothered. I hated soccer.

Baseball was my game. And I was damn good at it.

The EMT glanced around the too-bright room for a moment before grinning down at me. "Saw you play last year against Stilton. Took my boy over to the game and watched you hit for the cycle." He chuckled at the memory. "When you smashed that 3-0 count over the right field wall, Malcolm about lost his voice from screaming. Had to buy him a Hawks shirt. He wears it almost every day now. Wants to play for Westland, too."

Despite my pain, I smiled at his excitement. That had been one of the best games I'd ever been a part of.

"Can I ask you something?" He paused and waited for my consent. Most people usually just asked away. "Heard you got drafted out of high school. Why'd you turn it down?"

I snorted. It wasn't the first time someone asked me. The minute I stepped into our team meeting at Westland my freshman year, five guys asked me in five minutes. "I can do better than the thirtieth round."

"Then why didn't you go to a Division 1 school? I heard Texas and Iowa wanted you."

Texas and Iowa *did* want me, but they offered partials.

Westland offered a full ride. Besides, I'd dreamed of playing baseball at the same college my father had played. My parents only had to shell out the cash for food and a room. Everybody understood the money, but nobody understood the sentiment.

Trish had her heart set on Westland, too.

I shrugged with a grin. "Why do men always screw up their lives? For a girl."

That sent him into a belly laugh. "Ain't that the truth." He clasped my shoulder and squeezed. "You take care, Mr. Betts. Hopefully we'll see you on the field this spring."

The little drip of happiness our conversation gave me dried up. That had been my first thought as soon as my knee turned into scrambled eggs. The way it bent before separating and snapping back together, the fact that my kneecap wasn't in the right place anymore…I doubted I'd be out in centerfield this spring. But maybe I was wrong. I had to be. The draft was in June, and I was eligible again. Not playing would drop me out of the first round, probably even the second, if not completely. Every day I wasn't on the field lessened my chances.

Sighing, I glanced at the bandage holding the ice pack to the bowling ball that was now my knee. There wasn't anything I could do to change what had happened. Any of it.

That's the shitty thing about "the past." It's unchangeable.

Chapter Two

The ceiling fan clicked to the tune of "loser, loser, loser." It mocked me with its easy movement. Every time I twitched, pain swirled in my knee before exploding into my toes and up toward the backs of my eyes. I stared at my reflection in the black screen of my laptop as I waited for the video chat to ding a call. I used to have scrolling pictures of Trish as my screensaver. It had been black since the day of my injury.

The surgeon said to rest for a couple of days before putting pressure on it. He reconstructed my ACL two days ago, and I'd been sitting at home instead of in my dorm room ever since. Why didn't I pick something simple, less competitive? I'd only chosen soccer because it was fast and exciting compared to the golf game I'd been subjected to the last two years.

The video chat started up, dialing like the old rotary phone my parents kept in the kitchen. Crossing my arms over my chest, I settled back into my pillows and waited to be interviewed by the tutor. When Coach Hummel told me Monroe might flunk me, I thought he was joking. I'd called the history department and Monroe told me Coach wasn't bullshitting me. I hired the best tutor on campus the second I hung up with the prof from hell, but she required an interview. What kind of tutor interviewed students?

I rolled my thumb over the touch pad and clicked answer.

A girl with wild curls filled the screen. Actually, her hair filled most of the screen while her petite face frowned from the center. She had to be close to my age, even though the splattering of freckles made her look a few years south of legal. Not what I was expecting at all.

"I'm Mallory Fine." Her lips molded around each word. I opened my mouth to respond, but she didn't give me a chance. "If I agree to tutor you, I need your complete attention. I'm not going to waste my time on someone who isn't going to take this seriously."

She practically bit the last word. I fought the smirk, but it wasn't going to lose. Battling with my facial muscles had always been my tell.

"And I can see that you won't, Aaron. Good-bye," she snapped as she leaned toward the screen.

I sat up quickly, groaning at the pain in my knee. "Wait a minute. You haven't even given me a chance here."

She raised her perfectly crafted eyebrows, ones that didn't need to arch to question your very existence.

"Look, it's too late for me to drop the class, and Monroe won't let me turn in my work late, and my first paper was a solid D. I missed two quizzes and a second paper. The only way I can make up the grades is a twenty-page research paper in my worst subject. If I fail, they won't let me play ball in the spring. You're the best history tutor on campus, and I need the best to pass." I fell back into my pillows, wishing like hell I hadn't shredded my ACL. Since the game, I'd missed all my classes. Unfortunately, Modern American History was the one course with an unsympathetic prof. The rest cut me some slack. "I *will* take this serious, Mallory."

"Dr. Monroe can be…harsh." Her shoulders dropped, and so did her attitude. "I prefer payment weekly as a bank transfer."

Straight to the point. I liked that in people. "No problem."

"And my fee is not negotiable."

"I didn't think it was."

"When will you be back on campus?"

"Monday. The doc said I can start using crutches then." Even mentioning my injury made my knee throb.

"We'll need to meet at least twice a week, but I think three times would be better knowing Dr. Monroe's grading scale. We'll meet in the library on the third floor." She glanced at something on her desk. "I'll email you a schedule for the sessions. Any questions?"

I shook my head.

"Then I'll see you in a few days." She paused and sucked the right corner of her lower lip into her mouth, turning Mallory into the hot librarian so many guys fantasized about. Damn. "I'm not going to lie to you, Aaron. I don't think this is a good idea."

That yanked me out of my soon-to-be-X-rated fantasy. "Why?"

Her eyes darted down for a split second before turning hard when she raised them again. She reached forward. "I don't like baseball players."

My mouth dropped open, but before I could formulate a response, she signed out. What the hell? She didn't like *baseball* players? Of all the crazy-ass reasons—

My door flew open, and my little sister ran into my room.

"How'd it go?" Chelsea flopped dramatically onto my bed, jostling the mattress. It might've been cute when she was a little kid, but at eighteen, my sister wasn't little anymore. A wave of pain rolled through my leg.

"Shit, Chels. Be careful." I grabbed the sides of my leg, as if that would stop the throbbing.

She sat up, her gaze darting to my knee. "Sorry."

"S'kay." I lifted my ass off the mattress one cheek at a time to get some feeling back. Being bedridden was not fun. "And it went fine I guess. She agreed to tutor me."

"Weird. You always managed a solid C average without help in high school." Chelsea fidgeted, shuffling her feet on the navy-blue rug beneath her.

"Yeah, well, college Cs are high school As." I waited for the static to build and for her to zap me with her finger. But thankfully that didn't happen. She was too distracted. "What's going on?"

Her gaze darted around my room, pausing at the corkboard with a map of the world and pictures of me with Trish. I'd avoided looking at them since I'd been home, but they needed to come down. Trish made it clear we were over, but I just wasn't ready to let go yet. Not like she did. Four years don't disappear overnight. I almost told Chelsea, but for whatever reason, I kept the breakup to myself. Maybe I'd hoped Trish would change her mind. Maybe I wanted everything back that she'd taken away when she dumped me. The lines blurred lately. If I was honest with myself, I didn't miss Trish as much as I missed the clear path I'd set out on: college, marriage, MLB career, World Series ring, family, retirement, taking over Betts Family Farm and Implement. The only things that were certain now were college and Betts Family Farm and Implement.

"I sent them off." She turned to look at me. Her nerves almost made her vibrate. "The applications. For New York. I applied to every school for early action. Hell, I even applied to a few in New Jersey."

"Mom's going to shit." That was an understatement. This wasn't going to be easy for my sister.

"Ya think?" She rubbed her hands over her thighs and

stood to pace from the closet to the bed.

"And she'll get over it. Don't worry." I nodded to reassure myself as well as Chelsea. "She'll get over it. Give her time."

Chelsea stopped and stared at me with tea-saucer-wide eyes. "I hope."

"Remember how she freaked out when I was drafted in the thirtieth round? And when Texas A&M offered me a partial scholarship?" I shook my head. Being drafted, that was a dream come true, but I wanted to get drafted higher. A lot of players choose college over low A ball. And I was eligible again after this year; I just needed to get my ass back on the field. "She worried about me going a few hours away to Westland. She got over that."

"True. But Madison's in Iowa, not New York." Chelsea pressed her fingers against her eyes, rubbing them as if she just woke up. "At least you didn't go to San Diego or Texas."

"Nah, too hot there." I smiled. "You do understand why she's freaking out, right?"

Chelsea sighed. "Yeah, I know."

Mom had told the story of us getting mugged in New York a million times. One incident ten years ago and she was determined never to let us out of her sight. She'd taken us to New York, to Broadway, because she knew how much my sister loved the stage. That's the story she used on me when I was drafted. But I knew better. Mom didn't want us to grow up, move out, and leave her. "She'll let you go, Chels. And she'll worry every single day." I shrugged. "So will I. It's kinda our thing."

She finally smiled before bouncing over to kiss my cheek. "Thanks, bro."

"Anytime."

Chelsea ran out of the room, slamming the door behind her. The girl was a whirlwind of energy. Mom wasn't going to let her go without a fight. Her fears outweighed anything else.

But I had Chelsea's back. And she knew it.

I glanced over at the corkboard. Prom pictures, homecoming photos, courtwarming dances. All of the things Trish and I had done in high school. I'd left them behind when we both left Medill for Westland University. My dorm had the photos from our first two years of college. I'd boxed them up the day she told me it was over.

Four years with the girl I'd planned on marrying someday.

I closed the computer and put it on the desk by my bed. Four years I wasted. Thinking about everything we had and wouldn't have was a rabbit hole I didn't want or need to go down. Living in the past wasn't going to get me through a new future. Neither was living with the what-ifs. So my plan had to change when it came to her. I just hoped the baseball career wasn't going out the window, too.

I popped a painkiller and pushed my duffel off the bed with my good leg. It didn't take long for the ache in my knee to fade as the meds kicked in.

Chapter Three

At least my dorm room was on the first floor.

I opened the door and tossed my bag inside, grateful once again that Mom and Dad had gotten me a private room.

There wasn't much to it: a single bed, a desk for my laptop and books, a dresser where I had my trophies, and the closet. Pretty much the size of the average prison cell. Dorm rooms weren't made for comfort, but it was home. I hobbled over to the twin bed and fell back onto the blue and gold comforter. Dad sat beside me, staring out the window at the fading daylight.

"What happened to that poster you had over there?" Dad pointed to an empty spot between the closet and the window. Michael Arrington, a two-time gold glove centerfielder, had hung there.

I shrugged. "Didn't want a cheater hanging on my walls."

"Steroids are ruining the game." Arrington claimed his first positive test was a fluke, but he took the suspension in stride. The second one he blamed on recovering from an injury and not paying attention to what the doctor prescribed him. The third time banned him from baseball for life. Nobody cared what bullshit he spewed from his mouth. Michael Arrington cheated.

"You'll be fine, you know that, right?" Dad turned to face me, but the distant look in his eyes was enough to understand that he wasn't really talking about me.

"Yeah, I know. I don't want to redshirt this season, though." I scooted up so my back was against the wall. *This is what we've been waiting for, right? To get drafted again. To get drafted higher than the thirtieth round.*

"Another couple of weeks and you'll start PT with the trainers. Hummel's already talked to the doc about getting you ready. We'll see where you are after PT." He slapped my good leg. "Don't worry, Aaron. A knee injury isn't the end of the world."

Could be the end of baseball, though. Right, Dad? Like father, like son.

"Just don't do anything stupid." He tapped his bad knee and stood. With his hand on the door, he turned back toward me. His eyes darkened as a distant memory took over. "Be better than me, boy. With modern medicine, you can recover from this. You still have a shot."

He left without another word. Dad wasn't much of a talker, but I knew him as well as I knew myself. During his senior year in college, his drunk buddy knocked him down the stairs of the frat house they lived in. Dad broke his leg, blew out a knee, and almost broke his neck. The accident ended his playing days. He didn't set foot on a baseball field until I started T-ball. Then our life was baseball and nothing else. He held out hope I'd be scouted as much as he'd been. When I got drafted, he was the first person I told. Dad celebrated. Until I decided to go to Westland instead. It was the right decision. I would've been eaten alive at eighteen. Now I was ready. Now I could hold my own.

Shaking off the feeling of disappointing him again, I took my computer out of my bag and powered up. The first email I saw was from MFine. I laughed at Mallory's last name. She was pretty fine with that pixie face and hair a guy could get lost in. I opened it and smiled.

Dear Mr. Betts,

I hope you made it back to campus without any problems. We will meet in the library on the third floor by the microfiche. Nobody uses those except history majors and the area is always quiet. I'd like to meet on Mondays at three, Wednesdays at five, and Fridays at three. Our sessions will go no longer than an hour and a half; although I doubt we will need that entire time. Most of my tutoring sessions last an hour, but I always schedule extra time in case we hit a particularly difficult stretch. If these times are not going to work for you, please let me know immediately.

Sincerely,
M. Fine

I hit respond, amused by her formality. It was like talking to a character out of one of Chelsea's silly historical romances. Not that I would know anything about that. Okay, not that I'd ever admit to reading one. Once.

Dear Ms. Fine,

Those times are acceptable. For now. In a few weeks, I'll start physical therapy, so we may need to make adjustments depending on the doctor. Is there anything you want me to bring to the sessions?

Sincerely,
Aaron #4

I waited less than a minute for a response.

Dear Mr. #4,

Bring your books and your brain.

Leave your brain, and we may need the entire hour and a half.

Mallory

Maybe this girl wasn't as stiff as she pretended to be.

Hobbling around campus wasn't my idea of a good time. It didn't help when I got to Modern American History and saw Trish cozying up with Trent Hilton, running back for the football team. Trent was an all-right guy who had the brain of a turtle but the speed of a cheetah. Her eyes widened as she watched me maneuver into the room. I planted myself in the front row by the door instead of my usual seat as far in the back as I could get with Trish right beside me. Dr. Monroe couldn't miss my reappearance here.

"Hey, Aaron," Trish said softly to my right. I glanced down at where she knelt by my desk before refocusing my gaze on the front of the room. "How's the knee?"

"Fine." One-word answers should've been enough to deter her. Or so I thought.

"Listen," she whispered in a husky voice that I once found sexy. Now it cut me like a cheese grater against my skin.

I twisted to face her, not really wanting to hear what she had to say. My knee rotated along with my body, sending spikes of hell along my inner thigh and down my calf. Keeping the pain off my face was harder than Monroe's class, but I somehow managed it. Or Trish didn't notice. Either way, she didn't say a thing about the injury.

"Are we okay?" Trish shrugged her perfectly shaped shoulder. "I mean, I know that things are…awkward now, but we can still be friends, right? We've known each other forever, and you know me better than anyone."

"Apparently, I don't." I turned away from her, hoping to end this conversation.

Trish sighed and put her hand on my arm. "Aaron, don't be a dick. I'm trying to make this right—"

The laugh that erupted from my gut caused Trent to frown from across the room. "If you think there is anything you can do to make this right, Trish, you're dumber than I thought." I leaned closer so she would hear every word. "I wasted two years of high school and two years of college with you. There is no way I'm wasting any more time as your friend, especially while you're busy fucking the rest of the student body."

I'd be lying if I said I regretted the words that flew out of my mouth. The shock on Trish's face was worth its weight in gold.

"Leave me alone, Trish." I faced the front again as Dr. Monroe strolled in. "You've done enough damage here already."

She huffed as she stood and walked into Trent's waiting arms. I didn't need to watch her walk away. Trent glared at me over Trish's shoulder. He wasn't a guy I should piss off, but I didn't really care. Dr. Monroe cleared his throat, drawing my focus away from my ex and to his raised eyebrows. I smirked back, knowing he wasn't questioning the scene he'd just witnessed but my presence in class. After my video chat with Mallory, I felt like I could pass this class without Trish. I needed to prove I could do it.

Until Dr. Monroe started droning on about something

called Bay of Pigs. I imagined it was something like the
Boston Tea Party only instead of tea into the harbor, it was
pork into a bay. Images of pink pigs in Revolutionary War
attire swimming in the murky waters between tall ships
forced a smile to my face, which led to an unfortunate snort.
Dr. Monroe glared at me but didn't break his lecture stride.

My mind drifted to Trish and Trent, and it went downhill
from there. I was back in my dorm room the night before I
blew out my knee. Trish was lying beside me, buck naked,
and crying. We'd just had sex, and she was crying. Confusion
curdled like milk in my stomach.

"What's going on?" I had asked for the fourth time. "Talk
to me, babe."

She sat up, and I ran my hand down her spine. That only
caused her to leap from the bed like it was on fire.

"Okay, something's obviously wrong." I pushed myself up
on my elbows. "Did I hurt you somehow?"

"It's not that," she finally answered with her back to
me. She hooked the sexy new sheer lace bra. It was hot but
not like her. Trish was conservative and a constant lady. She
pulled on the matching thong, again not her usual style, but I
wasn't complaining.

"What is it?" My gaze never left her ass as she yanked on
her jeans. I threw my legs over the side of the bed and reached
for her, my fingers grazing the skin above her jeans. "Tell me
how to help."

Trish spun around, and a look of contempt covered her
face when her eyes settled on me. She bent down, grabbed my
shorts, and tossed them onto the mattress. "For Christ sake,
cover yourself."

You would've thought the alarm bells would've gone off
then, but they didn't. Trish never really liked it when I'd lie
around naked after sex. Her prudish nature wasn't a fan of
too much skin. I slid the boxers on without getting off the

bed, watching her cover her glorious boobs with a Westland Hawks Athletic Department tee. It was way too big on her, and not one of mine, but I didn't even question where she'd gotten it. Hindsight's a bitch.

"Better?" I asked, unable to hide the grin on my face.

She nodded, then sat at my desk. Her hands gripped the arms of the chair like it might take flight. "Aaron, I... God, how do I say this?"

Still no alarm bells ringing the warning. At least about us. I just figured it was an issue with a class or one of her friends or something. "I know I'm good, Trish, you don't have to call me a god though."

She didn't smile like she normally did at my stupid jokes. Her face turned hard as she met my gaze. "It's over, Aaron."

"What's over?" Call me stupid. I deserved it.

"Us, Aaron. This"—she motioned between us—"isn't working anymore."

"You're kidding, right?" I moved to the edge of the bed, leaning forward with my elbows pressed against my knees. "After what we just did, there's no way you mean that."

Trish stood and moved toward the door. She leaned against it, crossing her arms and staring at the floor. "I thought maybe if we'd... I thought it would change my mind."

"But it didn't?"

She shook her head.

I stood and paced between my bed and the desk. "Why? Why now? Why not two months ago? Six months ago?" I stopped and stared at her. "Why not four years ago?"

"Aaron, please, this isn't easy for me, either."

"Then tell me why. And don't fucking lie to me, Trish. I deserve more than that."

Her steel gray eyes met mine. "I'm bored. You...you're boring the life out of me, okay? All we do is watch TV and fuck."

I took a step back from her. Trish didn't curse. Ever.

"I feel like I'm forty and on the verge of a midlife crisis," she continued. "I'm only twenty-one, Aaron! I can't live like this. I want more. I need more."

I moved toward her. "I can do more—"

"No—" She held out her hand to stop me.

"Tell me what to do. Damn it, give me a chance here." It took everything in my power not to drop to my knees and beg.

"There's nothing you can do. It's not you, Aaron. It's me. I don't want this…us…anymore. I don't want the life that's been planned for us. I want more. I want to travel, see the world. I want to live in New York or L.A. or Chicago. I don't want to be a farmer's wife. I don't want to watch my life waste away like my mom's did." She spun on her heel and tore out of my room. Before closing my door, she said, "I'm sorry."

"Mr. Betts, I'm glad to see you've returned," Dr. Monroe said, dragging me from the depths of one of my worst memories. The rest of the class shuffled around us.

"A little knee surgery won't keep me away, sir," I said with a fake grin. It was time to cut my losses with Trish and stop thinking about the way she treated me. And the way she tossed me out on my ass.

He matched my smile. "That's good to hear. I understand you've employed the tutelage of Miss Mallory Fine. Wise move. However, I'm surprised she decided to take you on. Miss Fine isn't one to tutor athletes."

I snorted. She'd already made it clear that baseball wasn't in her wheelhouse. "I hope she's worth it."

Dr. Monroe took a step back as I struggled to free myself from the desk. Once I was upright and steadied by my crutches, he knelt and handed me my bag. "I must also admit that I'm impressed with your dedication to passing this course. I'd hate to see your baseball career suffer at the hands of academia."

Tossing the backpack over my shoulder, I adjusted the weight and secured the crutch. I kept the smile on my face without acknowledging the menace in his voice. Asshole thought he could push me down. I wouldn't stay down for long. Not by Trish. Not by Monroe. Not by anybody. One stupid class wasn't going to stop me from playing this spring. "Don't worry, sir, it won't."

He nodded in a way that made me think he didn't believe me. Apparently, Dr. Monroe didn't get one thing about me: I never backed down from a challenge.

Chapter Four

My backpack shifted to the left, sending me into the metal wall. The third floor might be quieter, but it was a pain in the ass to get to. Even with the elevator. The library wasn't exactly crutch friendly with tight corners and narrow halls.

I tightened the strap and maneuvered my way out of the elevator just as the doors opened. The elevator was in the middle of the building. I could go right toward the dusty stacks or left toward the buzzing overhead lights. Neither direction was a win, so I went left. If all else failed, I'd end up circling the entire floor.

The third floor was like any other part of the library, only dustier. The semicircular help desk didn't even have a chair behind it, but the dust on the oak counter was thick enough to practice my autograph. Bookshelves towered to the ceiling filled with tomes that may not have been opened in decades, standing like dominoes waiting for a push. Why would anyone bother coming up here?

Glancing around, I realized I had no clue where the microfiche section was. Hell, I didn't even know what a microfiche was. This wasn't starting out well. I turned right, away from the useless help desk, and headed into the stacks. The dust tickled my nose as I passed the elevator. Should've made a right. Story of my life these days. Always heading in the wrong direction.

I emerged from the stack maze and spied hair at a table in the corner. It was as bright as a Miller Lite fresh from the tap. The hair moved, and Mallory met my stare. I stumbled back, putting my left leg down to keep myself from falling. The pain shot around the knee and tightened, squeezing my breath from my lungs.

Holy shit, she was beautiful. Her hazel eyes were huge, and it looked as if someone had painted her skin in silk, adding the splatter of freckles as an afterthought. Mallory stood, but she didn't get any taller. She had to be almost a foot shorter than my six-two, although her hair added a couple of inches on its own. The exact opposite of Trish in every way. Trish's eyes were steel gray, her chestnut hair cropped at her shoulders, and she was taller than Mallory. Maybe that's why I thought Mallory was gorgeous. She wasn't Trish.

"Here," she said, her voice noticeably kinder than our previous chat, "let me help with that."

She reached for my backpack and slid her fingers under the strap. I shivered at her touch.

This wasn't good. Not at all. Either I was desperate for any chick's touch, or this woman was more dangerous than I imagined. I was going with desperate. Trish's fingers skimming over my chest popped into my head. I shook it off. It wasn't the time, and I didn't want to remember that shit anymore.

I followed Mallory to the table. She pulled out two chairs, one for me and one for my leg. I sat down, grateful to be off the crutches and awed at her consideration. It must have shown on my face.

Mallory blushed, and I just about lost control. I'd been

attracted to other women before, but having Trish stopped me from thinking past the "she's hot" stage. That wasn't an issue anymore, and my body seemed to know it. Physical attraction didn't mean shit. I'd had it with Trish, and look how that turned out. I covertly adjusted myself, focusing my thoughts on her kindness instead of her sexiness.

"What?" She sat across the table, arranging the books in front of her. Mallory raised her eyebrows, calling me out with that one simple gesture.

I shrugged, and her eyebrows disappeared farther into her curls. Biting my tongue, I decided to answer somewhat honestly. "Today's been kinda rough. For the most part, people haven't been all that…considerate about the crutches. I mean, it was really nice of you to take the backpack and pull out two chairs and…well, thanks."

Mallory rested her chin on her freckled fist. "I'm surprised that the famous Aaron Betts was ignored. Somehow, I figured your girlfriend would be at your beck and call. I half expected her to show up with you here."

I snorted at the idea of Trish in the library. "I don't have a girlfriend."

Mallory glanced at a paper in front of her. Without looking at me, she said in her less than pleasant voice, "We've wasted too much time already. Let's get started."

Thirty minutes and a thousand fried brain cells later, Mallory shook her head in frustration. I couldn't remember anything she tried to teach me. I had no clue who the Rosenbergs were or what the big deal was about the McCarthy hearings. All I heard was blah-blah-blah, and all I thought about was the American League Championship Series playing on TV.

"You aren't even trying," Mallory said as she leaned back in her chair and crossed her arms over her chest.

I slammed the book and pushed it away. "I just don't see

the point in learning this crap."

"Then why take the class?"

I refused to look at her. What would she think if I told her I only took the class because Trish was in it? Dumb reason to take any class, but it also filled a requirement, so I thought what the hell. Trish was on me all summer about spending time together. Of course, she dumped me two weeks into the semester. Then I blew out my knee and missed the cutoff date to drop the class.

"Okay, fine. Don't tell me." Mallory drummed her fingers on the table, and I glanced up. She sucked on the inside of her lip as she stared over my head. Her gaze dropped to meet mine. "Who was the last NL player to win the Triple Crown?"

I answered without thinking. "Joe Medwick, why?"

"What year?" she asked, leaning onto the table.

"1937. Why?"

"What team did he play for?" Her eyes never left mine.

"St. Louis." My curiosity hit a high note. "How do you even know all this? I thought you didn't like baseball."

"You do realize that all of that is h-i-s-t-o-r-y, right?" Mallory cocked her head to the left, ignoring my question. "Cy Young was inducted into the Hall in 1937, too."

"Yeah, I know." I pulled my bad leg off the chair and stood, grabbing my crutches for balance. I hobbled across the room and back. Pacing helped me think, and this was the best I could do. "What's your point?"

"A lot happened in 1937. FDR signed an act of neutrality. Pan Am flew the first commercial flight across the Pacific Ocean." Mallory stood and paced beside me with her hands clasped behind her back. "My point is maybe we can get you to think about baseball events and relate them to more national events. This might be the best way for you to remember the when, but the context will still be an issue."

I stopped, and Mallory spun around to face me. She

tapped her chin with her finger, lost in thought.

"We may have to work more than three days a week, though," she added, raising her head to meet my gaze. Her light hazel eyes were wide with challenge.

I wasn't really interested in learning every single event in U.S. history, but spending a couple more hours a week with Mallory Fine would be a distraction from all the other shit screwing with my life. And I could use a distraction.

"Yeah, okay. I'm in." I smiled, wanting to lift her up to eye level.

Mallory hurried back toward the table. "I need to come up with a new game plan." Her head shot up and she grinned at her pun. "Let's meet here tomorrow, say six?"

"Six sounds…" A nagging voice in my head reminded me that the NLCS started tomorrow night. It sounded a lot like our second baseman Chuck Mathis. "Wait, can we make it five? Or maybe meet at the student lounge."

"The student lounge?" Mallory tilted her head to the left again.

"Yeah, the Phillies are taking on the Cardinals—"

"I don't watch baseball," she said quickly. She gathered her papers and shoved them into her canvas messenger bag. It surprised me she wasn't putting them in order and making sure they were wrinkle free. "We can meet here at five, but I might be a little late. I have a study session at four with a group of freshmen flunking Comp. It's downstairs in the conference room, though. Maybe we can just meet there." Mallory glanced around the table, shoved my book back toward my seat, and hurried away. Halfway between me and the Ja-Jj shelf, she spun on her heel. "I'll see you tomorrow, Aaron."

I nodded as she turned her back to me again, disappearing around the help desk. The elevator *ding*ed a moment later. I reached down and set my bag on an empty chair. The excitement on Mallory's face clouded my vision as I shoved my textbook into my backpack. She knew who Joe Medwick was and when Cy Young went into the Hall. Obviously, she'd loved baseball at one point. I wondered what made her go cold against the game.

Yep, Mallory Fine was definitely the kind of distraction I needed to forget about my knee for a few hours and not think about how fucked up my life had become. She was a mystery. And one I wanted to unravel a layer at a time.

Chapter Five

Tutoring left me starving. I hobbled into the student union and headed straight to the cafeteria. Westland's SU was one giant pie, each slice having something different to do. Pool tables and darts, check. Study area, check. Gaming room, check. The sixty inch flat-screen, check. The cafeteria made up one slice with the booths and tables filling the center like a creamy circle. I ordered my usual burger and fries with a vanilla milkshake before heading toward the booth where Chuck, Barry, and Seth held court.

"Hey, Betts, where ya been?" Chuck Mathis laughed at his own joke. Of course he knew what happened to me. He was there. Besides, I'd seen the jackass twice already.

"Bite me, Mathis." I sank into the booth, glad to be off my feet after hobbling across campus. For the next hour, I only wanted to sit on my ass and catch up with my friends. "And thanks for the flowers."

"What flowers?" Barry Acklin asked through a mouthful of fries. I swear he gained more weight than a pregnant woman during the off-season. As soon as Coach started the serious work, he would drop fifty pounds in three weeks.

Chuck smacked him on the back of the head. "He's being sarcastic, dumbass."

Barry nodded and shoved more fries in his mouth. Every day I thanked God he was on our team. Barry was another guy who could've gone to a bigger school, if his SAT scores were better. As it was, he'd redshirted his freshman year for academic reasons. Once he learned how to study, he was a solid C student. He could've transferred, but he was a loyal kind of guy. Westland University gave him a chance, and he wasn't going to leave for greener pastures.

"How's the knee?" Chuck eyed a girl as she sashayed by our table.

I grimaced as I stretched it out. "Hurts like a bitch."

"What're your chances of playing this spring?" Seth Fisher asked. He leaned against the wall behind Barry. Seth was tall and lean. Despite the fact I took center field from him, he was one of my best friends. Seth wanted to win, and if that meant he had to move to right field, he didn't argue.

"Slim, if I go by what the doctor said."

Chuck laughed, but I didn't hear if he said anything else. My gaze toured the large dining area and settled on my new tutor. Mallory sat on the other side of the room at a small table with a hipster wannabe. Her hair was pulled away from her delicate face in a thick ponytail. I watched while she talked, her hands flying around the space between them. Hipster smiled, hanging on to her every word. He glanced at his phone, said something that she bobbed her head to, and stood to leave. He bent down and put his hand on her shoulder.

Was she dating that guy? He didn't seem her type, not that I was one to judge. From our brief time together, Mallory seemed like someone who needed a guy who would challenge her, make her think about life in a different way. But I'd been wrong about a lot of shit lately. I was probably wrong again. As if feeling someone spying on her, she tore herself from the guy and turned slowly around the room until meeting my gaze. I didn't glance away.

Someone stepped into my line of sight, breaking my staring contest. My eyes refocused on a denim-covered crotch standing way too close for comfort.

"What did you say to Trish?" Trent cracked his knuckles as I raised my head to look him in the face. Fluorescent light glinted off his shaved head, ricocheting off the silver ring hanging from his eyebrow. What a douche. He flexed his biceps, expanding the tribal tattoos wrapping his arms. Trent was the type of guy who probably didn't even realize he wasn't part of a tribe. And I was pretty sure those muscles were medically induced.

I leaned against the back of the navy-blue booth, playing it cool. "Oh, you know, Trent, I just told her that there wasn't anything she could say that would make me take her back. Guess that wasn't what she wanted to hear, huh?"

The anger in his eyes turned to confusion. "You serious?"

"As a heart attack."

Seth glared at Trent, waiting for him to make a move.

Trent seemed to realize I was lying. He reached down and grabbed my shirt, tugging me toward his face. "You sonnabitch. Stay away from my girl or I'll break your other knee."

"I wouldn't stick my dick in her if she paid me, buddy, so you've got nothing to worry about." I sneered so he'd know I wasn't afraid of his bullshit macho attitude.

Seth yanked Trent off me while Chuck got between us. The lounge went quiet as everyone waited for a fight to break out. Trent's eyes never left my face, and I kept my sneer in place. There was no way this musclehead was going to get under my skin.

Trent pointed at me, then slashed his finger across his neck. "You're lucky, Betts. I won't kick a man while he's down."

I laughed, knowing it would only antagonize him further and not really caring. "Man, you won't ever get the chance to kick me when I'm up."

"This ain't over." Trent continued to point while one of his buddies wrenched him away.

Seth and Chuck waited until Trent was out of sight before sitting down.

"What the hell was that about?" Barry asked before taking a bite of his second cheeseburger.

"Nothing. He'll forget about it by tonight." I swirled my fries in the ketchup/mayo mix on my tray. When Trent had grabbed my shirt, I'd rapped my knee against the table. The throbbing rattled my teeth. I reached into my pocket for the pain meds and popped one.

"Yeah, when he's banging your girl," Chuck added, getting a high five from Seth for the slam.

"She's not my girl anymore," I pointed out, emphasizing it with my fries. A glob of pink dripped onto the table before I shoved the mess into my mouth. I glanced back to where Mallory had been sitting. Two girls with tanned legs in short skirts occupied the table. For a moment, I imagined moving on from Trish with one of them. Just asking either of those girls out on a date. It wouldn't be hard. Baseball players were second only to the basketball players on campus. Winning a national championship does that. But the thought didn't last long. I didn't know them enough to date either of them. And I didn't have a lot of time on my hands to get to know someone new. With the knee injury, the physical therapy, the tutoring, watching tapes in my spare minutes, even one date was a daunting task. Moving on would have to wait until I could actually move.

I was twenty minutes early. Instead of settling into a cubicle to study for my Operations Management exam, I headed toward the conference room. Calling it a conference room didn't make any sense. It was a classroom, plain and simple. One for tutors like Mallory or, if a prof needed to make use of the library he could hold class. It was hidden on the north side of the building near the restrooms and away from any other study rooms or cubicles. The only thing between it and the open section of the first floor were the stacks.

Someone had left the door cracked open. I leaned against the wall and watched Mallory through the window of the door. She paced the front of the room, talking wildly with her hands as she explained the best method to introduce a thesis. A girl in front asked a question I couldn't hear. Mallory smiled, explaining what a thesis was. Probably not for the first time. She owned the room and the four students inside. When the study session was over timewise, she kept going. The students shared their latest papers and grades. Mallory explained why they'd failed in a way even I understood. I didn't wait any longer. Those kids needed her.

On my way across campus, I kept glancing over toward the library. Not the wisest move when maneuvering on crutches, but I only went off the sidewalk once and managed to keep my balance.

"Hey, Betts, how's it hanging?" Seth came around the side, wiping his mouth with the back of his hand. His rock star style and badass reputation made him both a source of jealousy and envy among most of the guys on campus. Whereas Trent tried to appear intimidating, Seth just was. Fortunately, anyone on the baseball team was on his good side.

"It's hanging." I was about to ask him what he'd been eating when some bottle-ginger walked out of the shadows, tugging her tight skirt down.

Seth laughed as she stumbled. Whether it was her too-tall heels or whatever happened between her and Seth, I really didn't want to know.

"Watching the game?" I asked, changing the subject before it even started.

Seth nodded, his gaze drifting down to my brace. "How's the knee doing?"

"Good as it can be, I guess. I'd rather eat gravel than have to crutch it for the next week." I tapped the metal crutch against the cement steps.

Seth propped himself against a half wall protecting the raised flowerbeds. "How long you out?"

"Depends on who you ask. I've read it can take four to six months. The doc thinks I'm in the six to eight month range." As much as I tried not to think about it, the length of my recovery weighed me down like a baseball doughnut in the on-deck circle before a big at-bat. The crutches cut into my pits as I leaned into them.

"Sucks. Remember when I tore my rotator cuff?" Seth stretched his arm above his head.

"Yeah, that's why I got the chance to play." Seth's injury was a freak accident during my freshman year. He'd gone after a long fly ball, slamming into the wall to make the catch. His head snapped back, but he managed to hold on to the ball. And he managed to keep his head in the game. He turned to throw out the tagging runner, bypassing the cutoff man. The minute the ball left his hand he felt a pop in his shoulder, and he went down hard.

"Well, they said six to eight weeks if not longer before I started throwing again." Seth grinned, and my gut instincts told me this was something I didn't want to hear. "I was practically healed at four."

That would've caused me to step back if I wasn't balancing

on metal poles. "And you had surgery."

"Yep." Seth pushed off the wall and strolled up the steps to the entrance. "Just remember that, Betts. It's the law of averages. Docs aren't always right. You can get better faster." He stopped with his hand on the door and turned toward me. "I mean, if you want to."

Seth pulled the door open with more force than necessary, using his surgically repaired shoulder.

He had a point. I'd only get better if I wanted to, but my knee was going to heal at its own rate. Nothing I did would make that happen faster. And Seth wasn't stupid enough to suggest anything chemical.

Shaking off the thought, I headed inside and made my way toward the rest of the baseball team gathered in front of the flat-screen TV. A few of the guys brought their girlfriends. Last year, Trish was among them. My mind flashed back, and I realized she never sat with me while we watched the games. She'd go off with one of the other girls and, well, I wasn't sure what she did, but she always came back for the ninth inning.

I tapped Tony Rosenthal's shoulder and motioned for him to get out of the recliner.

"Hey, I was sitting there," Rosenthal whined as I took over his seat.

"Shut up, Rosie," Chuck said beside me. "You're the reason Betts is on those damned crutches to begin with. Least you could do is give up your seat for the man." Chuck emphasized his point with a not-so-gentle shove.

Rosenthal's six-six frame slumped over. "You know it was an accident."

Chuck slapped him on the shoulder and guided him toward the middle of the couch. "That's the only reason I haven't kicked your ass yet, rookie. Now sit down, the pregame's coming on."

I settled into the chair as the debate raged on which team

was going to win the series. The Phillies had the reigning MVP while the Cardinals had the reigning Cy Young winner. The pitchers all thought the Cardinals would win. The freshmen went with the Phillies. The rest of us were split down the middle. My bet was on the Phillies, but I wouldn't count the Cardinals out completely. Jason Carter, a Madison hero who played for the Birds, had a hot bat and a good chance of being league MVP. Either way, it was going to be one hell of a good series.

The arguments got pretty heated in the bottom of the fifth. The game was scoreless and the Phillies were threatening with runners at the corners and one out. I almost didn't feel the gentle tap on my shoulder.

I caught the smirk on Chuck's face before I turned around. Mallory stood beside the recliner, staring at the screen. Her hazel eyes darkened. Guilt slid down my throat, even though I didn't make her show up. Why was she here? And what the hell did baseball ever do to her?

"Hey," I said, drawing her attention back to me.

She tried to soften her expression, but her eyes darted back to the game. "I just wanted to apologize for earlier. One of the freshmen had a meltdown that would rival Three Mile Island."

"Three mile what?" I asked, searching my brain and coming up empty. "Wait, isn't that an Eminem song?"

"Dr. Monroe was right, you didn't pay attention in class today." She shook her head as a grin lifted her cheeks. "Then again, he said there was some drama when he walked in."

Some guys groaned in unison while the others cheered, but I couldn't look away from Mallory. She, however, glanced at the screen, and her grin turned into a full smile.

"Why don't you grab a chair?" I asked, drawing her interest back to me.

She shook her head and dropped her gaze. "No, I can't

stay. I just wanted to apologize."

"You could've done that in an email," I pointed out.

"Maybe, but it means more face-to-face." A blush blessed her cheeks.

"Hey, Betts," Seth said, suddenly in front of me. "Introduce me to your friend."

Mallory didn't miss a beat. She held out her hand like it was a business meeting. "Mallory."

"Seth." He took her hand and lifted it toward his lips, but Mallory pulled free before he could kiss her. Seth raised his eyebrows, and she scowled in response. "Too good for a lonely right fielder?"

"I doubt you're lonely often. Besides, I don't date baseball players," she said. Her gaze shifted to me. "I'll see you tomorrow."

As she spun on her heel, I reached out and touched her arm. "Wait a second."

She stopped and turned, kneeling beside the recliner.

"Sorry about Seth. He thinks every girl wants to have sex with him," I whispered so only she could hear me. There wasn't anything to worry about. Seth had moved across the room to chat with some girl who stood next to the bottle-ginger from outside. He never was into pitching duels.

Mallory shook her head. "You're different than the rest of them."

"I'll take that as a compliment."

She grinned, ducking her chin in a failed attempt to hide it. "You should."

"Listen, I think Monroe has it in for me. Maybe we should up our sessions, meet during lunch or something. What do you think?"

"I don't think Dr. Monroe has it in for you," she said. I noted that she hadn't said no yet. "We can see how this week goes before jumping into twice a day sessions."

"He has it in for me, trust me on that." I pulled my cell from my pocket. "At least give me your number in case I get stuck on something." Inside I chastised myself for such a lame way to get her digits. But it was purely academic. Nothing more. "So I can text you."

Mallory stared at my phone for a moment before taking it and typing in her number. She handed it back, pursing her lips.

I let the phone drop into my lap. "Great. I'll text you if I need any help."

Mallory shook her head and walked away. She wasn't halfway across the lounge when I sent her a text.

Who won the AL Cy Young in 2008? Aaron

She stopped just before the door and pulled her phone from her front pocket. She read the text, shaking her head as a smile spread across her face. A moment later my phone buzzed with her response.

Cliff Lee. Who was the Republican nominee for president? George Bush?

Maybe try Google next time. ;)

I wanted to laugh, but Hipster showed up and put his arm around Mallory's shoulders. She shook him off, stepping away with a shy grin. He touched her arm, and she didn't move away from that. Weird. Were they dating? Were they just friends? Or did he want more and she didn't? I wondered what her type would really be. Somehow my gut told me it wasn't Hipster.

It was none of my business.

Turning back to the TV, I tried to focus on the game.

I have no idea who won.

Chapter Six

Mallory and I met every evening, adjusting our schedules as needed. I started randomly sending baseball trivia to her, and she always answered within a matter of seconds. Toward the end of the week, she started to send me history questions from our sessions.

Mallory: *Who was Richard Nixon's running mate in the 1960 election?*

Even using my favorite search engines, it took me ten minutes to find the right answer. I triple-checked my sources. Okay, it didn't help that I was looking up the matchups for the next game, either. I felt like an idiot for not knowing it off the top of my head like she always did with my baseball trivia, but I added more info than she asked for. I hoped it'd score me some bonus points.

Me: *Henry Cabot Lodge, Jr. Nixon was defeated by John F. Kennedy.*

Mallory: *Monroe will be glad to know you're paying attention. :)*

Me: *My tutor's a real hard-ass. She'd string me up if I didn't.*

Mallory: *A hard-ass, huh? You wouldn't happen to mean that in a different way, would you?*

Me: *Who me? I've never checked out your ass. Well...*

Mallory: *???*

Me: *Not that you know of.*

Nothing. I shouldn't have gone there. Then my phone dinged.

Mallory: *And vice versa. Have a good weekend. See you Monday.*

I read the text three times. Did she just admit to checking me out? I read it a fourth time just to be sure before I responded.

Me: *There's a party at the Gamma house tomorrow. You should come by.*

Mallory: *Frat parties aren't really my thing. Besides, I have plans. Sorry.*

So she had plans. Again. Did she mean to tell me this, or was she just using it as an excuse to blow off the invite?

Me: *Maybe next time.*

Mallory: *Maybe.*

I tucked my phone into my pocket and limped down the

hall of my dorm. I'd ditched the crutches a few days back, but the monster brace wouldn't be replaced until the doc okayed it.

The crisp October air bit at the back of my neck. I never understood what it was about October, but the minute the calendar changed, the weather flicked like a switch. Two weeks ago I'd worn shorts to class, now it was sweats and a hoodie. Maybe I'd get that new, smaller brace so I could wear jeans. I almost laughed at the thought. When did I start caring about what I wore?

Dad sat in his diesel pickup, looking every bit the disgruntled farmer he pretended to be. Our family owned the largest implement shop in southeastern Iowa. We farmed on the side, too, but the dealership was where the real money came in. Combines, tractors, balers, you name it, we sold it. On top of that, we customized paint jobs, adding family names or even crests, and had the best mechanics in the area. If there was an issue with a tractor, Betts Family Farm and Implement had the solution.

"Hey," I said after pulling myself into the cab.

Dad grunted and put the truck in drive.

"What's up?" I asked, knowing the telltale frown that covered his face better than anyone else in the family.

"What makes you think something's wrong, boy?" He glanced at me before making a left turn.

"Well, you're grumpier than usual, old man." I bent my knee as far as the brace allowed, stifling the groan that filled my chest.

Dad grunted again. He drove with his right hand while he rested his chin between his thumb and first finger on his left. His brows furrowed, drawing deep lines into his forehead.

"Mom okay?" I prodded.

"Your mother's fine."

"Chelsea?"

"Little sister's fine, too."

Tense silence filled the car. I wanted to ask about work, but his expression made me keep my mouth shut. It bothered me he wasn't talking. Not that my father was ever a big talker, but normally he didn't hide anything from me.

"Did you watch the game last night?" I asked, relying on the only thing we had in common anymore. "Carpenter smoked that ball in the eighth."

Dad nodded, becoming more animated as he started reliving the game. We took it play by play, inning by inning. Twenty minutes later, we pulled into the hospital's parking lot and had only covered a third of the game.

Madison Memorial Hospital was a small building where most people went for emergencies or to have babies. The surgery center wasn't that big and mainly focused on smaller surgeries like mine. Anyone who needed their hearts fixed or brains cleaned up went to Iowa City or Des Moines. Apprehension tightened my gut as I stared at the doctor's building where the offices were nestled on the third and fourth floors.

Dad didn't wait as he headed toward the entrance. I hobbled behind him, putting pressure on my repaired leg like I was told to do. It didn't hurt so much as it felt like a tight pinch in my knee. Until I tried to bend it too far. Then it hurt worse than fifty beestings.

Dr. Cooper's office was on the fourth floor. Dad remained in quiet, pensive mode even though we were the only ones in the elevator. Fortunately, the waiting room was empty, but we still had another fifteen minutes before the nurse led us back to an exam room. The waiting sucked. It smelled too much like hospital and not enough like recovery.

I sat on the table, watching my father thumb through a worn copy of *Outsiders Magazine*.

"All right, Dad, tell me what's going on." I scooted back

on the table, stretching my knee in front of me. The snaps along the side of my sweats were opened so my brace and still swollen knee were visible. I cringed at the red scars left by the staples.

The door opened, letting Dad off the hook.

"How's it going, Aaron?" Dr. Cooper asked as he stared at my chart with a perpetual frown. The lights ricocheted off his crisp white jacket and gleaming stethoscope, blinding me.

I blinked back the bright orbs dotting my vision and shrugged. "It's going."

Dad grunted.

"Knee doing okay?" Dr. Cooper sat on his stool and rolled next to the exam table. I didn't think it was possible for him to frown deeper, but he managed it once the brace was free from my leg.

"It's still there."

"I'm going to have to drain some fluid." His cold hand slipped under my knee, slowly bending it. How did doctors manage to have the coldest hands in the world? Was that a prerequisite for med school?

"Ow," I whimpered when the pain became too much. My knee was at a thirty-degree angle, but the lightning bolt began sizzling way before that.

"Aaron, I'm not going to lie to you. You're not healing as well as I'd like at this point." Dr. Cooper stared at me from over his half-moon glasses. "There's too much swelling, and you should be able to bend it to a forty-five-degree angle. When did you stop using the crutches?"

Disappointment sat on my chest like a broken anvil. I'd done everything he told me. I'd followed directions, taken my painkillers, stayed off my knee. Why wasn't it better? "Few days ago."

"I want you back on them for a couple more days. That's probably what's causing the swelling. And I'm going to up your prednisone." He rolled back to the desk and pulled some papers off the back of his clipboard.

"Not that," I said under my breath.

Dr. Cooper turned around on his stool. "You've been taking it, right?"

I shook my head. Dad grunted next to me, but he didn't say a word. I didn't want to take the prednisone. It was a steroid.

"Aaron, prednisone may be a steroid, but it's okay by the school's regulations." Dr. Cooper leaned forward, resting his elbows on his knees. "We've had this discussion. You know this. It's not cheating. It's going to help you recover. Take the prednisone, okay?"

I nodded. He was right. I double-checked with Coach and Dr. Ross, the athletic director. Prednisone was okay—it's not an anabolic steroid. I just didn't like the idea of using. But if it would help me get better, I'd get used to it. I needed to be back on the field. Sure, I could hold out until my senior year to get drafted, but that would put me off my schedule of making it to the big leagues by the time I was twenty-three. I needed at least two years in the minors to prove myself.

"I'm going to have Helen call the athletic department to schedule your physical therapy, three times a week." He rolled back toward me, offering the papers. "Here are some exercises I want you to do daily, but don't overdo it. If you feel pain, back off. If the swelling doesn't go down by Monday, call the office immediately. We may have to go back in. If it does go down, I'll see you again in two weeks."

"You mean I need another surgery?" I wasn't going to let that happen. It couldn't happen. If he cut me open again, I'd be done for sure.

"If I had to give an honest assessment now, I'd say it's unlikely. The swelling is probably caused by getting off the crutches too soon and putting too much strain on the repairs."

Doc smiled and glanced toward my dad, who I was sure held on to this conversation like it was his knee. "Stay off it. No unnecessary strain. I mention the possibility of a second surgery so you're prepared if that does in fact happen."

I nodded, swallowing hard. I needed to make sure that possibility went away.

Doc drained my knee, and I did everything I could not to watch him. It wasn't my idea of interesting. After the nurse came back in to check my vitals and scheduled the first PT appointment for Monday afternoon, Dad and I went to a nearby diner for an early dinner.

The 9er Diner was the type of greasy spoon favored by truckers and locals. It'd been around for as long as Dad could remember. He used to come here with his team after home games when he went to Westland. The waitress took our orders and shook her hips as she walked away.

"Wish you had better news," Dad finally said after our ice teas were dropped off.

"Me too." I used my spoon to steal his slice of lemon and shoved it to the bottom of my glass. "But it wasn't all bad. There's still a chance."

"Yeah, but I don't like how he had to drain your knee." Dad stirred sugar into his glass. "You been doing things you ain't supposed to?"

"Jesus, Dad, I'm following doctor's orders."

"Except the meds."

"Yeah, except that. I'll start taking them." I dropped my spoon to the table with a clatter. "And maybe it's just not healing by the averages. It's not like I've been through this before."

"Just worried about you, boy. That's all." He sipped his tea, adding an exaggerated sigh of pleasure at the end. The tea wasn't that good.

"I'll get better. I'll play this spring, get drafted in June." I tapped the table. "We just need to stick to the plan."

Dad grunted. He wasn't a fan of the plan. When I laid it out for him, he thought I was putting too much pressure on myself, that I'd make the majors when it was time, not on my own timetable.

It was easier to let it go, change the subject. "Now you going to tell me what's going on back home?"

"Ah, it's nothing. Dutch quit and left me in a bind today." He shook his head and spun his glass around in circles. "Your mother and Chelsea got it covered, but…"

"But what?"

"I hate doing this, but until I find someone to replace Dutch, I ain't going to be able to come here to take you to your appointments." Sighing, he fell back into the booth and ran his hand over his face. "You ain't going to be able to drive that stick of yours until after you see the doc again, so don't even think about it. That thing's hard on my knees, and I ain't had recent surgery."

I laughed and relaxed for the first time since getting into his truck. "That's what's bugging you? Dad, I've got friends who will take me. I'm sure Coach wouldn't mind helping out, either. And I can call a cab if I have to. Don't worry about it."

"You sure? I hate leaving you in the lurch like this. And your mother would feel better if one of us was with you during the appointments." Dad leaned forward, resting his elbows on the table.

"I'm positive."

"All right, then. But I want updates. Regular ones." He tapped the table before pointing at me. "And the business will be fine. Don't worry about that one bit. Focus on getting better so you can play. The scouts need to see you healthy."

The waitress appeared, bearing two plates of open-faced roast beef sandwiches smothered in gravy. My mouth watered just looking at them.

"Y'all need anything else?" she asked, winking at my father.

I think I threw up a little.

Dad shook his head.

Once she was out of earshot, I snickered.

"What?"

"You still got it, old man. She was all over you like flies on shit." I laughed louder as his face crumbled.

He glanced at the waitress behind the counter. "She ain't that bad, boy." He took a huge bite of his food. "How's that girlfriend of yours, anyway? You ain't talked about her in a while."

I hadn't told my family about Trish. There wasn't any reason to not tell him. The hope she'd change her mind shriveled up pretty quick once I got back to campus. Losing Trish was just another failure in my long list lately. I stuffed my mouth and chewed slowly, but that wasn't going to stop the inevitable. "She dumped me."

"She wasn't ever good enough for you, Aaron. Better to learn that now than after you got a ring on her finger." Dad pointed at me again, but this time with his fork.

I hadn't expected that. It made me feel a little better Dad didn't care. Mom might be another issue, since she loved Trish, but she'd have to get over it. "Thanks, old man."

Dad nodded. He started chatting about the usual. We fell into our old pattern of baseball, baseball, and more baseball. Seemed like that was all we ever talked about. At least we had that. Some people didn't.

Someone shoved a red cup into my hand, sloshing beer over my fingers. The frat house filled up faster than a feed trough with pig snouts. Girls slinked in wearing short skirts and revealing tops, sending most guys into a different kind of studying with a different kind of head. Mallory wouldn't have fit in with this crowd. Half of my brain was glad she'd turned me down.

The sweat, stench of alcohol, and the unmistakable odor of pot filled the air. It closed in on me. I've never been one for tight spaces, but a party didn't usually affect me. My heart galloped in my chest. I had to get out. I needed to get fresh air. And space. Lots of space.

"Hey, Chuck, let me borrow your car." I tapped my friend on his shoulder, almost knocking his drunk ass off-balance.

"You been drinking?" he asked.

"I can't until the meds are out of my system. Just give me the keys, dickhead. I'm a better driver than you are sober."

Chuck pulled his keys from his pocket and dropped them in my outstretched hand. "Just take care of her. She's the most loyal girl I have."

I slapped him on the back, knocking him into a blonde with tits on the verge of bursting from her too tight top.

"Well, hello," Chuck said with a shit-eating grin on his face.

I fought through the crowd toward the front door. Just in time to see Trent and Trish walk in. They were already pawing at each other like animals in a zoo. When we went out, Trish had a rule about public displays of affection. Guess that went out the window. I circled around them, hoping neither would see me.

Unfortunately, someone else did.

"Hey, you're Aaron Betts, right?" A tall brunette with too much makeup stepped in front of me. "Are you as good with a bat as they say you are?"

"Better." I smiled and made a move to go around her. "Excuse me."

"Leaving so soon?" she asked, stepping back into my path.

"Sorry, but I've got somewhere to be." I let my gaze take

in her tight body. It hadn't been that long since a girl like this hit on me, but I wasn't single then.

Nah, one night wouldn't be worth it. That wasn't me. I needed more than a quick release.

"Sounds like you'll be back." She pressed her body into mine. Rum mixed with her powerful floral perfume. And it didn't mix well. "Look for me, okay?"

I smiled and slid away from her. "Not likely," I muttered more to myself than to her.

Driving around Madison usually cleared my head. Seeing Trish practically screwing Trent in front of me, in front of pretty much everyone who mattered to me, set me on edge. I could've just screwed the first girl I saw. But I didn't. My parents didn't raise me to be a selfish prick. I needed to straighten out my head, except the drive wasn't working. Partying and shopping were just about the only things to do on a Saturday night. Neither of those appealed to me, and I needed to get out of the car.

Chuck's wussy car slipped into almost any spot. The two-door hatchback was bright yellow, and we quickly dubbed it The Lemon as soon as he drove it on campus. Thing was, The Lemon did not live up to its name. The car hadn't broken down once since Chuck bought it.

Climbing out of the driver's side, I glanced around Madison's hipster shopping district, a series of old warehouses repurposed into Bohemian shops on the ground floor and loft apartments above the stores, known as HighSide. It was old school meets new school with Christmas lights decorating the sidewalks all year long. The exposed brick and floor-to-ceiling windows of CuppaJo called my name. I'd discovered the place by accident when Chelsea showed up on campus last year after "running away." It was artsy and not my thing, but my sister loved it. Too bad I couldn't add a shot of Bailey's to the coffee, though. Caffeine wasn't a substitute for getting sloshed, but a couple shots of espresso would give me a buzz that wouldn't interfere with my meds.

I peeked inside the shop next door and saw the hair. Mallory sat behind the checkout counter near the front, her nose buried in a book. Plans, huh? Working qualified. But why didn't she just tell me she had another job?

Most of the school knew about UnShelved since they bought and sold used textbooks at a better price than the campus bookstore. The walls at the front of the store were stacked to the ceiling with various paperbacks and hardcover novels. Bookshelves filled the back with some well-worn and not-so-well-worn textbooks. The hours stuck on the window showed she had until ten before closing up. It was nine-thirty. I stared at her for a moment, noting how empty the store was at this time of night.

Who goes to a used bookstore at ten? Me, apparently.

Suddenly I felt like a stalker. It wasn't like I'd hunted her down, though. It was a happy accident. Still I stepped away from the store and leaned against the wall of the cafe. Talk about being an asshole.

I took a few breaths to calm my nerves and pulled out my cell.

Me: *Whatcha reading?*

Peeking into the window, I saw her pull her cell from her purse. She smiled when she read my text. I watched as she typed in a response.

Mallory: *What makes you think I'm reading anything?*

I chuckled quietly.

Me: *Just a hunch.*

Mallory: *Don't judge me, but it's a romance.*

Me: *A romance? Let me guess, a hot teacher falls for a sexy baseball player?*

Mallory: *It's not a book of advice.*

I laughed as I responded. *I don't need advice. Unless you've got some tips. It's been a while since I was in the dating game.*

Mallory: *Something tells me you won't have a problem. As long as you keep your ego in check.*

Me: *Ego? I'm offended.*

Mallory: *I doubt that.*

Me: *So…was reading a book part of your plans?*

Mallory: *Usually is. I'm at my other job. Not very exciting on a Saturday night.*

Me: *Is there anything you'd rather be doing?*

Mallory: *Maybe. Goodnight, Aaron.*

Me: *Goodnight, Mallory.*

I strode to The Lemon without looking back and climbed in. My cell chimed twice for text messages from someone else. I swiped to open them.

Chuck: *Getting laid tonight. Take the car back to the dorm.*

Chuck: *Some hot chick was looking for you, BTW. If you come back, take her to the dorm, too.*

I didn't bother to respond as I headed toward Donaldson Hall.

Chapter Seven

Chuck drove me to PT on Monday. The athletic department had its own team but kept them off campus and near the hospital. It was a state-of-the-art facility with everything a gym monkey and health nut could want. Plus, the therapists. Coach Hummel gave me an idea of what to expect — it wasn't going to be pretty. He even offered to go with me, but I knew he had a million other things to do, so I declined. Chuck told me he'd hold my hand during the torture, which was enough to know he'd make sure the entire team had a play-by-play of how I wussed out. He stayed in the lobby.

I didn't want anyone to see me suffer at the hands of the therapist. At least she was hot. Her long tan legs were the stuff songwriters wrote about. She smiled when I limped in, and there was a bit of cruelty to it, which made her even sexier. Unfortunately, I learned too quickly how truly cruel she was. It didn't help that a few guys from the basketball team watched. We worked through a series of strength training exercises, each one hurting worse than the last. Before the incident, I'd done two-fifty on the leg lift without a problem.

When Angela told me to press back against the pressure of her hands, I could barely bend my knee. At least the swelling had gone down.

"You aren't trying, Aaron. Push!" she ordered.

Sweat covered my forehead, dripping into my eyes, as I strained against her hands. I grunted as if I were in labor. This was fucking embarrassing.

Angela sat back on her heels with a smile. "Good job. We're done for today. Don't forget to do the exercises I showed you."

I nodded, too out of breath to speak.

"Great. I'll see you at the same time Wednesday." Angela rocked on her heels and stood. She grinned as she offered me her hand.

I let her help me to my feet, the ache pulsating in my knee.

Angela walked me to the lobby where Chuck sat reading some Hollywood gossip magazine. "The pain will fade in time, Aaron. You can't rush this, okay?"

"Yeah, I know." I tried not to let her see exactly how much it hurt. The last thing I wanted was another round of surgery. I'd miss the season for sure. As it was, I'd probably miss the first half, but there was hope. That was all it took to keep me going.

Chuck stood when he saw me limping his way. "Man, you okay? You're walking like you just got out of prison."

"Fuck you." I pushed open the door, grateful for the cooler air.

Chuck's laugh rumbled behind me. "Guess PT is a lot harder than I thought. You wanna grab a burger before we head back to campus?"

I stopped dead in my tracks. *Shit. Mallory.* "What time is it?"

"Ten till five, why?"

"I'm supposed to meet up with Mallory." I pulled out my

cell and confirmed the time. It would take twenty minutes to get back to campus. In all honesty, I hadn't expected therapy to go over by fifteen minutes. I was going to be late. And I hated being late anywhere. My coach in high school made us run ten laps for every minute we were late for practice. It hammered being on time into my head.

"Dude, why the freak-out?" Chuck asked, checking my phone as I composed the text. "And who's Mallory?"

"Remember how Dr. Monroe threatened to put me on academic probation because I missed almost three weeks of class?"

"Yeah. That guy's a massive dick without a hard-on." Chuck hit the remote to unlock The Lemon and strode around to the driver's side. "What's that got to do with some chick?"

I hadn't told anyone I needed a tutor. Apparently, that was going to change. "I hired a tutor so I wouldn't fail the class and not be able to play this spring."

Once we were both in the car, he started the engine and pulled onto the street. "I thought you were redshirting it anyway."

"Maybe. If I can avoid it, I will. And there's a small chance I could be ready in time. It just depends on how therapy goes. Besides, I don't want to drop in the draft. Or miss it completely." My phone *ding*ed a text and I read it fast.

Mallory: *Okay. Running behind myself. Sophomore meltdown this time. You aren't driving, are you?*

Me: *No. Got a ride. Can't drive yet.*

Chuck leaned over to glance at my phone. "That her?"

Mallory: *Good. See you in a bit.*

"Yeah, why?"

"The shit-eating grin on your face was a tell, man." He

smirked when he glanced over at me. "She hot?"

"She's my tutor. What do you think?"

"She's hot." He laughed and turned up the radio, singing some country song about lost love.

I stared out the passenger window. Sure, Mallory was gorgeous, but that didn't change anything. She was my tutor. Nothing more. So why did I have a shit-eating grin? I didn't. Chuck just had a good imagination.

Mallory sat at our table in the library with her laptop open and a huge grin on her face.

"I'm sorry I'm late," I said, sliding into the chair beside her.

She held up her finger. "Grandma, I need to go. He's here."

"Okay, dear," an older voice said through the small speaker. "I'm sorry about Thanksgiving. Chrissy's not doing well. I can't leave her."

"It's okay. Really." Mallory smiled at the screen. "I'll be working all weekend anyway. Thanksgiving is our busiest time. Great Aunt Chrissy needs you there."

"I know, but I hate leaving you alone over the holidays."

"I won't be alone." Mallory waved at the screen. "I'll call you later. Give her a kiss for me."

"I will, dear."

Mallory stared at the screen a moment longer before turning her attention toward me. She smiled, but it was guarded. "We can adjust our meetings by half an hour if we need to. You're my last of the day anyway, and my schedule at the store is flexible."

"You're the best." I groaned as I stretched my knee. It took everything in my power not to ask about her grandmother and aunt. Like everything else with Mallory, I reminded myself it wasn't any of my business. I was just curious about her life.

"How'd it go?" she asked.

I stared into her wide hazel eyes as I answered. "It wasn't what I expected. I mean, I knew I'd do certain exercises, but I didn't know my therapist would be a sadist."

Mallory rolled her eyes, trying—and failing—to hide her smile.

"I'd be lying if I said it didn't hurt like hell," I added. My knee still throbbed. I pulled a chair closer and rested my leg across it. Maybe an hour of hurting my brain with useless history would help the agony of my lower limb.

Her hand brushed over my forearm, and my skin flared. Chemical reaction. That's what I chalked it up to. Nothing but pheromones.

"You'll be fine," she said without realizing the effect her touch had on my libido. "Give it two weeks, and you'll be moving up to more difficult exercises. Before you know it, you'll be back to full strength."

"You've got some experience in this?" I asked.

Mallory's face tightened. "Something like that."

I put my hand over hers. A small gasp escaped her lips and she slowly pulled her fingers free. "Thanks, Mallory. So Great Aunt Chrissy?"

She swallowed, closing herself off before pinching her nose. "She's got Alzheimer's. Grandma takes care of her."

"Where do they live?" I prodded.

"Arizona." She closed her laptop and pulled a book toward her. "Now where were we?"

"Oh, the usual. You tell me I'm a moron in an hour because I can't remember anything." I shrugged. The idiot factor doubled when it came to this shit.

"You're not a moron, and it's not that bad." She smiled before ducking back into her book.

"Yes, it is. And you know it." I leaned against the table, curiosity getting the best of me. "Let me ask you something. Why tutor?"

"Well, I'm a history major, so this is natural. But I'm also majoring in secondary education." The hair fell around her face as she dropped her gaze to the book. A worn black bookmark held her place. Her shoulders relaxed and she sucked her lower lip into her mouth. "Teaching in high school will get me some experience as I work toward my doctorate. I really want to teach at a collegiate level. Maybe write some books eventually."

"So you want to become Dr. Monroe?"

Mallory raised her head and cocked an eyebrow. "Maybe not as…mean."

"Monroe's mean? No." Sarcasm dripped from my lips.

"Well, you claim he is." She grinned. "He treated me like a queen."

"As you should be."

Her freckles disappeared into a blush. "Um…we should probably get to work."

"As you wish, Your Highness." I bowed my head, causing her to smirk.

An hour later, my brain felt worse than my knee. Whipped. Sadly, the brain pain didn't distract me enough. Instead both ends of my body were miserable. My stomach growled, adding just another bit of agony to my life. I hadn't eaten much lunch, and dinner called my name.

"Since I made you stay late, how about I make it up with dinner?" I asked without looking at her.

"Oh," she breathed.

What? It's just food. And maybe a little conversation. Not a date.

"I…I'm sorry, but I have plans."

I just nodded. *Shit. She thinks I'm asking her out.*

"Maybe next time," she offered.

"Yeah, sure," I said, knowing a blow-off line when I heard one. My stomach churned. Whether it was from hunger or the fact Mallory shot my not-date request down was beyond me. My cell *ding*ed a text, giving me a way out of the room without even looking at her.

> Chuck: *Get over here now. That hot chick from the party is looking for you.*

> Me: *On my way.*

I gathered my books and hustled toward the elevator. My foot caught on a slip of rug, twisting my bad leg in a way it shouldn't be twisted. At the rate I was going, I'd have to redshirt my junior and senior year. Ignoring the sharp knife julienning my tendons, I slammed my finger into the call button, punishing it for taking too damn long.

Mallory had caught up. We waited in silence for the doors to open. When they finally did, I realized I'd have to ride down the world's slowest elevator with a girl who just rejected me. Even if I wasn't asking her out, a rejection's a rejection no matter which way you spin it. Great, just fucking great.

"I really do have plans tonight," she said as soon as the doors closed.

"No big deal." I tried to sound nonchalant, but there was a quiver of hurt in my voice that I couldn't hide. It didn't help that my knee throbbed and my stomach growled, making me doubly irritable. "Really."

"Dinner plans," she emphasized. She put her hand on my forearm. "It's a history department thing. I can't back out—"

"Stop it, okay? It's not a big deal." Finally I turned to face her. She stared up at me with those perfect hazel eyes. Damn it, why did she have to think I was asking her out? That was the last thing on my mind. "You don't want to have dinner with me. Just come right out and say it. I'm a big boy, I can take it."

"Aaron—"

"What?" I snapped. "I said it's not a big deal, and it's not a big deal. It's not like I was asking you out, Mallory. It was a simple gesture of me trying to be nice."

Thankfully the doors opened on the first floor before she could say anything. I limped out of the elevator as fast as my throbbing knee would take me. Once I was sure Mallory wasn't anywhere near me, I slowed my pace and headed toward the student union.

That girl had a lot of what Grandma Eddie would call gumption. Just because a guy asked her to dinner, she decided it was more than two people hanging out. It pissed me off the more I thought about it. I had to shake it off or I'd let her assumption ruin my night.

The guys were in their usual spots by the flat-screen with a baseball recap show on. The World Series started in two days, and it was the matchup of the century. The St. Louis Cardinals were taking on the New York Yankees. No other teams had more World Series rings than these two, and both were coming off hundred-win seasons.

Rosenthal stood from the recliner and let me sit. 'Bout time the rookie did something right. The cheap pleather formed to my ass. The pity covering Mallory's face filled my vision. The damn TV wasn't enough to block her out.

"Hey, Seth, heard you used to play center." One of the rookies leaned against the wall to my left. I closed my eyes. "Think you'll get back out there this season now that Aaron's out?"

Seth laughed. "Ironic, right? I lose my spot to him with an injury, he loses it back the same way." He slapped my shoulder. "How was therapy?"

"I'm hurting more now than I did before I went in."

"You think?" Seth smirked. "Did you get that hot chick? Man, she can hurt me whenever she wants." He held out his fist for a bro bump and I complied. "You know I'd gladly ride the bench if it means winning Nationals. Means I get more tail."

"And ride the bench you will, buddy." I kicked back in the recliner as Seth laughed and walked toward four girls on the other side of the room.

The stats flashed on the TV screen, and I played manager. How would I match them up? Who would I shift the defense against? How many pitches allowed to the starter? Who would be out of the pen first against their lineup? So many possibilities. God I loved this game.

The brunette from the party sat on the arm of my chair.

"Hey, Aaron." She leaned down so I had a clear shot of her cleavage, and what a beautiful shot it was.

"Hey," I said, nodding approval. "Didn't catch your name the other night."

"Candy," she said, sliding down so she sat half on me and half on the chair. I glanced up at her angular face, the kind plastered on billboards and magazine covers. Her sea-green eyes drifted down to my crotch before meeting my gaze.

I let my arm fall around her waist and pulled her completely onto my lap, careful to keep her away from the brace. She pressed her hand to my chest, splaying her fingers across my Westland Hawks shirt. I nipped at her ear, hoping it would elicit some kind of response from my bat. It didn't. Maybe it was the physical reaction I'd had from Mallory touching my arm.

"I have a thing for baseball players, you know," she whispered.

"Really? Do you prefer infielders or outfielders?" I could play the game. Maybe I'd just been on the bench too long.

"All of the above," she answered. Her lips skimmed over

my cheek.

The answer shouldn't matter. She only wanted to get laid, and I didn't think that was a bad idea. This wasn't the type of girl who wanted happily ever after, she wanted happily for now. I tried happily ever after and failed. Big time.

I brought her lips to mine, slashing my tongue over hers. She tasted like a fucking ashtray. I pulled back as her tongue started probing my mouth. The least she could've done was suck on a mint before she came over.

"Who won the AL Cy Young in 1992?" I asked, hoping like hell she knew the answer. If she did, I could put up with ash mouth for twenty minutes.

Candy leaned away from me. "Are you serious? I have no idea."

Nope, not happening. "Then you aren't into baseball players."

"Excuse me?" She shoved off my chest, bumping my knee. I pushed her away as gently as I could. She stood in complete shock that I was turning her down. "You can't be serious. You're going to give up all this because I don't know some stupid baseball fact?"

"It's not stupid to me," I answered through gritted teeth. She'd barely touched my injured leg and pain shot through my muscles. "By the way, it was Dennis Eckersley, one of the greatest relievers of all time."

Candy huffed, tugging her dress down as if it would give her back her dignity. I had a feeling she gave two shits about it, too. She stomped away, and a tiny gnat of guilt nibbled at my conscience. It wasn't that she wasn't attractive, but she didn't have girlfriend quality. God, I was pathetic. Guess I hadn't given up on happily ever after. Such a dumbass.

Barry leaned over from the couch. "Dude, what the hell was that about?"

"She's not my type," I answered, taking a swig from the

water bottle he offered. It was filled with straight vodka and went down smooth. This was the type of painkiller I needed tonight. Screw the meds and the rules.

"Do you care if I…" He motioned after Candy, wiggling his eyebrows.

"She's all yours, just leave the bottle."

Barry grinned. "Deal."

I didn't bother to watch him hit on Candy. There wasn't any way she'd turn Barry down if he told her he played first base. Hell, Barry would probably hit a home run tonight. The pun made me laugh. I sipped the rest of the vodka and let the alcohol dull my senses, not really caring anymore. I thought about Trish and the ideal. The more I thought about her, the less it hurt. The less I missed her. But the ideal, that was a different story. I gulped a shot. Getting over Trish wasn't hard, but giving up on what I wanted was. Fuck me. Fuck happily ever after. I was no fucking prince.

My phone *ding*ed a new text message. I didn't even glance at it.

Chapter Eight

Needless to say, I had a massive hangover. I suffered through the morning, thankful for not taking an early class this semester. At least I didn't have Monroe. The swelling in my knee ballooned, but I blamed the alcohol. Chelsea had sent me some water retention pills she took once a month to help. There were things about my little sister I never wanted to know, and that was one of them. I preferred to think of her with pigtails and a gap between her teeth instead of the eighteen-year-old who wanted nothing more than to move to New York.

The pills helped with the swelling. The pain I ignored, something I'd gotten pretty damn good at lately. I'd also doubled up on the prednisone as the doctor ordered.

I entered the student union for lunch and saw Barry sitting with Seth at our usual spot.

"How'd it go last night, Barry?" I asked as I plopped into the booth. Seth grinned before stuffing his face with a chicken leg.

Barry didn't bother to look up from his notebook. "Be

glad you didn't hit that, Betts."

I swallowed the laugh that his morose tone solicited and cleared my throat. "Why do you say that?"

"It was like driving a Beetle into the hangar of a seven-forty-seven, dude."

"That's harsh," I said before erupting into laughter. Seth's cackle joined mine. When I finally got control of myself, Barry glared at me. "What?"

"What was up with you last night? Turning down a chick willing to put out. And you looked like someone maimed your cat." He tapped his pen on the table.

"Guess I haven't been single long enough."

Seth shook a clean chicken bone my way. "Yeah, whatever, dude. I'm not stupid. Trish is a bitch, but you aren't dead. Get laid."

"Maybe," I answered. But I wasn't looking at him or Barry anymore. Over Barry's shoulder, Mallory sat with Hipster. That made the previous night's rejection all the more painful. Why did I even care? I turned back to Seth who was picking through his green beans. "Anything going on tonight?"

He shook his head. "Nah, unless you want to head into town for some shots at O'Malley's."

"Sounds like a plan. Come by around six thirty."

Seth raised his eyebrows. "You serious, dude? 'Cause I'm in, but you don't normally go for this sort of thing on a school night."

"Fuck you, man."

"All right then, son, let's get stupid tonight. I'll tag Chuck to DD." He raised his fist at the same time I did for a bro bump. "'Bout time you came around to the real college experience. You in, Barry?"

Barry nodded, too busy scribbling in his notebook. He kept studying and flipping pages in his textbook. I shook my head and let my gaze fall back toward Mallory.

Two girls, one with long straight hair and the other with too-big glasses, stopped by her table. Mallory's face lightened, then they all laughed at something. Mallory stood and threw her messenger bag over her left shoulder. Hipster reached out to touch her, but she shrank away from him. The smile stayed on her lips as she stepped back from the dude to add space. Hipster didn't seem to get it. He made a move toward her, but the glasses girl stepped in between them. Mallory made a hasty getaway. What was up with that?

You know what, I didn't care. It wasn't my business.

"Yeah." I turned my attention back to Seth. "It's time to get stupid for a change."

The elevator door *ding*ed and I walked out onto the third floor. Mallory wasn't there yet. That was surprising.

I sat in the chair opposite of where she normally did. My phone vibrated in my pocket. I barely glanced at it when I saw a familiar number without a name. Trish. I'd deleted her out of my contact list, but I knew her number by heart. I hesitated for only a second before hitting decline, sending her to voicemail.

The little message icon showed two new texts. I clicked open and saw both were from last night. My mind circled before remembering I'd ignored it because I was too busy drinking vodka. I scrolled back to the oldest one I hadn't read.

Mallory: *Who won the presidential election in 1952?*

Like I'd know that. Hell, like I cared.

Mallory: *Are you okay?*

I scrolled through the rest of the messages between us. They looked like two people trying to one up each other. Two people with a constant competitive edge. Shaking my head, I cleared them all, wishing there was a way to get out of this tutoring thing. The mystery of Mallory Fine was one I had no interest in anymore.

"Hey," she said behind me. I spun in my chair to face her. Her hair was pulled into a massive ponytail and her eyes flashed to my face before darting back to the blue-gray carpeting. "How…"

"We should get started. I've got something to do later." I turned in my chair and opened a book.

"Fine." As soon as she sat down, Mallory became all business. "Did you find out who won the 1952 presidential election?"

I snorted. "Ah, so that was homework?" Shaking my head, I fought the childish and girly eyeroll. "No, I was busy last night."

She eyed me for several seconds. "Then we'll start there."

An hour later I still had no idea what we'd been talking about. She slammed the book closed, bringing me out of my stupidity.

"What?" I asked, stunned by the anger radiating off her.

"You're not concentrating. I can't do this without you, Aaron. You need to focus." She shoved the books into her bag and stood so fast her chair tottered behind her before resting back on its legs. "Let's pick this up tomorrow. And bring your brain next time."

Anger welled inside me, waiting to spring on her. I grabbed my stuff and scurried to catch her at the elevator. By the time I got near her, I felt like a limping zombie, but damned if I was going to let a little agony stop me. She pushed the call button five times before crossing her arms over her chest. Her breasts heaved beneath the shirt, and the silver locket around her neck rose and fell with each breath. She tapped her foot against the padded carpet until the door *ding*ed.

After hurrying into the tiny space, she held out her arm so I couldn't get in. "Take the stairs, Aaron."

"Like hell I will." I pushed inside, pressing her against the wall. When the doors closed, I stepped back. My breathing huffed like I'd just run a marathon. "Like I can."

The elevator creaked before stopping somewhere between the second and third floors. Not an uncommon occurrence, but it would more than likely jumpstart in a minute or so. The football field had new sod, but the library couldn't get an elevator fixed. Priorities.

Mallory reached for the red emergency button. Her hand hung for a moment before falling back to her side.

"Look, I'm sorry about yesterday, okay? I really did have plans that I couldn't get out of and, quite frankly, I didn't want to get out of." She let her bag drop to the floor as she paced in circles around me. "You can't let that get in the way of the tutoring session."

I put my arm out to stop her. She stared up at me, a question in her eyes. It was probably "what the fuck" because that was going through my head. As in "what the fuck am I doing?"

She pressed her hands against my chest. My body went on autopilot. I wasn't thinking, only acting and reacting. My hand moved to her face, my fingertips gliding down her cheek until my thumb slipped over her lower lip. Her hands slid up to my neck. Her lips quivered under my touch. I leaned in and brushed my mouth against hers. Every cell in my body lit up at the contact. I moved my lips gently, more so than I wanted to, and Mallory responded by kissing me back.

The elevator lurched to a start, sending us to opposite sides. I slammed into the wall, knocking the wind out of my chest and sense back into my head. God, what in the hell was wrong with me?

Mallory righted herself, smoothing down her shirt before

lifting her bag back over her shoulder. She glanced at me out of the corner of her eye, her fingers on her lips. In that moment, I knew she was as confused as I was.

"Aaron, we can't do this," she said, tearing her gaze from me. Her voice trembled. "I'm sorry, but I can't do this with you. I don't…I won't date a baseball player."

If I was confused before, this only made things worse. "Just baseball players? But wannabe hipsters with faux hawks are okay?"

"What're you talking about?" She shook her head, still facing the elevator doors. "Never mind, I don't want to know. Just…this won't happen, okay?"

I nodded, still sorting through everything that just occurred. Did I even want to date her? Hell, I didn't know I was going to kiss her until I did it. "Okay. If that's the way you want it…"

"That's the way it has to be," she said.

"This is…this is stupid." I stretched my arm above my head, pressing it against the wall. "I'm the one who should be apologizing to you. I… I'm not looking for anything here. I just got out of a relationship and I'm not interested in starting another one, okay? That…that kiss was a mistake. I won't let it happen again."

Mallory nodded once as the doors opened to the first floor. Without glancing back, she rushed from the elevator and around the corner toward the exit.

Her lips still burned on mine, and they'd barely touched. I replayed her words as I finally exited the elevator. She didn't date baseball players. On purpose. There was so much more to this girl than I imagined. She knew more about baseball than most of the guys I played with, but she claimed she didn't watch the game. Whenever I saw her on campus, she was with that Hipster most of the time. What was it about him?

My phone buzzed a text message. Hoping it was from

Mallory, I pulled it from my pocket.

Seth: *You ready to get stupid tonight, bro?*

A smile spread over my face. Seth was right earlier. It was time I started living a little, started having some fun. In all my years with Trish, I'd been the good boy to her good girl. If she was going to go bad, why couldn't I?

Me: *Yeah. Let's get stupid.*

Chapter Nine

The last thing I remembered was doing shots at O'Malley's. I groaned as the light infiltrated my room. Then I wondered how the blinds got opened. Living on the first floor of the dorm, I kept my blinds closed. Learned the hard way my freshman year when a drunk girl climbed in the wrong window.

"Hey, sweetie," a soft feminine voice said on the other side of my room.

I flipped over, groaning at the pain that encircled my head. It was nothing compared to what shot from my knee. What the hell?

A blonde sat in my chair, tugging on a pair of well-worn cowboy boots. She smiled, and her face flashed before me from the night before. The waitress at O'Malley's was in my room, obviously getting dressed. She stood and strode toward me.

"Thanks for a great night," she said as she bent and kissed my forehead. "Mallory's one lucky girl. See you around."

She sashayed out of my room and closed the door behind her. As soon as the latch clicked, I fell back against my pillows, grabbing my head. I vaguely remembered her feeding me shots. I vaguely remembered her running her red nails down my arm. I vaguely remembered… Holy Shit. I didn't even know her name.

I rubbed my eyes and looked at the clock. Twenty until ten. History class didn't start until ten after. So I had time. Icing my knee seemed like a good idea.

My cell buzzed on the desk, vibrating itself right onto the floor. Chelsea's face flashed on the screen in one of her classiest poses: tongue sticking out and eyes crossed. I grabbed it and swiped to answer.

"Hey, Chels," I said, trying to seem wide awake and not at all hungover.

"Fun night in the cesspool of college life?" My little sister rarely missed a beat. "You sound like you ate gravel with breakfast."

I cleared my throat. "Funny. What's up? Aren't you supposed to be in class?"

"Aren't you?" A nervous laugh followed, setting me on high alert.

"Seriously, what's going on? Is everything okay?" I tried to sit up, but that lasted all of two seconds before my head hit the pillow.

She sighed; the burden of the world weighed it down. "You remember Amanda?"

"The one you were glued to forever? Of course." They were so close, Amanda even joined us on a family vacation the summer before Chelsea started high school. Things went downhill after that. "What about her?"

"She started spreading this rumor that I'm smoking pot behind the gym at lunch. Mr. Evans even asked me about it. Thank God, he's not the type of teacher to rat me out to Mom and Dad. At least he believed me." She gulped down another sigh. Or maybe it was a sob. Chelsea kept her emotions in check when she needed to. She'd hold it in at school, but it would all come out later. I felt sorry for the shitstorm Mom and Dad were going to end up in. "The thing is, I don't have any idea why Amanda started hating me to begin with."

I knew why, but I never wanted to hurt Chelsea. Amanda came on to me one night during a party. She was drunk off her ass, but that didn't stop her from grabbing mine. I turned her down and made it clear nothing was ever going to happen between us. Unfortunately, she took her anger out on my sister instead of me.

"I just… It's not even that big of a deal, but it still bothers me, you know? I mean, she was like my sister."

I stuck my arm under my head and stretched. The strain on my leg actually felt good. "Betrayal sucks."

"Yeah, it does." Chelsea sighed again, her favorite silence filler. "Speaking of betrayal, how's life without Trish?"

I snorted. "Great."

"Good. I hated her anyway." A bell rang in the distance. "Shit, I have to go. Thanks, I just needed to get that out of my system."

"Anytime, sis."

We hung up, and I thought about Trish. Actually, I thought about how I hadn't thought about Trish. Chelsea mentioning my ex's name didn't cause any great flare of pain or remorse. I felt nothing. I stretched again, and the knee sent a shot of lightning through my nerves.

Ice and an aspirin then off to Monroe's class. Twenty minutes for a ten… Fuck! I didn't have time. I was going to be fucking late to history. Rolling off my bed and landing on my good leg, I reached for the sweats, noticing not one but two empty condom wrappers on the floor. Great, I got laid twice, and I didn't remember either time. Just fucking great.

It took me all of five minutes to get dressed, grab my bag, and limp out the door. I was halfway down the hall when Seth fell into step beside me.

"Guessing you got lucky last night," he said, glancing down at my limp. "You're limping pretty bad, Betts. I can help with that."

"Not a good time. I'll talk to you later." I popped a prednisone and an aspirin, downing them with the water I'd grabbed and sped up my pace, which wasn't easy. And it wasn't a good idea. As soon as I cleared the front doors of the dorm, my knee buckled the wrong way. But I couldn't be late. And I couldn't miss class. On top of the agony, I'd forgotten my jacket. The cold, cloudy air drizzled just enough rain to be an annoyance.

I got across campus to Brexin Hall with less than a minute to spare. Yanking the door open, I slammed my knee into it. The slew of curses spewing from my lips would've made a sailor blush, but I couldn't let a little pain stop me. I used the wall for support as I hustled toward the room. Dr. Monroe strolled from the opposite end of the hall, his head down in a newspaper. If I walked into the room after him, he'd chastise me in front of the class and deduct stupid participation points from my grade. Which I couldn't afford to lose.

Sweat broke out on my forehead as my knee threatened to come apart. I wasn't supposed to be doing anything this physical yet. My therapist was going to kill me. My doc was going to kill me. Not to mention my dad. At least I made it into the room before Monroe. I slid into my desk, fighting the urge to reach down and grab my knee.

Dr. Monroe glared at me for a moment before setting his worn-out briefcase on the table and jumping into a lecture. He talked for the entire fifty minute period. I swear he didn't even take a breath. I tried to listen, but my tendons and muscles sawed away at my nerves. It was easy for my mind to wander back to the chick in my room.

Then it hit me like a piano from the eighth floor. She

knew about Mallory, or at least her name. What in the hell did I say last night? I already knew what I did, but what did I fucking tell her? I had to get to O'Malley's to find out. But what did I ask a girl whose name I couldn't even remember?

Hey, remember me? I know we were getting busy last night, and I don't have a clue who you are, but do you mind telling me what stupid shit came out of my mouth? Doubted that would go over well.

Dr. Monroe cleared his throat, forcing me out of my daze. Most of the class was gone or almost out the door.

"Is there a problem today, Mr. Betts?" He rocked back on his heels, clutching that ugly ass leather case in front of him.

I shrugged. "No, why?"

"You seem…distracted." A smile lifted his salt-and-pepper mustache. "Again. I hope this class isn't boring you too much. Miss Fine says you're coming along quite nicely in your tutelage, but it appears you are somewhere else during my lectures. Please, do your best to make an effort to pretend to listen."

I stood and almost crumpled as my knee gave. The groan slipped from my lips.

"And try not to be late. In your condition, it doesn't do well to run just yet."

I glanced at my professor. There was something about this man that made me hate him, actual physical hate. The kind that seeped from your pores and made you want to vomit venom all over his cheap shoes. He smirked and strolled out of the room, without a care in the world.

It took me longer than normal to get to lunch. My entire leg throbbed, and I longed for my crutches and a handful of painkillers. And a bottle of Jack. I would've gone back for them, but the food was closer. Seth, Barry, and Chuck sat at our usual booth when I plopped down without bothering to get food. I needed a break.

The guys weren't alone, either. Candy sat by Barry and the blonde from the party clung to Chuck. If Dr. Monroe made me want to hurl chunks, the presence of these girls made me downright bulimic.

Seth's face lit up. "You give new meaning to 'let's get stupid,' dude."

"Yeah, I've never seen you get drunk like that," Chuck added as he tugged Blondie closer. "This is Hailey, by the way."

Hailey stuck her hand out and limply shook mine. "Nice to meet you, Aaron. I've heard a lot about you."

Barry smiled at me like he had a secret. By the way Candy was inching closer to him, I bet he did.

"Where's your lunch?" Chuck asked.

I pulled a chair up and lifted my leg. My knee was definitely swollen. Two bowling balls swollen.

"What'd you do this time?" Seth asked. He leaned over with one eyebrow raised. "This wasn't from last night's... exploits, was it?"

Chuck and Barry burst into laughter. The girls stared at the four of us like we'd lost our minds.

"Had to get to class on time. It hurts like a bitch." I tried to straighten it, but pain tugged the muscles closer to its center. "I just needed to sit down before I get a burger."

"Gotcha covered, Betts. My treat." Chuck turned to Hailey. "Babe, could you and Candace get a burger, fries, and a Sprite?"

"Both of us?" Candy asked with her eyebrows raised.

"Yeah, if you don't mind. We need a minute with our boy here to discuss something," Barry answered. He reached out and touched her cheek. "I'll make it up to you later."

I suddenly lost my appetite. Seth apparently did, too, by the way he pretended to hurl. The girls left and stood in line. Thankfully, it was a very long line.

"What happened to a Beetle in a seven-forty-seven hangar?" I asked Barry.

He shrugged as a huge grin spread across his face. "Everybody's gotta park somewhere."

"Man, that is just *wrong*." Seth dropped his hot dog back onto his plate.

"Speaking of parking, did you find a new spot to pull into?" Chuck wiggled his eyebrows as if I didn't get his meaning.

"You could say that, I guess." I shifted in my seat, not really wanting to discuss this with any of them, but they knew exactly what went down.

"What do you mean you guess?" Seth asked. He took a long pull off his soda, and I could see the light ding in the attic. Now he got it. "You don't fucking remember? Man, I knew you were drunk, but damn."

"I can't believe nobody'd remember bagging that fine piece of ass," Barry added. He glanced over to check on the girls. They chatted away, oblivious to his stare.

I ran my hand over my face. "Just tell me what happened. Fill in the blanks."

"Dude, I wasn't there for *all* of it," Seth said with a laugh. Chuck joined in. Barry shook his head and scribbled into his ever-present notebook.

If I had the energy, I would've hit all three of them. "You know what I mean."

"Well, she was eyeballing you the minute we got there, but you needed some liquid courage." Chuck slapped my shoulder. "Tequila, to be precise. She kept bringing you shots. Man, every time you downed one, you kept saying 'Let's get stupider.' Seth stopped after the fifth shot, but you kept going. That waitress came over, talked you up a bit, then gave you the old 'I get off in an hour' line and you were all 'Maybe we both will.'"

"Please, tell me I didn't say that," I groaned. Cheap lines and alcohol, I never thought I'd stoop so low.

Seth laughed. "Yeah, *that* I do remember."

"Then she changed her tune. The bar was dead, so she clocked out early and said she'd take you home. That was the last we saw of you until now." Chuck slapped my shoulder again. "You wanted to get stupid, you got stupid and laid."

"Yeah, I've done worse." Seth tapped the table. "I think."

"Blow it off, big guy. You didn't do anything wrong." Barry drummed his pen against the table. He dropped it and headed toward the food line.

He had a point. I wasn't seeing anyone. I wasn't tied down. Why not have a good time? The grin spreading over my face made them laugh.

"Guys, just tell me one thing. What in the hell was her name?" I asked, feeling foolish but desperate for the information.

Chuck and Seth stared at me as if I'd just come out of the closet. Then they broke into laughter loud enough that several of the tables around us stopped to enjoy the show. I joined in, a little self-conscious, but I couldn't stop myself. It didn't take me long before I felt like a complete ass. Over Seth's shoulder, I spied Mallory sitting at her usual table. Instead of reading, her eyes were focused on us.

"You're too much, Betts." Seth stood and stretched his arms over his head. A girl walked by, distracting him faster than a squirrel distracts a dog. He took off after her without another word.

"What, or rather who, are you staring at, young whippersnapper?" Chuck asked in his terrible fake accent that sounded like absolutely nothing on this planet. Of course, he thought he was impersonating Jimmy Stewart, although it was highly unlikely he'd ever seen one of Stewart's movies.

Chuck leaned closer, stinking of sweat and cheap

cologne, and peered over the back of the booth. Mallory's eyes widened, and she dropped her head back into her book.

"Ah," he whispered. "She's the reason you feel guilty. She's cute. Not your usual type, but cute." He moved back into his own space and shoved a handful of chips into his mouth.

"What's my usual type, Freud?" I wasn't about to tell him he was wrong.

Chuck shrugged as Hailey bent over him, shoving a tray of food in front of me. The smell of greasy cheeseburger wafted up to my nose, rumbling my stomach in both good and bad ways. I sipped the Sprite and waited for Chuck to answer my question. I knew he would in a matter of time. Normally when I least expected it.

"Hot and innocent," Chuck said as soon as I stuck the burger in my mouth. I almost choked on the damned thing. He might have planned for that. "Not cute and hiding from the world."

As soon as I swallowed, I asked, "What're you talking about?"

Hailey stared at us in rapt attention. Barry and Candy were oblivious in their own little touchy-feely world across the table. I wanted to tell them to get a room, but they'd probably take me up on that. Or ask for the key to my dorm.

"Look, Trish had this whole sweet angel thing going on, which was totally fake, but you fell for it. And she's got a smoking bod with a rack that could feed a starving nation. That girl over there is cute in a girl-next-door way, not a bang-your-neighbor way. Besides, just look at her. There's no reason for her to sit alone unless she wants to be alone. She's hiding something, man." He glanced over Barry's shoulder again. "And she's not going to let you in on it easily."

"Wow," Hailey said in complete awe of Chuck's insight. She stared at him with idol worship in her eyes.

"Bullshit. She's seeing some dickhead with a faux hawk."

I, on the other hand, was used to Chuck's insight. There was a reason Chuck was majoring in psychology. "What else you got?"

"Faux hawk?" When I nodded, he glanced at her again. "Hmm, that might put a damper on things but, considering she's checked you out a few times, I'd say patience is your best friend."

Nodding, I finished my burger, occasionally checking to see if Mallory was looking my way. I never caught her. Maybe Chuck was giving me false hope. He was good at that, too. Last season during a slump, he'd convinced me that my swing was back before a game. That was the night I hit for the cycle. I'd only realized what he'd done after the fact.

If patience was my friend, confusion was my lover. Me and Mallory? I barely knew her. And she didn't even want to get to know me. It didn't make a whole hell of a lot of sense.

But what did make sense these days?

Barry took me to therapy that afternoon. He decided to hang around and see if Angela would let him observe. Like me, Barry was a junior. Unlike me, Barry didn't have a clue what he was going to be when he grew up. He'd been contemplating physical therapy since last spring when his mom got into a car accident. She was fine, but her arm was broken in two places and she needed therapy. Barry went with her over the summer and thought that he might have found his career.

"What in the world did you do?" Angela asked as she examined my swollen knee.

My face burned with embarrassment. "Unintentionally jogged." *Possibly hurt it during a one-night stand. Oh, and I hit it with a door.*

"Yeah, to beat his prof to class," Barry added. I would've

smacked him if he was closer.

Angela shook her head and spent the next five minutes chiding me for my stupid behavior. Once she ran out of words, she let her job punish me. Hell, she even let Barry observe my torture. He was over the moon.

"Aaron, I have to tell you this isn't good." Angela tossed a towel over her shoulder. She put her hand on my arm, stopping me in the middle of the room. Barry headed toward the water fountain near the exit. "I'm going to recommend you lay off physical therapy for a week and rest. If the swelling doesn't go down by tomorrow, schedule an appointment with Dr. Cooper. He may need to drain it again."

I nodded, thankful Barry didn't hear any of that.

"If you don't take care of yourself, you'll regret it later."

Dad's limp popped into my mind. He didn't get it unless it was cold or wet, then his leg showed its age. I didn't want that to happen to me. Modern medicine made it possible for a better recovery.

"She's hot," Barry said once we were safely in his car.

"What about Candy?" I settled into the torn bucket seat, trying not to think about Angela's warning. The problem was the season. I'd have no choice but to redshirt. That wasn't an option. Too long of a recovery could be seen as "injury prone" to scouts, even if this was my first real injury.

He ignored my question. "I'm going for it, man. That was amazing. Everything she mentioned about muscle atrophy and flexibility… She totally blew me away. When's the next appointment?"

I stifled the yawn. "Should be the same time next Friday." *If I wasn't taking a week off. Or more.*

"Shit." He slammed his hand against the steering wheel. "I've got a lab. Maybe next time after that. Am I taking you back to the dorm?"

"Library. I've got…a study group." I stared out the window,

wishing the constant throbbing would go away sooner rather than later. All I really wanted to do was go back to my room and fall into unconsciousness from pain meds.

"That sucks," Barry said.

Not really, I thought as he turned up the radio, putting an end to any conversation and any chance of a fifteen-minute nap for me. Not that I'd be able to sleep without the drugs anyway. Maybe there was a safe, non-med way to get better. Seth had done it. He'd recovered from a torn rotator cuff faster than anticipated. Maybe he knew something.

A smile crept over my face as I turned my thoughts toward spending the next hour with Mallory Fine. No, tutoring didn't suck at all.

Chapter Ten

My fingers clawed into my scalp as if that would release the answers from my brain. Mallory had decided I needed a pop quiz. Or that's what she called it. It was more like a final exam. How was I supposed to remember all this shit?

Okay, think, Aaron. I tried to recall the day we talked about this. Mallory's brilliant idea of mixing my baseball knowledge with historical events helped. If I could remember anything. Test anxiety never bothered me before, but this was an unusual situation. It didn't help that the drumming in my knee intensified the harder I tried to remember. It also didn't help to think about baseball.

Bay of Pigs invasion. Pigs. There was a movie about a pig. Babe, *that was it. Roger Maris broke Babe Ruth's home run record in 1961.* The light bulb dinged in my head. *That was the year of the Bay of Pigs invasion.*

My head almost fell off at the next question: *What year was JFK assassinated?*

I spent several minutes trying to sort through it but came up with nothing.

The next forty minutes went the same. I finally handed the test back to Mallory, more exhausted than after dead lifting for an hour. Leaning back in my seat, I propped my leg on a chair and closed my eyes.

Mallory shook me awake a few minutes later. I yawned, stretching my arms over my head.

"Are you okay?" she asked.

She bent toward me and put her hand on my forehead. I inhaled her scent, a soft perfume of wildflowers and meadows. It took what little energy I had left not to lean in to her neck. The gentle touch of her palm on my forehead didn't help any, either. I closed my eyes, imagining her hand sliding down my face. God, even my imagination was turned on.

"No fever." She lifted her hand from my head.

I opened my eyes and stared at her, holding her with my gaze. "I'm just tired after the day I've had."

"What happened?" She sat back in her chair.

The usual. Hurt my knee again. Oh, and I woke up from a one-night stand with a woman whose name I can't remember. Yeah, telling her that was not a good idea. "Was almost late for class and ran to beat Monroe into the room."

She nodded and bit her lower lip. "He hates it when his students are late."

"He hates *me*, Mal," I said.

Her eyes widened as if I'd slapped her in the face. I assumed it was because she idolized Dr. Monroe. I was wrong.

"Please don't call me that," she said. Each word laced with distress. The kind that only comes out when something unexpected happens. The kind that bears emotional scars that don't ever heal.

"Okay." My fingers curled into the fabric of my joggers. It was the only way to keep them to myself. "But can I ask why?"

She stared past me, lost in whatever memory the nickname

conjured. Her eyes aged while I watched her. The twenty-one-year-old girl with a brilliant mind turned into an old soul, like she'd seen more in her brief life than I ever would in mine. When she didn't seem capable of returning to the here and now on her own, I took the risk and reached out, resting my fingers on her forearm.

"Mallory?" I whispered, not wanting to startle her.

Her head snapped toward me, as if only now realizing that I was there. She glanced down to where my fingers touched her skin and pulled her arm out from beneath my hand. The trance was broken, but so was she. I'd thought I'd seen it before, but the darkness that filled her eyes confirmed it. "My…dad used to call me that."

I zeroed in on the key words: *used to.* As in not any more.

"So how'd I do, Miss Fine?" I asked to change the subject. Little nuggets of information were all I needed. Take down the wall one brick at a time.

She sucked her lower lip into her mouth and focused on the test, blinking as if it was the first time she'd seen it. "Not as good as I'd hoped." Back to business. "You passed, but you can do better."

For the next ten minutes, she went over the questions I got wrong, careful to praise the ones I got right. We were only halfway through the test when I yawned again. Then my stomach growled. I hadn't eaten anything since the burger at lunch.

Mallory smiled, the anguish that held her face captive a moment ago disappearing. "Sounds like you need to eat."

The idea to ask her to join me again jumped into my head. I couldn't be as direct as last time, so I decided to go with honest. "Mallory, listen, I got your message the other day. And I'm not asking you out, okay? Just so we're clear."

Her face stayed passive while she waited for the other shoe to drop.

Taking a deep breath, I continued, "But I would like us to be friends. And friends hang out, right?"

At that she nodded, still wary of where I was going with this. The tension in her face drew lines into her forehead that could cut ice from the Arctic.

"So, as friends, why don't we go get something to eat? You can continue to chastise me about my test scores if you want." I mentally begged her to say yes. She got me. She listened when I talked. She gave a shit about what I said, too. And I wanted to know more about her. I needed to know everything about her.

"I…" Her head dropped, and she twisted her fingers into a pretzel. I leaned down to get a better look at her expression. It wasn't pained, but it wasn't happy, either. It was like she was working out a puzzle. "I don't know if I can."

"Why?" I asked as gently as I could. My need to understand her was an incurable disease.

Mallory lifted her head, locking onto me like a missile. "I'm not good at this. At friends."

"You seem to be fine around those other girls. And with Hipster…your boyfriend?"

"My… What're you talking about?" Her eyebrows furrowed together, creating a mini Grand Canyon between them.

"Faux hawk dude." I ran my hand over my head as if that explained the hair.

Her face brightened. "You must mean Chandler."

Chandler? He even has a hipster name. I kept my face relaxed, grateful the ability to read minds stayed in comics.

"Chandler's just another education major. We're… acquaintances."

"Not friends?" I tapped my fingers on the table in a poor attempt not to show how happy this new information made me.

"I don't have a lot of friends, Aaron." Mallory slouched in her seat. "Not like you mean. Most of the people you've seen me with are just in my classes, and we sometimes study together."

"You do fine around me," I encouraged.

She huffed. "I'm tutoring you. Study buddies."

"Then why teach?"

"I told you, I want to share what I know, and I want to teach college. But I need to get a job to get through the master's and doctorate programs." With a huge sigh, Mallory sat up and squeezed her hands together. "Tutoring won't pay enough for that."

"You're a great teacher. I watched you… That sounds creepy, but I got here early that one day we were going to meet, and I saw you with the freshmen comp kids. You were amazing." She smiled, and I took that as a sign to push a little. "Come with me to the lounge. I'll eat, you tutor. If you feel like eating, great. If not, that's fine, too. If you decide you can't stand being around me in public, then you can leave and it won't hurt my feelings. No commitment. No worries. Nothing you don't want to do." I moved to the edge of my chair, ready to throw it all out there. "I really like you, Mallory. You don't put up with my bullshit. I don't have enough people in my life like that. If that means I can only be your friend, I'm okay with it. But I'd like to be something, anything you want me to be. We can take our time. Get to really know each other."

The debate waged in her eyes as she stared at me. I didn't look away. She needed to know I wasn't lying to her. If she couldn't be anything more than my tutor, I'd take another history class and fail it. Just to hang around her. Mallory made me smile. She made me laugh. I liked how easy she was to hang out with. No pretensions. No ideals to live up to.

"Okay," she said. "But no promises."

The grin exploding on my face could've lit the plains of

Africa. "No promises."

We gathered our books and waited for the elevator in silence. When the doors *ding*ed, the memory of the last time we were inside it rushed to my head. The feel of her lips on mine, her hands on my shoulders. I shook it off. Maybe I'd get to taste her lip gloss again, but not now. And it would have to be her move, not mine.

"And I like you, too," she said. "You're not the jackass I expected you to be."

"Thanks." I grinned and glanced at her out of the corner of my eyes. "I think."

The doors closed and the agonizing descent began. We both stared forward at the carnival mirrors. I watched her reflection in the unpolished chrome. She rocked on her feet, a move I already knew meant she was nervous and maybe even a little scared.

"I never see you around campus at night," I said in order to start a conversation that didn't revolve around baseball or history.

She sucked her lip into her mouth. God, I wanted to suck it back out. "I live off campus."

"Student housing?"

"No," she said, shaking her head. Her eyebrows furrowed for several minutes before she elaborated. "My grandmother's house. When she left to take care of Aunt Chrissy, she planned on being gone for a month at the most. It's been three years." She took a deep breath as the elevator stuttered to a stop. "What about you?"

"Um, I'm in Donaldson Hall."

"That's right, the athletic dorm."

"Yeah, the athletes-live-on-campus rule sucks, but it's cool that my teammates aren't far away. History lesson for you." Mallory raised her eyebrows. "That rule was enacted a few years after my dad fell down the steps at his frat. Blew out his knee and ruined his playing career."

She squinted at me. "Is that true?"

"Every last word. Keeping the athletes on campus made it easier to enforce the curfews, too. Dad's accident was just the first in a string of events that led to the rule change." I tried to catch her eyes in the reflection. The elevator lurched again, heading down to the first floor. "See, this isn't so bad, is it?"

Mallory laughed, and my heart swelled. I needed to hear that more. I needed to be the one to make that happen again. And it made me want to hear her moan beneath me. My body responded in its natural way, and I tried to put out the fire by thinking about the ethics paper due in a few days.

"How's your knee?" Mallory asked, thankfully distracting me from my horny thoughts.

"It hurts, but it's getting better, I think." I leaned against the wall, wishing I hadn't lied. My chances of playing diminished each day. But she didn't want to hear any of my personal hell. "My therapist was pissed at me for running to class today. Barry didn't help. He was more than happy to help her bitch me out."

Mallory turned to face me as the doors opened to the first floor. She stepped out and waited until I was beside her. "Who's Barry, and why was he with you?"

"He's our first baseman. He drove me, since I can't drive my truck yet."

She raised her eyebrows.

"It's a stick shift."

She furrowed her brow, then nodded as if she got it. "Oh. That was nice of him."

"Teammates stick together. Like a second family, you know?" I held the door for her as we stepped into the chilly October night.

"Yeah, actually I do." Mallory clutched her sweater

tighter around her chest.

The lounge wasn't far from the library, but the cold seeped into my skin as soon as the doors closed behind us. We took our time. She led the way at a slow pace, which I suspected she did deliberately. We walked in silence for several minutes when my phone buzzed a text message.

"Shit," I said as I read it.

Mallory stopped in the middle of the sidewalk. "What is it? Do you need to go?"

I glanced up at her. Her expressions were so varied that I couldn't tell what she was really thinking. "No, but I forgot that the World Series starts tonight. I lost track of what day it was. The guys are going to be at the lounge. We don't have to sit with them, though."

My gut tightened. She could turn around and walk away. I wouldn't blame her. She'd made it clear how she felt about the game. I didn't want to force her to do something she was uncomfortable doing. Mallory's expression shifted a million times before settling on one that I recognized so well. Determination.

"Okay. I think I can deal with that," she said.

"Can I ask you another question?" Instinct told me to tiptoe around this subject, but curiosity ruled my brain. "Why don't you like the game?"

Mallory stopped and faced me. Her eyes closed as she took a deep breath. This was going to be big. At least for her. When she opened them, the determination tightened the skin around her mouth.

"For a…huge part of my life, it seemed as if that was all anybody cared about. My dad spent more time with the game than he did with me. No matter what I did, what I accomplished, the game came first. I tried but…" Her fingers closed around the silver locket resting on her chest. "Softball… for him, it wasn't the same."

"Yeah, I get it." My gaze shifted away from hers as I confessed something I'd never said to anyone. "My dad…he was heading to the pros before he blew out his leg. He pushed me hard to improve. Don't get me wrong, I love baseball. Sometimes, though, it's like he's trying to live out his dreams through me."

Mallory touched my arm, and I stared into her eyes. Her fingers slid down until they wrapped around mine. Her lip quivered as she squeezed then let go.

I smiled, saddened by the fact that this was harder for her than I realized and thrilled that she was making the effort. Chuck, as much as I hated to admit it, had been right. This girl was damaged. I just hoped she wasn't beyond repair.

Chapter Eleven

Most of the team was already camped out around the TV, watching the pregame show. No surprise there. I checked the time—twenty minutes before the first pitch.

Mallory stayed by my side, almost as if she was terrified to be in a room with this many baseball players. Her eyes darted around, taking in every detail. She clenched her jaw as her gaze settled on the TV. Guilt welled inside me.

"We can go somewhere else if you want," I whispered just above the noise.

She turned and stared up at me. Her shoulders relaxed as she shook her head. We got our food, three slices of pizza for me and a grilled chicken salad for her, and found a four-person table near the far wall. I expected her to sit on the opposite side, but she took a chair beside me.

I pushed the plastic container with my fork. "Do you always eat salads?"

She considered this for a moment. "No, not always. I usually do here now that I think about it."

"Why not a burger or pizza?" To make my point, I folded

the New York style slice and shoved half in my mouth. Mallory rolled her eyes, but the smile that played at her lips was worth the gluttony. The grease that dripped down my chin made me feel more like the pig I pretended to be.

"The burgers and pizza here are too greasy. I gave up on them about a week after I started classes." She glanced at my chin. "Apparently, nothing's changed."

I grinned back. "Nope. My mom would freak if she knew what I ate around here."

Mallory tensed, her fork halting for a moment before bringing the lettuce to her mouth. She kept her head down as she chewed. I'd hit a nerve, but the way she diverted her gaze stopped me cold. Instead of asking why she froze, I opted to simply change the subject.

I took a long pull off my water. "So, you're a senior, but you're my age, right? How'd you manage that?"

Her shoulders dropped, and she lifted her chin with pride. "I took some basic classes from Madison Community College while I was still in high school and had my Associates the summer after graduation. I've been in school pretty much nonstop since then."

"Really? That's dedicated."

She laughed. "I don't know if it's dedicated, but with two majors it felt necessary. And I have goals. I mean, I know where I want to go, what I want to do, and how to get there."

"I get it. My plan's been derailed lately. I need to take a step back and figure out what my next move is." I pulled off a slice of pepperoni and popped it in my mouth.

"Besides getting drafted?"

I nodded, chewing the fluffy crust.

"Life doesn't always go the way we plan, though." She shrugged. "I didn't think I'd need to work two jobs even with a full-ride scholarship. But it's what I have to do."

"Doesn't leave a lot of time for anything else," I said, the rest of my pizza forgotten on my plate. Listening to Mallory talk about her education was like listening to a waterfall in the jungle, relaxing and exciting at once.

"Not really. I make it a point to see my best friends whenever they're in town. We video chat as much as we can, but our schedules make it hard." She twirled her lettuce on her fork.

"Where do they live then?" I barely spoke to my best bud in high school. He went to college in Oklahoma and rarely came home. I saw his Facebook and stuff, but that's not the same as being friends.

"St. Louis and L.A." She smiled and set the fork down. "Amie always wanted to be an actress. The day after graduation, she hopped in her car and drove to L.A. She's doing great, too. Last week she shot her first commercial and she's done some stage work."

"What about the friend in St. Louis? That's not too far." I drummed my fingers on the table, taking in every new detail, letting each piece of the puzzle fall in place.

"Hey, Mallory." Chandler stopped beside our table. He didn't even acknowledge me. "Got a minute?"

She turned her eyes toward me. "I'm in the middle of something, Chandler. Can it wait?"

"Oh," he said, glancing out of the corner of his eye. "Yeah, sure. I'll call you later. Okay?"

"Or I'll see you in class." She smiled politely at him, but returned her gaze back to me.

"Yeah. Class."

I didn't see him walk away.

"Sorry. He's an education major, too. A lot of classes together over the years." She shrugged and changed the subject.

"You do realize he's got a thing for you, right?"

"Chandler? No, he doesn't." She glanced toward the food

line. Chandler waved at her.

I laughed. That guy needed some moves. "I can't believe you didn't notice that."

"Oh, and you did?" Mallory raised her eyebrow in challenge.

"Yep. He's always trying to touch you in some way. He's constantly staring at you." I pointed toward where he stood still staring at us. "Like right now."

Mallory glanced over her shoulder again, and Chandler smiled at her. She turned back around, her eyes wide.

"Told ya." I tapped the table. "Let the guy off the hook. He's got it bad."

"I never noticed before. He acts like that to a lot of the girls we both know." She shook her head and started to turn around again.

"Don't look or he's going to get the wrong idea." I leaned forward. "It is the wrong idea, isn't it?"

Mallory stiffened. "He's not my type."

"What is your type then?" I steepled my fingers.

"Someone who knows what they want in life." Her gaze held mine. "Chandler doesn't. He's an education major because he wants summers off."

That sounded like me, but I kept my response to myself and decided to get her mind off Hipster and back onto safer ground. "Ask me anything. I'm an open book tonight."

"Just for tonight?" Mallory grinned, Chandler already forgotten. "Okay, I never asked before, but what's your major?"

"Ah, now mine is boring," I said, eliciting a wider grin from her. "I'm a business major. My plan is to finish my degree online after I get drafted this summer. Then once my baseball career is done, I'm heading back home to take over the family business."

"And what's the family business?"

"My dad owns the largest implement dealership is southeastern Iowa. You name it, we sell it. Tractors, combines, balers. We also customize 'em and fix 'em when they break down."

Her eyebrows furrowed as she considered this. I loved how she took the time to think about our conversations. She didn't rush in with her opinion or tell me I was stupid. Well, she'd tell me I was wrong about history in a heartbeat, but that was different.

"What?" I asked when she didn't say anything.

"It's just." Sighing, she turned her body toward mine. "I'm not trying to be nosy—"

"Friends can be nosy," I interjected.

Mallory smiled. "Okay then, let me ask you something. Is that what you really want to do or what you're expected to do?"

I tilted toward her, resting my cheek on my fist. It was something I'd asked myself a lot over the past few weeks. Whether I came back to the same conclusion because that was what was in my head for so long or because I really wanted the future I'd planned was the real question. One I didn't know the answer to. I wasn't sure if I wanted to know, either. Mallory wanted to know what *I* thought, what *I* wanted.

A light blush crept over her cheeks. "I'm sorry. I shouldn't—"

"No, it's okay," I reassured her. "It's just that the truth isn't so easy."

"You can tell me the truth," she said, leaning closer.

I shifted so we were facing each other. Her knees rested just inside mine, and our heads bowed together. It was like there was some big secret we were sharing.

"I don't know." I inched a little closer to make sure she got my full meaning. "It's not so simple, is it? But taking over the shop, that's all I really know. It just makes sense. Up until a month ago, I knew exactly where I was going. Within twenty-four hours, everything changed. It's not as clear as it used to be, you know."

"What if you're meant for something else? Besides baseball or the shop." Mallory's eyes never left mine.

I didn't move, hoping she would be the one to kiss me this time. Something in her eyes made me believe she wanted to. She even shifted her head to the left a little. The hope spun in my chest, but I still didn't move.

At least not until someone cleared her throat beside us.

Mallory shot away from me like a cheetah. It took all my strength not to drop my head in defeat. I glanced up and wished like hell I was in some terrible nightmare.

"Hey, Aaron." Trish stood with her hand on her hip and a glare on her face. Unfortunately, Mallory was her target.

"What?" I made my voice as cold and hard as possible. She needed to know she wasn't welcome anymore.

"Is that any way to treat an old friend?" she asked with added emphasis on the word "friend."

"We aren't friends." I turned my back to her, hoping that she'd get the hint. Mallory glanced over at me, confusion flooding her face.

"Aaron," Trish said, putting her hand on my shoulder, "we really need to talk. I've done some…thinking and—"

"There's nothing to talk about, Trish," I said, holding Mallory's gaze.

Trish dropped all her pretenses and the fake sweet lilt that she used whenever she wanted something. "After all we've been through, this is how you're going to treat me?"

"I'll be back," I said to Mallory. Pushing off from the table, I stood and led Trish a few feet away. Far enough so Mallory wouldn't have to hear this. "What do you really want, Trish?"

"I miss you," she said, crossing her arms under her breasts.

I raised my eyebrows. "And?"

Trish sighed and threw her head back. I knew this move. It was the "you're too stupid to understand" move. I'd seen her use it on her mom and her friends. "And I miss talking to you, hanging out with you. I… Can't we try this again? As friends?"

"Are you shitting me?" was the first thing that popped into my head and out of my mouth.

"No, I'm not shitting you." She rolled her eyes.

I ignored the jab but not the reason she wanted to talk. "Look, Trish, I can't do this with you. We had a plan. You decided not to be a part of it anymore. I can't just turn on a dime and let you back into my life when you don't really want to be there."

"You were my best friend, Aaron. And I thought you loved me," she whined.

"I did. Once," I said, shaking my head.

"But not anymore?" Tears welled in her eyes.

"No, not anymore." I knew it hurt to hear that. But she needed to. Just like I needed to say it. I wanted to comfort her. A great deal of my high school life had revolved around her. She'd always be part of me in a way. Even if it was only as a memory.

Trish nodded, and the sweet innocence disappeared. Her eyes narrowed into tiny slits, but she didn't say anything. She moved back to the table and leaned over Mallory, whispering loud enough that I could hear her. "I taught him everything he knows. Remember that the next time you're lying in his bed. I was there first." Trish eyed Mallory up and down then smirked. "Every time he's fucking you, he'll be thinking about me."

I reached out to put an end to this, but Mallory beat me to the punch. Well, actually the slap. Her palm on Trish's cheek echoed throughout the lounge.

"Get away from me," Mallory said, the anger and

confusion clear in her voice. "And stay away from Aaron. He deserves better than you."

Trish rubbed her hand over her reddened cheek. "Like you?"

"You should probably go. The football team needs their goalpost back," Mallory snapped. She spun back into her seat and began eating the remains of her salad with new fervor.

The quiet in the lounge erupted into hooting from the baseball team. Mallory reached into her hair and pulled out the ponytail holder so her curls would hide her face. Trish's skin turned the color of a new bruise as she backed away from us.

I didn't know what the hell to do. So I sat down, facing Mallory. Her body shook, and I hated that Trish did this to her. Without really thinking, I reached out and brushed her hair from her eyes. As soon as my fingers touched the golden curls, I had to fight myself from sliding my hands deep into their softness. Who knew hair could feel like satin?

Ducking my head, I tried to catch her gaze.

"I'm sorry," I said.

She turned slightly. Instead of the tears I expected, she was laughing. Hard. I smiled and joined her.

"Goalpost?" I asked.

"Wide and open. All they have to do is punt," Mallory said once she caught her breath.

Chuck sat down beside us, a grin covering his face. "That was the best damned thing I've seen in a while. Man, even Trent starting roaring."

I glanced to the pool tables where Trent stood with a few of his buddies. They were all whooping. He raised his bottle of Coke in salute, and I nodded. Trish had dumped him for the quarterback after three weeks. She'd moved onto a noseguard not long after the quarterback.

"I'm Chuck," he said to Mallory, offering her his massive

hand.

"Mallory," she responded, barely touching his fingers.

"Nice to meet you. Come over after you're done. The game's coming on soon. I'm sure Hailey and Candy would like someone else to talk to. Besides, the stakes are high on the game."

Mallory turned to me with a grin. "Please tell me you didn't bet on the Yankees."

I held up my hands. "No way. Betting's against NCAA regs. I'm not getting suspended over a technicality."

"No danger, no fun, Betts." Chuck turned his jackal grin toward Mallory. "No betting on teams and no betting money. Only on our picks for who the MVP will be, how long the series will go, who will hit the first home run. That kind of stuff."

Mallory nodded. "It'll go seven. The Yankees have some young starting pitchers, but the bullpen's deep. The Cardinals have veteran starters but a weaker pen."

Chuck raised his eyebrows at her. "Are you a betting lady?"

"What did you have in mind?" she asked, matching his tone.

"If I win, you edit my research paper. If you win, I'll make you the best dinner you've ever had." Chuck smirked. "You game?"

Mallory tapped her chin and stared down Chuck. I waited to see which way she'd go. Chuck could cook, and he wouldn't skimp on anything.

"I'm not doing your research paper," Mallory said with a shake of her head.

Chuck snorted. "I'm the king of research. And at writing my own shit. I just suck at the technical shit like commas."

"What're you cooking?" Mallory asked.

"Whatever you want."

She seemed to consider that a little longer before asking, "You're sure you won't get in trouble?"

"No money, no reason to get in trouble." Chuck held his hands in front of him. "You in?"

"You're on."

"Then it's settled." Chuck slapped his hands on the table and pushed to his feet. "I could use a break on my fingers." He air-typed and grinned. "I'll save you a spot on the couch."

I waited until Chuck was gone before I said anything. We stared at each other, grinning. Her hazel eyes darkened, but the little smile never left her face. Maybe I had a chance with her. And I was going to make the most of it, no matter how long it took.

"He may think he's won, but there is no way this series ends in six." I slid my free hand under my thigh to keep from reaching for her.

"Sounds like he got the best end of the deal, though. I don't think a dinner of ramen noodles is the equal to typing a paper."

"Don't underestimate Chuck. He made chili for a fundraiser last winter and had old ladies begging for the recipe. If he wasn't determined to become a shrink, he'd be chopping veggies for a living. His mom owns the Trainwreck Diner." I broke our stare. The betting bothered me. It was the first rule of baseball. The original commissioner banned anyone associated with gambling; even those acquitted in the 1908 Black Sox scandal were banned. It wasn't worth the risk. "I just hope he doesn't get in trouble. He's walking a fine line. One thing the pros hate is gambling."

We cleaned up our table and made our way to the rec area. True to his word, Chuck cleared a spot on the couch for us. Mallory sat between me and Devin Miller, one of our better starting pitchers, just as the first pitch was thrown. I didn't understand her hatred for a game she knew so well.

Each swing of the bat, each slap of the ball on leather, I watched her, ready to bolt if she got too uncomfortable. If she knew I supported her, maybe she'd open up. Maybe. By the third inning, her eyes were glued to the screen, and her body relaxed against the back of the couch.

"Curve," she whispered.

I turned to the screen and watched McGrath throw a nasty curve that caught the inside edge of the plate.

During his next windup, she whispered again. "Slider."

McGrath missed outside with a slider.

I waited, my body inching a little closer to hers.

"Fastball. Dumbass," she muttered.

Sure enough, McGrath hurled a fastball down the middle and Harold smacked it out over the right field wall. The guys started high-fiving each other, but I didn't take my eyes off Mallory. She must have realized I was staring, because she turned to face me.

"What?" she asked, innocence covering her face.

"You called his last three pitches. How?" I shifted on the couch, curving my body around toward her.

She shrugged and stared at the TV again. "It wasn't hard." McGrath was in his windup. "Curve."

The umpire called a strike as the batter swung at a curve on the outside of the plate.

"Seriously, tell me how you're doing that." I felt like getting on my knees and begging her for this information. If I could've bent my knee. "Are you reading the signs?"

"No. I'm reading the pitcher. Breaking ball." She turned toward me again after McGrath threw a breaking ball that hung in the middle of the plate. It was crushed into right center for a standup double. "He's tipping his pitches. Just watch, the Cards are going to break out this inning."

Mallory leaned a little closer to me and called the next four pitches. The Cardinals scored another run and loaded the bases. The pitching coach came out to settle McGrath down.

"Okay, you have to tell me how you're doing that," Devin said from the other end of the couch. He started to scoot a little closer to Mallory until I glared at him.

I glanced around. Apparently I wasn't the only one who'd heard Mallory. A couple of other guys leaned on the back of the couch. Mallory tensed almost immediately when she realized what was going on. I touched her arm, and she met my gaze.

Angling in so none of the eavesdroppers could hear, I asked, "Do you want to leave?"

She nodded, sliding a little closer to me. Her thigh pressed against mine and heat shot through my pants straight to my groin. "Yes, but I don't think I should."

I bent a little closer, my mouth so near her ear that I felt her shiver. "What do you mean?"

She responded the same way. "Because this feels like something I need to do, okay?"

Nodding, her hair tickling my face, I said, "Okay. Let me know and we're gone."

"Thank you," she said. The "you" felt like a warm breeze against my ear. It took every bit of strength I had inside me not to wrap my arms around her.

Mallory straightened, and the fear on her face was replaced with that determination I'd become so familiar with. She took a deep breath. In that moment, her expression changed again. Mallory turned into the girl I first saw online, a take no shit teacher.

McGrath was getting settled on the mound when Mallory said, "Watch his position." McGrath dug in a little to the right of the rubber. He pulled his glove up. She pointed toward the screen, a little cockiness tainting her voice. It was sexy. "See, there. He's tilting his glove to the left, and you can see his index finger. That's a curve."

This time his curve went wild, bouncing in the dirt outside and past the catcher. Another run scored. The rest of the inning, Mallory continued her education of McGrath until he was pulled from the game. The guys took in her every word. It really was like watching her command a classroom.

"Betts, your girl's awesome," Devin said. A few other guys chimed in their agreement.

I started to open my mouth to tell them Mallory and I were just friends, but she shook her head slightly, and I closed it. They settled down when the game started back up with the relief pitcher ready, peppering Mallory with questions. She answered them all, amazing everyone. She called pitches, told us what the managers would do, and knew which way the ball would go when hit. Her knowledge blew me away. Devin left, and the rookie took his place. On the couch, sitting too close to Mallory. In the seventh, Rosenthal leaned in to her and put his hand on her knee. I reached out and pushed it off. He shook his head like he'd only just realized where his hand had been. Bullshit.

Mallory pressed herself closer to me and brought her lips to my ear. "Now, please."

As much as I wanted to keep her that close, I stood, offering her my hand, and pulled her to her feet. My body froze the second hers left mine. I loosened my grip on her hand, but she wove her fingers between mine. Talk about mixed signals. Not that I protested.

We squeezed through the masses, ignoring the jabs about leaving early. I didn't say anything, and I didn't let go of her hand as we made our way out of the building. The wind hit me in the chest once we were out. My grip tightened around Mallory's fingers.

"Aaron," she said once we were a few steps from the building, "Thank you."

I smiled at her and squeezed her hand, expecting her to

let go. She held on halfway across the quad before loosening her grip. I let my hand fall away. We walked toward the other side of the campus in silence. Each step brought a new agony to my resistant knee.

"Knee bothering you?" She slowed further, and half of me was grateful. The other half was pissed I couldn't keep pace with a girl a foot shorter.

But I wasn't going to lie again. "Yeah, a little. It's pretty tight."

Her head bounced as her gaze returned to the path ahead.

I wished I could read her mind. I had no clue what she was thinking about. All that I focused on was the way her lips felt near my ear, her breath tickling my skin, the way her hand fit so perfectly in mine, and the heat that radiated from her. At the fork in the sidewalk, I turned with her toward the library instead of heading to my dorm.

"Don't you need to go that way?" Mallory pointed behind us before sticking her hand back into the sleeves of her fleece jacket.

"Not until I know you're safe in your car," I said.

"That's really sweet, but—"

"No buts, Mallory. I'm walking you to your car." With a grin, I added, "Deal with it."

She smiled and stepped on the edge of the sidewalk, twisting her ankle and losing her balance. Shit. I grabbed her arm before she hit cold ground and pulled her upright, straight into my chest. If she didn't know how much I liked her before, she damned sure should've known then. The instant she touched me, my entire body went on high alert. I was saluting the troops.

Mallory's face turned redder than a fire truck, and she pushed me away.

"You okay?" I asked, shoving my hands in my pockets and trying to covertly adjust myself.

"Yeah, thanks." She started walking again, but at a slower pace than before. We practically stood still. "I'm sorry about earlier. I should've let you tell those guys we're just friends."

"That's okay. I'm glad you didn't."

"Why?" She stopped in the middle of the sidewalk again and stared up at me.

"Because of guys like Rosenthal. Even after we let them believe you're my girl, he still tried to hit on you." The image of his hand on her knee flashed in my head, and my anger flared along with it. "I'll take care of that shit later."

She nodded, lost in her own thoughts again, and began walking.

"Can I ask you something?" I nudged her shoulder with my arm. "Were you any good? At softball?"

Mallory laughed. "No, I was terrible. I can't hit. I can't field. But I was a great first base coach. Dad taught me how to read the fielders, the pitchers, the shift. I knew where the ball was going before the hitter even swung the bat. Our coach relied on my instincts. You know the old saying: those who can, do; those who can't, teach."

"I would've liked to have seen that."

A sad smile was her response, but nothing more. I didn't push it.

The quiet continued until we got to her car. Then I couldn't help myself. She used a remote to unlock the doors of a black Jeep Wrangler. My jizz almost exploded in my pants. The seats were heather gray and the spotless interior was as if it just came off the assembly line. I climbed into the back, checking out every inch of it.

"I take it you like my car," Mallory said, stifling a giggle with her hand.

I leaned forward between the front seats and gaped at her. "Are you kidding me? I've been dreaming of this Jeep since before I could drive."

She dropped her hand away from her mouth, suddenly serious. "Me, too."

The confusion clouding her face was all I could focus on. I locked eyes with her and climbed out, stopping in front of her. There was something under that confusion, fear maybe. Maybe a little regret. What did she have to regret?

I touched her arm. "Friends give friends rides in their dream cars, right? Maybe you can show me what this baby can do."

"Friends do that," she agreed. "But not tonight. I've got an early class tomorrow."

Mallory climbed into the driver's seat and strapped herself in. She waved as she pulled out, but she didn't look back. I waited until her taillights disappeared around the corner before turning to my dorm.

Friends. Yeah, right.

I stopped outside the dorm, far enough from the entrance to need a break. The throbbing had gone from a toy drum to an entire drum line. The last thing I wanted was another surgery. Watching Mallory as she dissected the game tonight revealed how much I wanted her to see me play. I wanted to come off the field after the ninth and catch her eye in the stands. I wanted to leave the locker room and walk straight into her arms. I wanted her. Simple.

But not so simple.

Seth whistled as he strode toward the dorm.

He had an answer.

He had the key to my season.

If I wanted it, it would be mine.

The debate inside me raged. It wasn't cheating. Not really. Herbs and natural remedies didn't make them PEDs.

And I was already taking prednisone. This would just be an additional supplement. Nothing more.

"Seth, man, wait up," I shouted before I even made up my mind. He stopped, confusion turning quickly to understanding as I limped toward him. We fell into step the rest of the way. "Tell me, how exactly did you return from rotator cuff surgery so fast?"

His hand clamped onto my shoulder, pushing me down a road I never thought I would take. "Step into my office. I'll tell you everything."

I followed him into his double room. Lucky bastard. I'd loved to have a double to myself. He had a navy loveseat next to his desk and a double bed with a black comforter. There was no doubt what atmosphere Seth wanted. Seth pulled a stash of bottles, syringes, and vials from his closet. Definitely not herbal.

"This isn't a good idea," I said the minute I realized exactly what I was doing.

"It's only cheating if you're doing it to play better. You just need a little boost to heal, Betts. That's all." He took a bottle of clear liquid and a syringe out of the plastic bag. "Quit juicing before Thanksgiving. It'll be fine."

I hated to admit it, but I wanted to believe him. If this helped me heal, maybe it was worth it.

"Why?" I shifted on my feet. *It's only cheating if you're doing it to play better.*

"We win with you. And, to be honest, the scouts coming to see you are seeing everyone else. It's a slim chance, but they may take me, too, Betts. That's something I don't want to fuck around with." Seth held out the bag. "Look, I'll let you have the first one for free." He opened a syringe packet and filled it with liquid. "Drop your pants."

I swallowed hard, staring at the needle. If I did this, there was no turning back. "You're sure this will help."

"Can I throw a runner out at the plate from right?" Seth smiled like a hyena. Hell, yes, he could. With a surgically repaired rotator cuff.

Nodding, I turned away from him and let my sweats fall to my ankles. The pinch of the needle on my thigh caused me to yelp. Seth chuckled. After a minute, he slapped my back, and I pulled my pants up.

"There are anabolics and HGH in the bag, which you can have," he said as I faced him, "for a price, Betts."

I closed my eyes and nodded. The lights of Fenway. Digging my cleats into the batter's box and facing a Cy Young winner. Watching that first pitch sail over the outfield wall and giving the crowd a curtain call. Maybe it was nothing more than a fantasy, but I'd pay the price.

I'd pay any price.

Chapter Twelve

Doc canceled physical therapy for a week and chewed me out worse than Coach did after an error on the field. He wasn't happy with how I kept pushing too far too fast. It didn't help that Coach Hummel gave me a second ass-chewing the minute I set foot back on campus. I took it easy on my knee as the week flew by. When I wasn't in class or in Coach's office watching tape, I was with Mallory. It didn't feel like we ever had enough time.

Mallory and I walked toward the lounge for game seven of the World Series.

"Favorite music?" I kept my hands in the pocket of my blue Westland hoodie to fight back the chill in the air.

"Country. I love Jason Aldean, Little Big Town, and Maddie & Tae."

"Luke Bryan?"

She shuddered as a cool November wind bit against her skin. "Him, too. What about you?"

"Country's good, but mostly alternative. Imagine Dragons, Twenty-One Pilots, bands like that. They help me think."

Mallory shook her head. "I don't get that. Music distracts me. I can't read or study with it on. The TV, though..." She bounced a finger at me. "That I can have on while I study."

I faked a gasp when my phone actually rang. I yanked it from my pocket and glanced at the caller ID.

"Who is it?" Mallory asked, clearly recognizing the grin on my face as a good one. As much as she hated me asking her questions, she had no problem interrogating me.

I simply answered the phone and Mallory's question at the same time. "If it isn't the world's most annoying little sister."

"Very funny, Aaron," Chelsea replied with a sniffle. Either she'd been crying or she was getting a cold. My bet went with crying.

I froze, waiting for the bad news. "What's wrong?"

"You know how I applied for early admission into NYU?" Chelsea sniffled louder. "Well, I got in."

The tension raced from my body, and I breathed out. This wasn't a bad thing. She'd dreamed of New York since I could remember. "If you got in, why are you crying?"

Chelsea broke into full-on tears then. Between her sobs, I managed to decipher, "Mom won't let me go."

"Calm down, Chels. I'll call Mom tomorrow and talk to her. Just rein in your temper for the night." Without thinking, I put my arm around Mallory's shoulders and pulled her closer, tucking her against my body. "Trust me, it'll be fine, and you'll get to go. Mom's probably freaking out like she did when I was drafted."

"But you didn't go to Arizona. I *am* going to New York." Chelsea blew her nose into the phone.

"I know. And you'll be great. Let the shock die off tonight."

"Yeah, okay." She heaved out a loud, dramatic breath. "You're the best even if you smell like a cow patty."

I laughed. "We have the same body odor genes, you know."

We hung up, and I glanced down at Mallory. She wasn't fighting to get away from our close proximity. Not that I wanted her to, but the fact she hadn't shoved me into the grass was a good sign.

"Is everything okay?" she asked.

My arm dropped from her shoulders. "It's fine."

I wouldn't bring up the family drama unless Mallory dug deeper. And I knew she would. Her curiosity was infinite. We started walking again. I shoved my hands deep into my pockets to keep from reaching out for her. The entire left side of my body was cold. I wanted to feel her against it again but took comfort in the fact that she hadn't pushed me away.

We hadn't gone ten steps—yeah, I counted—when curiosity got the best of her.

"Do you want to talk about it?" she asked.

Playing coy, I shrugged. "Not really. It's not a big deal."

Her head bobbed as if considering my vague answer. "I didn't know you had a sister."

"Yeah." *Let the interrogation begin.*

"How old is she?"

"Eighteen."

"Why was she upset?"

"Mom." Giving one-word answers drove her nuts. Mallory craved information and always more than a simple answer during our sessions. But I was afraid to tell her too much. I was afraid she'd shut down like she normally did when it came to family.

She nodded and took a deep breath before the next question. "What happened?"

"Chelsea got into a school. Mom doesn't want her to go."

"Aaron, you're not being very verbose."

I snorted. Time for a little truth, even if it hurt. I stopped in the middle of the sidewalk and stared at the lounge for a moment. "Friends tell each other the truth, right?"

She turned around to face me, and I dropped my gaze to meet her eyes. "Yes."

I dug my fingers into my palms to keep from touching her. "We don't really talk about much. Family seems like a… hard topic for you. We keep everything simple. The last thing I want to do is make you uncomfortable." Her eyes widened as she opened her mouth, but I couldn't let her interrupt me now. "It's okay. Really. But don't be mad at me if I try to…if I don't want you to feel like you can't be around me because of it."

She turned away and started toward the student union. I just stood there, not sure if I should follow her and beg for her to talk to me or if I should hustle back to my room. She stopped halfway to the entrance.

"Are you coming?" she asked over her shoulder.

Smiling, I hurried to catch up and took my place by her side as we went into the lounge together. Secretly, I thanked my little sister for calling me and giving me a chance to confront Mallory gently.

We sat in our usual spots on the couch. Mallory wrung her fingers together, her jaw locked tight. She turned toward me. "Why doesn't your mom want Chelsea to go to that school?"

"It's not just a school. It's the city. Mom doesn't like New York. When we were kids, she took us because Chelsea loves musicals." I tapped my hands on my legs. "I didn't want to go, but Mom insisted that I needed 'culture.' We were mugged. Mom's been overprotective since. But that's just the excuse she's using. Mom doesn't want us to grow up. It scares her."

"That actually makes sense. Grandma didn't want to leave me alone when she left." Mallory relaxed and opened up. "I went to New York when I was five. It was Dad's idea to see all the stadiums. We went to Yankees Stadium and Shea. I wanted to go to the history museum, but we didn't go."

"Why not?"

"He said there wasn't enough time." Mallory shrugged. "But he made time to spend an extra hour in the gift shop at Yankee Stadium."

"You'll get there."

Mallory smiled sadly. "Maybe."

Chuck sat on the arm of the couch and quizzed me about the tape Coach had me watch earlier in the day. When I glanced at Mallory, Rosenthal sat too close as he peppered her with questions. By the tight jaw and narrowed eyes, I could tell she was getting more and more uncomfortable.

I leaned over her and shoved him back. "Mind your space, rookie."

"I was just talking to her, Betts. You need to relax," he said with a sneer uglifying his pimply chin. I couldn't wait to face him in live batting practice this spring. Rosenthal was a cocky shit, and he needed to be taken down a notch or ten.

"Go talk to someone else," I said. Devon and Seth nudged him from behind, forcing him to stand. Seth took his spot, smiling at Mallory but making sure he was pressed against the arm of the couch. I leaned in close. "Are you okay?"

She kept her eyes glued to the TV and nodded.

I sat up, letting her have the space she needed. Honestly, I wanted to pummel that little shit. Rosenthal knew she was off-limits. He knew she didn't want to talk to him. He knew not to get too close to her. The more I thought about it, the more I wanted to get up and put my fist in his face.

"You're moving around easier, Betts." Seth smiled and nodded toward my knee. "Getting better?"

"Yeah, much better." *Because I'm doing what I'm supposed to do. With a little extra help.*

Chuck leaned over the back of the couch between me and Mallory and asked in his usual no-filter way, "You two need to set a date for dinner. I've already got the place, and I know what I'm making. Just tell me when. Or do you want to go double or nothing?"

You two? When did I get involved in this?

Mallory's mouth crooked up in a lopsided grin. She didn't glance back at Chuck when she answered. "What did you have in mind?"

"If I win, no dinner and type two of my papers. If you win, I'll make you and Betts dinner." He paused dramatically. When I was about to stick a cattle prod up his nose, he added, "And breakfast."

The world could've swallowed me whole.

"That's interesting," Mallory said without a missing a beat. She finally looked at him. "It's a lot of effort to deliver to different places early in the morning."

Chuck stared at her as the slam on me sunk in. Well, it felt like a slam to me. Why else would she say something like that? I was proud of her for it, too. He laughed loud enough to cause half the room to turn our way. Again, the floor could've opened up beneath my feet and I wouldn't have given a damn.

"That's ripe, Mallory," Chuck wheezed between fits of hilarity.

She beamed back and dropped her gaze to mine. The embarrassment must have shown on my face, because that little spot between her eyebrows wrinkled together, and her smile disappeared. I hated that, but she'd actually hurt me in a way I didn't think possible.

I turned away from her and settled more deeply into the corner. Chuck slapped my shoulder a few times before pushing off the back of the couch, signaling his departure. Mallory's eyes stayed on me through the first pitch and well into the top of the inning.

After the Yankees went down one-two-three, she asked, "Are you okay?"

I snorted but didn't answer.

"Aaron," she said, putting her hand on my thigh and leaning in so that her sweet body pressed against mine. When her lips were on the edge of my ear, she whispered, "I'm sorry. I didn't mean…"

I closed my eyes, memorizing how she felt against me. Her hand squeezed my thigh, and I thought the world was melting from the heat. Opening my eyes, I turned my head toward her and my lips found the edge of her ear.

"Forgive me, please," she added.

"Always." I meant it completely.

Mallory was shy, quiet, brilliant, but she was also awkward and off-balance. Standing in front of a room of students wouldn't faze her; standing in a room of people who want to really get to know her was not in her comfort zone. If she asked me to run away and live in a cabin in the wilds of Montana, I would've done it in a heartbeat, knowing how comfortable she was without other people near her. Her body made my mind go numb, and I planted a soft kiss on the skin just beneath her ear. She shivered at the contact. This girl was seriously testing my powers. I pulled my head away from hers slowly, letting our skin barely touch until all that was left was the burn of where we'd been connected.

Mallory moved back into her spot in the center of the couch. Her face flushed a sweet pink. Hope spun like a whirlpool in my chest. Maybe this whole patience thing would pay off after all. Seth glanced at me with a huge grin.

We watched the rest of the game in intense silence. The Cards would take the lead, then the Yankees would take it right back. In the bottom of the ninth, local hero Jason Carter stepped to the plate. He'd graduated high school in Madison about six years before and went straight into AA. When he was nineteen, he made his Major League debut and won Rookie of the Year. Not that I'd admit it, but the guy was kind of my hero.

He fouled off the first two pitches. Mallory and I both moved to the edge of the couch, wondering if he could do it, if he could win the series with one swing.

The next pitch was low and outside.

The fourth pitch was high and tight. With the count two and two, the pitcher had little leeway.

Then the pitcher threw the heat straight down the middle. It must have come at Carter in slow motion. He kept his head down as he dropped his shoulder, swinging in one fluid motion. The sound of the ball meeting the ash of the bat was all anyone needed to know the game was over. The crowd erupted as the ball soared through the air. Mallory's hand found mine, and she squeezed the life out of it. Both of us knew it was gone, but until the ball cleared the fence, we weren't going to believe it.

Those three seconds felt like an eternity.

The right fielder leaped, his glove clearing the fence, but the ball bounced off the end of his mitt.

Jason Carter hit a walk-off home run, giving the Cardinals a World Series title.

Mallory and I jumped off the couch, screaming. I couldn't have cared less who won, since the Sox weren't in it. But, as a player, that was one of the best games I'd ever seen. Mallory must've felt the same by the way she was celebrating. She high-fived my team and beamed from ear to ear. Her eyes lit up with pride.

She turned toward me and wrapped her arms around my waist, resting her head on my chest. Initially, it felt like a friendly hug. But she didn't let go. She held me tight. My left hand snaked up her back, entangling my fingers in her wild hair. I couldn't hear her sigh, but I felt it. I felt how her body relaxed into mine. My head dropped, burying my nose in those soft locks. God, she smelled like fresh roses. Somewhere the celebratory hug turned into something more. I didn't want it to end.

Unfortunately, Chuck's a dumbass sometimes. As insightful as he was, he often failed to see things right in front of his face when he wasn't looking. He grabbed both of us, pulling us into a bear hug.

"Damn straight, boys and girl," he screamed.

When he let go to torture other unsuspecting people, Mallory and I fell away from each other. She stared at me, confusion covering her face once again. I hated that. The careful control she held so high had disappeared for a moment. And she was truly happy. I knew it in my gut as I knew that the last walk-off home run in game seven of the World Series happened in 1960 when the Pirates won.

I smiled, anything to defuse the tension rolling from her. "Do you want to watch the rest or leave?"

She sucked the corner of her lip into her mouth as she considered her options. "I always liked it when the commish gives the trophy to the team."

"Okay then."

We sat on the couch, casually discussing the game. In the back of my mind I wondered how many moments we'd had where it felt like there was more than just friendship between us. There had been quite a few, but Mallory only really ran when I initiated anything. If I told her the truth, she didn't run. If I acted on my feelings, she shut down. When she initiated it, like the hug we'd just shared, she got confused and tense. That was what I had to let her work through.

Chuck pushed Seth out of the way and sat beside Mallory during the postgame. When it came time to announce the MVP, we all cheered for the obvious hero. Jason Carter won a sweet new car to go along with the trophy. He beamed like a kid in a schoolyard.

"Jason, congratulations on winning the World Series and

being named series MVP." The announcer was interrupted by the cheers of the home crowd. "How does it feel?"

"Surreal. I feel so blessed right now. These fans are why we're here today. Without them, there's no way we could've won this game." Jason waved at the crowd who started chanting his name.

I glanced at Mallory. She stared at the screen with a calmness on her face that I'd never really seen before.

"You got a tattoo before the playoffs and said if you won the World Series, you'd share the meaning behind it."

Jason tugged up the sleeve of his left arm. On his bicep was the 23V32 tattoo that brought a lot of speculation, especially since he got it the day after the Cardinals clinched the division. Not the best time to get a tattoo.

"I lost some people very close to me once and promised myself that if I ever made it this far, they'd be with me." Carter pointed to the sky, and I swear there was a tear in his eye, but it could've been sweat. "Coach V, Danny, I never would've gotten here without you. I miss you every day."

He kissed two fingers and saluted his fallen friends.

I glanced at Mallory, expecting the usual girly tears from such an emotional declaration. That's not what I saw. Her face was as pale as a corpse as she stared wide-eyed at the screen. She wrung her hands together in her lap, scraping her nails over the reddened skin. I reached toward her and covered her hand. Her head snapped toward me, and our old friend fear reflected in her eyes. No, not fear, complete terror.

"Do you need to leave?" I asked slowly, enunciating each word.

She couldn't speak even as she opened her mouth to answer me. So she nodded. I helped her to her feet, held out her coat, and let her lead from the lounge. We walked the old familiar path to her car in silence. Her hands were shaking so badly that she dropped her keys three times before I took them from her and unlocked the door with the remote.

"Talk to me," I whispered, leaning against the driver's door so she couldn't climb in and get herself killed.

Her voice still hadn't returned, and she shook her head again. I watched her for a minute. She kept her head down and shuffled her feet with nervous energy. Reaching out, I touched her shoulder and opened my arms. Mallory glanced up at me with wary eyes.

"Come here," I whispered.

Whatever was warring inside her mind, the need for comfort won out. She collapsed in my arms, sobbing uncontrollably. I held her close and ran my fingers along her spine, making shushing sounds and telling her it was okay even though I had no idea what caused the sudden onslaught.

Her tears slowed, and I pulled my head back to look down at her. "Let me take you home."

She sniffled and finally found her voice. "I can drive."

"Maybe, but I don't think you should, and I would never forgive myself if you were in an accident. Please, Mallory, let me take care of you."

Her lip sucked into her mouth, but for once, she didn't think too long. "How will you get back?"

"Don't worry about that. Seth or Chuck will come get me." I steered her to the passenger side and helped her in. Once I settled into the driver's seat, I turned the key, enjoying the low rumble of the engine as it roared to life. "I knew you'd let me drive it sooner or later."

Mallory let out a small laugh. "Just take it easy, cowboy."

"Cowboy?" I raised an eyebrow at her. "I like the sound of that."

She rewarded me with an eye roll. Her phone rang in her pocket. She pulled it out and stared at the screen for a moment. I waited to back out until she gave me directions. Whoever was on the other end made her hesitate. Finally, she swiped the screen.

"Hey." She turned away from me while she listened. "You shouldn't have done that."

Why'd she turn away from me?

She sucked a sob back in. "We'll talk about this later, Cutter. Just… Not now."

Cutter? Why'd she feel the need to hide?

"I'm sorry. That was… Anyway, turn right out of the lot." She sat ramrod straight in her seat. "My house is pretty easy to get to."

Mallory lived on the edge of town not far from the campus. The closer we got to her house, the more tension built in her body. Whether it was from the phone call or from me being so close to her house, I didn't know.

As instructed, I parked in front of a small shotgun style house that had a room sitting on top of the back. It looked like an *L* that was tipped over from the right and was nestled between two small A-frames.

I followed Mallory, feeling eyes on me from every direction. When I glanced around, there wasn't anybody in sight. It was creepy even though I knew it was just a nosy neighbor. Mallory unlocked the front door, took a visible breath, and stepped inside, flicking on a light.

She dropped her keys into a tortoiseshell bowl and hung her coat on a hook in the short hallway. A gray tabby leaped on the bench and meowed. Mallory scratched it behind its ears as she set her bags beside it. The cat jumped down and disappeared into the small living room, but not before glaring at me. Mallory followed it. The room had a plum couch and matching chair. It didn't fit her. On the far wall was an old TV surround by photos in ornate frames. I took in every part of the house; each bit seemed more old lady-ish. A crocheted afghan hung over the back of the chair and lacy doilies centered every table. Just past the couch was an open kitchen with almond countertops and appliances. Beyond that was another short hallway, steps to the upper floor, and three doors. I wanted to explore the rooms to see if there was any space that was hers and not her grandmother's.

"Take off your coat," Mallory instructed, motioning to the coat rack.

I wasn't expecting her to let me stay for very long, but I also hadn't texted Chuck to get me yet, either. After hanging up my coat, I followed her to the couch. There was one single personal touch in the room that screamed Mallory. Her books were stacked on the table and beneath an end table. Her cat watched me from its perch on the back of the couch. The photos around the TV were clearly family. Curiosity got the best of me and I stood, stepping over to them. An old black-and-white photo of a beautiful brunette in a wedding gown holding hands with a guy with wild hair stood in a silver frame next to a similar photo of a woman with wild curly hair, holding the hand of a trim, athletic man.

"My grandparents." Mallory pointed at the black-and-white photo then moved her finger over to the other one. "My parents."

I glanced over my shoulder at her. Mallory's gaze stared off into another place, maybe another time. I picked up one of Mallory in a red graduation gown holding her high school diploma. Her expression was blank, neither happy nor sad. The rest of the photos were of her parents or her grandparents. There weren't any more of her.

Mallory sniffled, and I drew my gaze back to her. She curled her legs to her chest, resting her cheek on her knees while she watched me. One last tear trickled from her eye.

I opened my arms to her. "Come here."

She shook her head.

"Then talk to me." I paused before adding, "About anything you want. You don't have to tell me what set you off tonight, but for the love of all things, Mallory, talk to me."

I couldn't say how long we sat like that, staring at each other. Waiting was torture, but that was the only thing I really knew how to do with her.

"I'm not good at this," she said.

"Good at what?"

She didn't answer. The silence pressed on my chest. I stood to relieve the pressure of the frustration building inside. It had been growing for a long time and I didn't want to let it out now. Five weeks and I still knew so little about her. I paced the room for several minutes before kneeling in front of her. My knee popped, sending electric shocks of complete agony through my heart. The only thing I could do was to ignore it. Focus on Mallory. I could see myself and the desperation on my face as I stared into her eyes.

"Why won't you talk to me?" I asked.

Neither one of us blinked as I waited for her answer. "I don't... Aaron, I don't really talk to people."

Closing my eyes, I released a frustrated breath. *Bullshit. She talks to her friend in L.A. And her friend in St. Louis. The Hipster, the people in her classes. And Cutter, whoever that was.* "Don't or won't, Mallory?"

Her body started to shake again, and I moved beside her, pulling her into my arms. The tears erupted as soon as her face was buried in my chest. Christ, even if I could get her to talk, what would she tell me? There was something dark lurking just beneath her surface. She fought it every day. She made herself an island.

"It's okay, Mallory," I whispered into her hair. "Whatever it is, it's going to be okay. I'm here. I'm not going anywhere."

I meant it. Every fucking word. I wasn't going anywhere. I'd started this thing with Mallory Fine to solve the mystery of her, but it had grown into so much more. Solving the mystery was one thing, but unraveling all the knots that tied her up was another. I wanted to do both.

"My parents died when I was fourteen," she said through a round of sniffles. "They…they were on their way back from a baseball game in Iowa City when a tractor trailer rear-ended them." She raised her head, meeting my gaze. "I…I was at a softball tournament in Council Bluffs when…Grandma came to the field and told me."

Her head fell against my shoulder. I couldn't imagine what she must have felt. My parents weren't perfect, but I still had them. But why weren't they at her tourney? Why did they go to Iowa City for a baseball game? A piece of Mallory kicked into place. Her mom and dad chose baseball over her. And it cost them their lives. If they'd chosen Mallory, they never would've been on that road, never would've been in that accident. No wonder she hated the game so much.

An hour and a half later, I left Mallory asleep on her couch. The gray tabby reappeared, curling up beside her and hissing at me. I covered her with the afghan, barely missing the claws of death swatting my way. The cat glared at me as I left the house. I caught a cab back to the dorm. I fell into my own bed, colder than I'd ever felt. For the first time since grade school, I had nightmares. When I woke the next day, a cold sweat covered my body and all I could remember was Mallory walking away from me no matter how much I begged her to stay.

Chapter Thirteen

For the next couple of weeks, Mallory acted like nothing had happened the night the Cardinals won the World Series. I let her. She curled back into her cocoon almost completely. We didn't discuss baseball. We didn't really hang out like we had been, either. During our tutoring sessions, we focused on the twenty-page paper I had to turn in to make up for the missing work, low grades, and stupid participation points. I swore Dr. Monroe was the only prof who actually tracked that shit.

The best thing that could've happened was the visit to the doctor. My recovery was now ahead of schedule. After all the setbacks, the doubts, staying off it the extra week made a world of difference. Four weeks of physical therapy, and it was over. Angela wasn't going to torture me anymore, but I had to keep up a prescribed regimen through the athletic department. The rest was up to me. Well, and Seth's help. As much as I hated the needles, it helped. I'd be able to play sooner. Maybe not at the beginning of the season, but in enough time for the scouts to see me.

Barry was more disappointed than I expected. He'd

finally found his calling, at least. My knee wasn't 100 percent yet, and it probably wouldn't be for a while. I just needed to keep up the boost through the end of November to be ready for training next semester. I felt stronger every day, and my knee was improving better than I had hoped.

The Tuesday before Thanksgiving, I finally broke the new, silently enforced "no personal talk" rule.

"What're you doing for Thanksgiving?" I asked as Mallory marked over the latest draft of my paper with a purple pen.

Her head shot up, and the deep crease returned between her eyebrows. That wasn't good. She shrugged, going back to my paper. I waited until we were in the elevator to bring it up again. This time I welcomed the lift's screeching halt between the second and third floors.

"I don't know what I did, but I'm sorry," I said as I leaned against the wall opposite her.

She kept her eyes forward, and her body held the same tension it had for the last few weeks. I hadn't seen relaxed Mallory since before the game. "You didn't do anything, Aaron."

I rubbed the back of my neck. "Friends don't lie to each other." The elevator shuddered as it lurched downward. I waited until we were past the second floor before I hit below the belt. "But I guess you don't want to be friends anymore."

She reached in front of me and slapped her palm on the stop button, bringing the car to another halt. "That's bullshit."

Anger. An emotion I didn't think she had. I raised my eyebrows, knowing it would antagonize her. "Really? That's not how it feels. You're shutting me out again. You have since—"

She slumped against the back wall. "I know. I'm sorry. I just…"

Her anger might have disappeared in an instant, but mine flared. I slammed my fist into the button for the lobby a half a floor away. For once, it eased into its descent. "Of course you are. Protect yourself, Mallory. No matter who it hurts."

"I'm not protecting myself, I'm protecting you." Her voice was so calm, so clear, I had no doubt she believed that.

"I don't need you to protect me," I said as I lifted her chin. "Whatever you're hiding from, I can handle it. Just let me in."

The doors conveniently opened, and Mallory bolted out of the library in a sprint. I debated about going after her. What could I say?

I didn't need anything from her but her trust. And that was something she wasn't willing to give easily.

I'd been lying in my bed, staring at the ceiling when a light knock interrupted my pity party. Weighing my options to either ignore it or answer it, I caved to another light rap and forced myself to the door. A little bubble of hope grew when I thought it could've been Mallory.

Nope. Should've known better.

Trish stared at me with wide eyes. I knew this look. She wanted something only I could offer. After we first broke up, I shredded through every memory we shared, searching for signs that she wasn't into me. When I looked for them, they were pretty obvious. Playing on her cell during baseball games, flirting with other guys in front of me, disappearing during school dances for longer than it really takes to use the restroom. Yeah, there were good times, but those were early on. We'd grown apart, grown up, and changed. It wasn't just Trish who had changed. I had, too.

I blocked the door so she wouldn't just barge into my room. "Can I come in?" she asked.

"I don't think that's a good idea."

She chewed on her bottom lip and bent her head down,

gazing at me through her lashes. A few months ago, I would've fallen to my knees to give her what she wanted.

"Why are you here?" When she didn't answer, I started to close the door in her face, but she caught it with her hand.

"What, did your little princess dump you already?" she sneered. I glared back. She pinched the bridge of her nose. "I'm sorry. That was uncalled for."

"Yeah, it was."

"Look, I need a favor." When I didn't bother to respond, she launched into one of her no-breathe, nonstop explanations. "I need a ride back home. I never told my parents we split, and they are expecting you to stop by, and I wish we could at least fake our way through the holiday. I promise I will tell them, but not yet, and I really, really need you to do this for me."

I crossed my arms. "Why haven't you told them?"

Trish huffed out a sigh. "Because I can't stand to hear them tell me how disappointed they are. Again. You know how it is. You know how pissed Dad was when I told him I wanted to major in secondary ed. You know how furious Mom was when she…caught us fooling around in the barn. Which was my fault, of course. Everything I've done has been a failure in their eyes. Except you. You they love."

Staring over her head at the door across the hall, I pretended to contemplate the idea. Trish's parents were hard on her. Our relationship became clearer, too. She'd stayed with me because of them, not because she wanted me. It didn't hurt anymore. That was over. It just made me sad for her. But she needed to tell her folks the truth—I couldn't do it for her. "I've thought about it. Answer's no."

Then Bitch Trish came back with a vengeance. "After everything we've been through and you won't even fake it for this weekend?"

I leaned down so we were nose-to-nose. "You were faking

it for years, Trish. Maybe it's time you stopped."

"You son of a bitch," she snapped, slapping me hard across the cheek.

I would never hit a woman, but it took every ounce of my control not to slap her back. Rage boiled through every pore. She stared at me, smug, knowing I wouldn't touch her. I hated myself for wanting to wring that look off her face. I hated myself for being a colossal dick to her, too, and I struggled to control the wrath surging through me. My fists clenched, digging my nails into my skin, which was not an easy task, since they were bitten down to the quick. I ground my jaw tight and pressed my tongue to the roof of my mouth.

"You think you're so fucking superior to everyone else when you're just a scared little boy who can't think past being exactly like his daddy." Each word was punctuated with a finger to the chest. "Grow some balls, Aaron. You're going to need them someday."

She spun on her heel and stomped down the hall. I stayed in the doorway, forcing the anger out of my body using a trick, ironically, Trish had taught me when she went through a new-age kick last year.

Then I realized what she said.

Grow some balls, Aaron.

The laughter bubbled from deep in my gut until it was loud enough that a few of the guys on my floor finally looked out to see what was going on.

"You okay, Aaron?" Seth shouted from a few doors down.

That only made it worse. When I could breathe, I yelled, "Never been better."

"Glad to hear you've grown some balls," he shouted back, causing the rest of the guys to join in my hilarity. The door to the hall slammed, making us laugh harder.

"Need anything?" Seth nodded to his room. I shook my head. He'd stocked me just last week. "Let me know."

Turning around, I let the door close with a soft click. Trish had no idea how much I had changed since she freed me. I stood up for myself. She just didn't like that I'd done it with her. She didn't like that she'd lost the one guy she could control, and there was no way in hell he was coming back anytime soon.

Chapter Fourteen

I drove home first thing Wednesday morning. It felt great to be behind the wheel again. I'd missed my truck. And we had two hours together. Twenty minutes after I left, my phone buzzed a text. I glanced at it, half expecting to see Chelsea's face in a not-so-flattering photo. She'd already sent me up-to-date warnings about the family. I thanked God every day for my little sister. She kept me sane at times like Thanksgiving.

The name I saw almost caused me to drive off the road.

Mallory.

I pulled over onto the gravel shoulder before responding. I'd learned my lesson before my senior year in high school when I was texting Trish and ran my truck into a shallow ditch. I got lucky.

Mallory: *I'm sorry.*

I debated about how to respond when another text came up.

Mallory: *I don't want to hurt you.*

Me: *Friends don't lie.*

Mallory: *Are we still friends?*

Me: *I don't know.*

There was a long pause and I put the truck in gear when I heard the ping. I threw it back into neutral.

Mallory: *I hope so.*

Me: *Can we talk about this when I get back? I'm driving home now.*

Ten seconds after I hit send, my phone rang.
"Hel—"
"Please tell me you aren't texting and driving." Mallory's panicked voice ripped through me.
I had to remain calm. "Relax, I pulled over."
She exhaled audibly. "Thank God. But you could've waited until you got to your house."
"No, I couldn't. You would've freaked out." I paused for a moment. "I couldn't do that to you."
"Thank you." Her voice was steady, but the quiver underneath it was undeniable.
"Hold on a sec." I turned on my Bluetooth and put the earpiece in. One day I'd have a truck with built-in Bluetooth, but there's something about driving a classic. I slipped the truck into first and eased back onto the highway. "Can you hear me?"
"Sure. Are you driving now?"
"Yeah, I've still got an hour and a half before I get to the farm." The Iowa landscape rolled by. Field after field of harvested corn and soybeans peppered by the occasional barn and house. A few tractors sat in the middle of their fields, abandoned for the weekend celebrations. God, I loved Iowa.

"Maybe we should hang up. I don't want you to get in a wreck or something." The quiver in her voice was unmistakable.

The last thing I wanted to do was hang up. "You realize this is the first time you've called me?"

"I had to. I thought you were being stupid."

"Well, that's a given."

"Very funny, Aaron."

I smiled at the quick change in her voice. "If I'd known that was all it took, I would've done something stupid earlier."

She coughed to cover her laugh. "I heard about what happened last night. Are you okay?"

"You mean with Trish? How'd you find out about that?"

"I ran into Chuck at Markum's this morning. He was picking out a turkey."

"Ah, the gossip king of Westland. If his therapy career fails, he might have a future as a member of the paparazzi."

"You didn't answer my question," she said.

"You don't answer any of mine." I let that sink in even though it was a little assholey. "Sorry, that was—"

"No, don't be. Friends don't lie."

I hated ever saying that to her, but I wasn't going to take it back. "No, they don't. And, to answer your question, I was pissed at first. But she said something, well, that I needed to hear. She told me I needed to grow some balls." Mallory inhaled sharply, but I kept going. "But the fact is, I had. She used to walk all over me. She thought she could manipulate me into driving her home and playing like we were still together."

"I heard she slapped you," Mallory said, anger raising her voice to a higher pitch. It was kind of sexy.

"Chuck must have spies everywhere." I laughed. Seth had probably shared it with him. He was just as bad as Chuck. "Yeah, she did. It stung, but it didn't hurt."

Mallory's anger hadn't abated one bit from my joke. "What a bitch. She was in the lounge last night. I guess it was before she came over to your room. Anyway, she was at a table with that Candy girl. They were talking in great detail about…"

"About what?"

"I shouldn't tell you this," she said.

"I think you should." She sighed, and I wanted her to sigh in my ear sometime. I was such a lovesick wuss.

"Okay, but don't say I didn't warn you." She didn't speak for several seconds. I could almost see her sucking her lip into her mouth. "They were talking about how bad you are in bed."

I almost drove off the road.

"And they were doing it loudly enough that I could hear them."

Words failed me. Nothing sarcastic. Nothing even slightly humorous. I couldn't think of a damned thing to say to her. The need to explain, to justify their accusations, overwhelmed my vocal cords.

"Aaron?"

"Uh…"

"Well, I was still mad about…earlier. When they started going into graphic detail about certain…parts of your anatomy, I went over to their table and put an end to it. Candy looked a little embarrassed, but Trish acted like I'd stolen her high."

"What did you do?" I forced the words from my mouth.

"Um… I told them that if they hadn't fucked half of the school, they'd know what a real man is like and that you're one."

The image of five-foot-nothing Mallory facing off against Trish and Candy took some tension from me. But that white elephant still sat on my chest. Taking a quiet, deep breath, I ripped off the Band-Aid. "I never slept with Candy."

Mallory didn't say anything right away. I waited for her to respond. "It's not really my business, is it?"

"Isn't it?" My voice sounded all throaty and breathless. It wasn't me at all, but it felt right in a way. That's how Mallory made me feel. If it was possible to see tension across the digital cell line, this would've been visible. I cleared my throat. "Thanks. For standing up for me. I don't think anyone's ever really done that for me before."

"You're welcome." A distinct sniffling sound came through the line. "I'm sorry. For the way I've been the last few weeks. I'm trying to be better at this. It's just...it's so easy to shut myself down."

"Yeah, I get that." And I did. Mallory had been alone in that house since she was eighteen. She'd cut herself off from the world. Letting me in even a little was monumental. I loved that she trusted me enough to try.

"Aaron, when you get back, maybe we can...talk. I mean really talk."

"I'd like that."

"I think I would, too."

"So, what's your grandma doing for Thanksgiving?" I changed the subject to the only thing that popped into my head. Probably wasn't the best subject to change it to, though. Until Mallory chuckled.

"She's cooking for Aunt Chrissy and a few of their neighbors." Mallory's voice lit up at the mention of her grandmother. It wasn't what I expected. "I wish I could see her, but I have to work all weekend, and a round trip ticket to Phoenix isn't cheap. At least I know she's enjoying herself with her new friends. She deserves it."

"All grandparents do." I pictured Grandma Eddie and Grandma Jean showing up at a neighbor's house. They'd hate it if they couldn't do their own cooking. They have a hard enough time letting Mom do most of the work. "So, what's up with the cat?"

Mallory laughed. "You mean Mickey? He's a troublemaker but a good kitty."

"You seriously didn't name your cat after Mickey Mantle." It was hard to keep the amusement out of my voice.

"No, he's named after the famous mouse. When I found him, his ears were too big for his head."

"Found him? Tell me about it." I settled into my seat.

"After…after I moved in with Grandma, he showed up on the steps." Her tone darkened for a moment. "I snuck him into the house and hid him in my room, but you can hide a cat for only so long. Grandma found him the next day when she went in for my laundry."

"Was she mad?"

"Yes and no." Mallory sighed. I loved how she opened up more to me every day. "It felt like he was sent to me. Grandma understood, or just played along. Either way, Mickey moved in."

"He hissed at me. Not sure how much of a good kitty he is."

Mallory chuckled. "He doesn't do well with strangers."

We stayed on the phone for the rest of my drive. Our conversation steered toward simple things, even a little history quiz. Mallory told me a few historical facts that would've bored me to tears if someone else shared them. She made history come alive with her passion. I didn't want to hang up when I pulled onto the gravel road leading to the farm. I slowed to almost a crawl until the truck crested the small hill and the two-story white house with wraparound porch came into view.

"Mallory…I have to go, love." The word slipped out, and I wanted to take it back because there was no way Mallory wanted to hear that.

The familiar Mallory Fine pause filled the space. "Have fun with your family, Aaron."

"Thanks. What're you doing besides working?" I put the truck in neutral, letting it idle while my mom waved from the back door. I waved back and motioned that I was on my phone. Mom shook her head, and I couldn't stop the smirk spreading. Mallory didn't ask me not to call her love. It felt like a huge victory.

"I'm behind on my reading."

That was impossible. I laughed, and Mallory's giggle joined me. "I'll call you later, okay?"

"Or text."

I laughed. "Or text."

We said good-bye, and like some lovesick junior high girl, I waited until I knew she had hung up before I took the Bluetooth from my ear. I turned to open the door and almost shit my pants. Bright blue hair filled the view out my window. My sister grinned like she had eaten the last of the pie. That's when I saw the lip ring. And the fucking nose ring.

Oh this was going to be a great Thanksgiving.

Mom and Chelsea weren't talking, but I had known that for weeks. Dad wasn't home from the shop yet, and my grandparents weren't due until later this evening. My aunts and uncles had rolled in throughout the day and were hiding in their hotel rooms in town.

My Thanksgiving weekend with the family was starting out just great.

I took my bags to my room and immediately realized some redecorating was in order. I'd finally gotten Trish out of my heart; it was time to get her completely out of my life. Taking the stairs faster than I had in months, I went into the kitchen to grab a trash bag.

"I talked to the Hendersons yesterday. They were excited to see you and Trish this weekend." Mom kept wiping the already clean counter. "I thought you two had split up."

I tugged the bag free from the box, letting the cabinet door beneath the sink slap shut. "We did."

"I don't understand, honey. Why hasn't she told her parents?" Her cleaning frenzy moved to the doors of the stainless-steel fridge. "I know boys will be boys and you wanted to see other people—"

"Trish ended it with me, Mom. Not the other way around." I leaned against the counter and watched her disinfect the door handles. "I told you that."

She stopped and opened the door, tossing a water bottle toward me. "I know what you told me, Aaron. I just thought that you were trying to…"

"Trying to what? She wanted to see other people. I didn't." I put the trash bag on the counter, walked up to her, and planted a kiss on her forehead. "But it was the best thing that ever happened to me."

Mom sighed. "You may think that now, but you two were—"

"I know you liked Trish, but she treated me like shit. That's not how I want to live my life." I grabbed the bag and started toward the stairs when I stopped, turning around to confront her. "Are you ever going to talk to Chelsea?"

The frustrated scrubbing moved to the already clean sink. "She won't listen."

I snorted and spoke before thinking. "She's not the one who won't listen."

"What?" Mom spun on her heel, her face reddening with anger.

"Tell her the real reason why you don't want her to leave, Mom. Tell her what you told me after I was drafted. Tell her that you're scared. She needs to hear you say it instead of just telling her how dangerous it is. Tell her you don't want to lose her. But let her go to New York. Let her have her dreams."

"New York's dangerous—"

"Yep, so's Madison. So's Iowa City. So's Cedar Rapids. She'll be fine. Don't let your fear stop Chels from living her life. Just trust her." I took off down the hall and up the stairs before she could respond.

Chelsea sat on the top step, grinning at me sadly. "Thank you."

I patted the top of her head. "Get rid of the blue hair. Mom'll come around, but you need to stop acting out like a kid."

"I *am* a kid."

"Kids don't get to go to New York."

"Fine. I get it." She stood and pointed at the trash bag. "What's up with that?"

"Throwing out some bad memories. Want to help?"

"Hell yes. I've wanted to do it myself for months."

I threw my arm around my little sister and laughed. "Wish you would've."

We spent the next hour removing all the stuff Trish-related. Chelsea went to the basement for a box to keep the things she didn't think I should throw out. I let her pack up that shit. The love notes, some photos, and a couple of stupid T-shirts (that I never wore) got tossed into the trash bag. Once my room was devoid of my ex-girlfriend, Chelsea and I went out to the burn barrel. I grabbed the lighter fluid and the box of matches. Chelsea was a little too excited to empty the trash bag into the barrel, and she laughed when I put more lighter fluid onto the memories than I needed to.

"You ready?" I asked, poised to light the match.

She smiled, but it faded fast. "Wait. Can I tell you something and you won't be mad at me for not telling you sooner?"

I raised my eyebrows, promising nothing.

"You remember Mitch Larsen?"

"Yeah, he was a year ahead of me."

She took a deep breath and a step back. "Remember your senior year when you missed the spring bonfire?" I nodded. I'd been down with the flu and missed the first week of baseball season. "I saw her. With him. In a way a sister should never see her brother's girlfriend, if you get my drift."

Unfortunately, I did. "You'd think it would bother me more, sis, but I'm not surprised. Sad, but not upset." I shrugged. "It's the past. I'm ready to start a future."

"I should've told you, but...well, I—" She closed the distance between us, pulling me into a bear hug. "I'm sorry. I promise I'll tell you if your next girlfriend is hoe-skank."

"Thanks. I think." I grinned as I let her go. "Let's burn this shit."

Chelsea laughed, and I struck the match. Neither one of us really expected the big *whoosh* followed by a wave of heat that erupted as soon as the match hit the lighter fluid. It almost knocked me on my ass. Chelsea's laughter grew hysterical, and I joined in. We watched until the flames died down.

"Guess I'll go fix my hair," Chelsea said, a hint of sadness coloring her voice. "You know, I did this today to piss Mom off. It washes out."

"Yeah, I know why you did it. Ditch the nose ring and lip ring, too. Grandma Eddie might kick your ass all the way to New York if you don't."

Chelsea popped off the magnetic rings and slid them into her pocket. "She's not going to let me go, is she?"

"She will. But you have to understand why she doesn't want you to. The real reason, not the bullshit she keeps throwing at you."

"Thanks, Aaron."

My cell rang and I pulled it free from my back pocket. The shit-eating grin on my face was a dead giveaway.

Chelsea leaned over and raised her eyebrows. "Who's Mallory?"

I didn't respond as I walked toward the barn, answering the phone. "Hi."

"Hey." She sounded distant, like she was hiding behind something.

"Is everything okay?" I pulled open the side door and stepped into the darkness. The lights flickered on like the lights of Fenway, slowly then—bam—the entire inside of the barn lit up. The combine and two tractors shone red with fresh wax. Dad always waxed his implements for winter. I used to think it was stupid, but Dad told me it was his way of thanking them for another good year. His baseball superstitions bled into farming. He used to do something similar with his glove, a habit I picked up.

Confusion clouded her voice. "Yeah, I just…I don't know why I called."

"You don't have to have a reason, you know." I climbed into the cab of the combine and settled into the leather seat. "Anything exciting going on in Madison?"

"Other than the usual, no." She laughed. "How's the family? Your sister?"

My heart almost stopped. She always avoided family. Instead of holding back, I told her about the drama between Mom and Chelsea. She listened, not once interrupting me.

"You have a great relationship with Chelsea." There was something I never thought I'd hear from Mallory. A hint of jealousy in her voice.

"Yeah," I said, knowing I'd need to tread lightly here. But it wasn't like she had any siblings of her own. "We fight sometimes, but we've always had each other's back."

"That's nice. That you care so much for her." She inhaled deeply into the phone, and I half expected more, but she changed the subject to the book she'd finished reading. She told me the entire story. Her voice soothed me as she talked about a torrid love affair gone wrong and the injustice of the fictitious murder. I told her about burning the past.

"Sometimes that doesn't help," Mallory said. The joy that had just been in her voice was gone.

"It doesn't change anything, but it felt like I finally closed that door. I needed that." I held my breath before letting the words out as gently as I could. "I'm ready to start my life with the right person. With someone who loves to read. Someone who loves history." I let out my breath. "With the only someone who gets me."

"What if she's not?" Mallory asked.

"Then I'll wait until she is."

"What if she's never ready?" God, her voice sounded so small I wanted to wrap my arms around her and hold her to my chest. Anything to take away the pain she hid. Anything to make her happy.

"Mallory—"

"I should go. I'll…I should go. Bye, Aaron."

I opened my mouth, but she'd already ended the call. Why in the fuck did I go there?

Chapter Fifteen

Thanksgiving at my house was not a small affair. It was the only time the entire family sat around the same table. My aunts and uncles, along with my younger cousins, drifted back to Chicago and Cedar Rapids for Christmas, but Thanksgiving we're always together. The grandmas liked to race to our house first thing in the morning to see what they could do. Grandpas Len and Vincent long ago gave up trying to convince Grandma Eddie and Grandma Jean that Mom didn't need their help. Never stopped their competitive spirit. Neither did the annual pumpkin pie debate. Both grandmas would bring three pies apiece, and nothing was ever left over.

I spread out on my bed, like I did every year to avoid the overcrowding situation. Our house wasn't small until Thanksgiving. Then it was microscopic. Thank God nobody tried to spend the night. The local hotel with indoor pool was too inviting.

"Hiding, boy?" Dad leaned against my doorframe, smirking like he just ate one of Grandma Eddie's pies all by himself.

"You know it, old man."

Dad stepped into my room and glanced at my trophy shelf. He stepped over to them, touching the plaques I'd gotten for being team MVP my sophomore, junior, and senior years. "How's the knee?"

"Good." I sat up and bent my knee a few times to show him. My brace was still necessary, but the pain was nothing more than a mild discomfort now. Seth was a genius.

"Doc seemed mighty concerned about it last time we spoke." He refused to look at me, and my stomach turned into a whirlpool filled with boulders. "Didn't think you were healing quite right."

"Yeah." My palms were slicker than oil. "It wasn't going well, but I took another week off putting pressure on it and started being more careful. Followed my PT routine, took all my meds. You know, giving myself more time to get to class and making sure I didn't do anything stupid like running."

"You were running?" His head snapped toward me, and a blaze of anger flashed through his normally calm eyes.

I held up my hands in surrender. "Once. Not on purpose, but I was going to be late for Monroe's class, and he'd dock me for sure. I strained it pretty bad."

The fire dissipated as fast as it flared. "But you're doing better now?"

"Great. I may even be ready for the season." I tried to smile, but this entire conversation set me on edge. Did he know something? I didn't bring anything with me, so there was no way. But Dad tended to know things without knowing things. It was some kind of weird sixth sense or something.

"Don't do anything stupid, Aaron." He sighed, and the weight of life pushed him beneath his six-foot frame. "Nothing's worth sacrificing your health or your education. The scouts look at your integrity, too. See if who you are will fit in with the organization." He bent his knee, and it crackled like a fresh log on a fire. "Trust me on this."

"Yeah, Dad. I trust you." I bit the words as my heart slammed against my ribs. *What have I done?*

He nodded and shuffled out the door.

I fell back on my bed and stared at the smooth white ceiling. The fan didn't spin, just collected dust. I closed my eyes and dug deep for answers. Why did I start juicing? Because I wanted to play. Because I wanted to heal. Because I wanted to get drafted. Because I wanted to succeed where my father had failed. And because I wanted Mallory to watch me from the stands, proud of her man. But she wasn't mine. Not yet. And she wouldn't be if I got busted.

I'm done. No more.

Seth told me to stop by Thanksgiving. I'd dump the stash when I got back. I bent my knee to my chest, feeling the strain of the stretch but no pain. *I don't need that shit anymore.*

Our youngest cousin Angela kept Chels trapped in her room, because Angela wanted to try on makeup. The best part was that it was easier to avoid Chelsea. She'd been trying to pin me down since Mallory called. It was not a conversation I wanted to have with her. Fortunately, she had enough sense to avoid the topic around my parents. Unfortunately, she also had an attack plan. By the time we sat down to eat around two, there were about thirty people crowded into the dining room, kitchen, living room, and family room. Chelsea planted herself right next to me. Thank God, she had let her hair return to its natural blond.

"Who's Mallory?" she whispered the minute after Grandpa Len finished saying grace.

I ignored her and continued to butter a homemade roll. Grandma Eddie and Grandma Jean might've fought every year about who made the best pumpkin pie, but they learned a long time ago that nobody could beat Mom's homemade rolls.

"You can ignore me all you want, Aaron, but I'll keep pestering you until you break." She snatched the roll from my hand. "You're already hot and bothered over her. Just tell me who she is."

"My tutor," I said through gritted teeth.

Chelsea's laughter drew too much attention from the other end of the table.

"What're you two whispering about down there?" Mom asked. Everyone's eyes turned toward us, and I wanted to sink under the table.

Chelsea, however, had always been a superior liar. "Aaron was just telling me about his physical therapy. He called his therapist a sadist. I thought it was funny."

The conversation turned to my knee injury, not that I thought for a moment my sister had given up.

"How's the knee doing, young'un?" Grandpa Vincent heaped a pile of potatoes higher than Kilimanjaro. My arteries clogged at the sight. They damn near became impassable when he scooped a lump of butter and doused it with gravy.

"Good." I couldn't take my eyes off the trainwreck of food. Any red-blooded American boy loved mashed potatoes, but this was something Pastor Walters would question. Gluttony at its best.

"Gonna play?" Grandpa Len asked. He shook his head at Grandpa Vincent and took a respectable serving of potatoes.

"I hope so."

"Aaron will be fine. He's a smart boy." Dad slapped the table and changed the subject.

"Good," Grandpa Vincent said before shoveling the potatoes into his mouth. "Think you'll get drafted?"

"Of course he will," Mom said as she passed the green

bean casserole to Grandma Jean.

"Scouts will know how long it took you to recover." Grandpa Len stared at me through his too-thick lenses. "You sure you're good? I'd hate to see you go and get hurt again."

"If he says he's fine, he's fine," Dad snapped. "He'll get drafted, Dad. Don't worry about that."

My gaze darted around the room. *Do they know? Do they suspect anything?* Panic welled in my chest. It was impossible, but I couldn't stop the thoughts from ricocheting around my head.

Grandpa Len stared at my father with doubt and regret. He knew how close his own son had come to the pros. And I knew he didn't want the same shit to happen to me.

Dad knew it, too. He quickly changed the subject. "Did I tell you about the Harpers, Dad?"

"No, you didn't." Grandpa Len smiled at the gossip. He was as bad as Mom and Grandma Eddie. And Chuck.

I finished my meal ignoring my cousins and my sister. It was easier than answering her constant barrage of questions. It was easier to keep my head down and pray they didn't see the guilt in my eyes. Unfortunately, by eight, everyone was gone.

The first thing I did was check my phone when I got to my room. Nothing. No text. No missed call. Zilch. I thumbed in a quick message and waited. And waited. And waited. I was still staring at my phone, willing Mallory to respond to the text I sent almost twenty minutes ago, when Chelsea piped up.

"Why don't you just call her?" Chelsea stood in my doorway, leaning against the frame like Dad had done earlier in the day. My little sister had Mom's looks and Dad's imposing stature.

"Don't you ever knock?"

"Why start now?" Chelsea moved into the room and sat on the edge of my bed. "When'd you start crushing on your tutor?"

"Is it that obvious?" I still wouldn't look at her, but I wasn't going to lie, either. She could read me like a billboard. Besides, she had all the fibbing skills in the family.

"The minute your phone rang yesterday, I knew. Does she?"

I nodded. After what I'd said on the phone yesterday, Mallory had to know. I'd all but told her. I wasn't sure if she'd let herself love me, though. Or if she even wanted to.

"So what's the holdup?"

I poured my heart out to my little sister. Nothing stayed hidden. It felt good to get it off my chest. And Chelsea wasn't a kid anymore, no matter how much I wanted her to stay the little girl in pigtails. We'd never lied to each other, that I knew of, and I needed someone to tell me what to do, because I sure as hell didn't know.

"Sounds like you really do care about her," Chelsea said softly. "What're you going to do?"

"Be patient, I guess. But I don't know how much longer I can last." Finally, I glanced up. Chelsea had a faraway look in her eye. "How long is long enough?"

"I wish I could tell you. She's obviously got some serious problems to work through first."

My phone *ding*ed a text message. I stared down at it, not wanting to appear like a lovesick fool in front of my sister, but apparently it was already too late for that.

Chelsea laughed. "She's really gotten under your skin. The minute you got that text, your whole face changed." She stood and moved toward the door. "If it were me, I'd leave tomorrow morning and head back to school. If I were her, I'd be thrilled the guy came back early for me."

"When'd you get so smart about this kind of shit?" I asked, a bemused smile covering my lips.

"You aren't the only one who's got a thing for someone,

Aaron. But you're the only one of us who can make it work."
She closed the door behind her before I could even ask what
she was talking about. My little sister? With a major crush?
That didn't seem possible.

Glancing at my phone, I opened the text, rereading the
simple message I'd sent earlier.

Me: *Happy Thanksgiving.*

Mallory: *Thank you. I hope yours went well.*

I started to tap out a response and stopped. Chelsea's
first question came back to me. I'd never called Mallory.
There wasn't any reason other than texting was just easier.
I pulled up her number and hit send. The line rang several
times before she finally picked up.

"Hey," she answered.

Everything inside me lightened at the sound of her voice.
The near disaster at dinner, the doping weighing on me, the
look Grandpa Len gave Dad. Everything disappeared.

"Hey," I said. "So, tell me, what did you do today?"

Mallory detailed her own disaster of making a turkey.
"I just… I wanted a real Thanksgiving this year. It's…been
a while."

"You should've come here. We have enough leftovers to
feed the entire campus."

Mallory laughed. "I'll bet."

"Maybe next time," I said. "Just throwing that out there."

"Maybe," she said without hesitation. "I…I'd like that."

We talked for the next hour about turkey, Thanksgivings
past. Mallory didn't bring up her parents, but she did share
details about her life with her grandmother. They had a great
relationship. I made up my mind then to go back the next day.
I needed to see her and to clear the air once and for all.

Chapter Sixteen

Mom tried to get me to stay home longer. I let her lull me in for a big breakfast of sausage, biscuits, and gravy, but finally broke free just after ten in the morning. She muttered under her breath the entire time I packed my clean laundry. She muttered as I hugged her and Chelsea good-bye. She even muttered when Dad offered to carry one of my duffels as he walked out to the truck with me. We tossed the overloaded bags in the back and slammed the tailgate closed. Mom stood at the screen door in her bathrobe, chewing on her nails. Guilt dug at me. Mom hated watching me leave, but she did it anyway. I yanked open the driver's door, and Dad grimaced at the screech of the metal. I really needed to get that door fixed.

"Your mother's freaking out that you're getting ready to flunk out of college now," he said.

I'd made the excuse that I needed to meet with my tutor to go over my paper one last time before turning it in. Truth was Mallory had already read it and sent me revision notes. "I'm not. Not even close, but I do need to make sure I pass this course. If I've got a chance to play, academic probation is the last thing I need."

Dad shook his head. "Whoever she is, boy, I hope she's worth it," he said with his face drawn into a frown. "And I hope she doesn't… Don't let some girl ruin your dreams."

"That's not going to happen, Dad," I said, forcing myself to stay calm. He didn't need to go there.

"And I hope you know that your mother will never like her." Dad grinned, breaking the tension.

I laughed, knowing he was partially right. Mom wasn't going to like anybody. As if I was going to let that stop me. "As long as you do, old man, we'll be good."

He smiled then and clamped his hand on my shoulder. "I'm not the one who has to, boy. Remember what I said, don't let this girl derail your life."

I shook my head and slipped the truck into reverse. There wasn't anything I could say to get it through his head that the only thing that would stop me was death. I was going pro.

Two hours of thinking lay ahead of me, along with the smell of Mom's leftover Thanksgiving dinner as an added distraction. I turned up the radio as loud as I could. Marshall Travis's voice bounced around my cab, wailing about his lost love and how he found her in time to lose her once again. As much as I loved the song, I couldn't listen to it much longer and switched over to a sports station. The debates about who would trade whom over the course of winter kept my mind off everything but baseball for the rest of the drive.

I pushed eighty and shaved twenty minutes off my usual time. Probably not smart, but I knew where the cops liked to nail speeders. No way they were going to bust me as I hauled ass back to Madison. I needed to see Mallory, to tell her exactly what I wanted, what I needed. There wasn't anything else on my mind. Just her. I parked behind the Jeep outside Mallory's house. That Marshall Travis song wormed back into my head. It almost made me second-guess myself. Almost.

The lights were on in the living room. It was a quarter after noon but dark as dusk. The chill in the air promised the threat of an early snow. She'd hung a Christmas wreath on the front door since the last time I'd been here. The *only* time I'd been here.

Do you really want to do this, Aaron? Do you really want to tell her? Are you willing to risk losing her?

Yes, the answer was yes to all three questions. A tiny bit of fear dug its fingers into my heart. I couldn't keep pretending. I couldn't continue to let my emotions, my intentions, slip out only to have her ignore them. She didn't always ignore them, though, did she?

It was time to throw it on the line once and for all. I needed to get this out of my system, to get her out of my system, regardless of how it played out in the end.

I climbed out of the truck, careful not to tilt the two complete meals my mother packaged up. She didn't ask why I wanted two, but she grumbled under her breath. Maybe if my mother met Mallory… No. Dad was right. Mom was going to hate her if they ever met.

If. Such a tiny word with huge implications.

I opted to knock instead of ringing the doorbell. After waiting for several minutes, the tension causing my heart to hammer so hard in my chest it felt like I was being pushed toward the door until it finally opened.

Jason Carter stood in front of me with the look he'd give an ump who called a strike when it was clearly a ball. His jeans hung off his hips and the championship T-shirt stretched over his chest like it was a size too small. What he didn't have on were shoes and socks. This was not how I wanted to meet my favorite ball player.

And it was not *where* I expected to ever meet him.

"Can I help you?" he asked, crossing his arms and taking

on a defensive stance.

I closed my eyes to compose myself. There was no way I was leaving without at least seeing her. Not now. Not after Jason fucking Carter opened her door. I knew I was being irrational. I knew there was a logical explanation to this, but I couldn't stop the jealous rage rolling through me. I couldn't stop the idea rooting in my brain that she was the mystery girl that kept him coming back to Madison. Why didn't she tell me she knew him?

Son of a fucking bitch.

I held out my hand, willing it not to quake. "Aaron Betts. Is Mallory home?"

"Jason Carter," he said as he shook my hand in a firm grip. There may have been an extra hard squeeze. A meow sounded at his feet. Mickey flicked his tail as he wove a figure eight through Jason's legs.

"There you are," Mallory said behind Carter. Mallory peeked around his large frame with Mickey in her arms, her eyes going wide when she saw me.

"Hey, Mal," I said, knowing the nickname would set her off. I shouldn't have, since I told her I wouldn't call her that anymore, but Jason Carter was in her house. It was the nicest way I could tell her I was furious without pissing off the pro ball player making himself comfortable in her house. Too comfortable.

"Aaron? What're you doing here?" It was an accusation. I could hear it in her voice. Like this was all my fault. Like I was the one who'd lied.

As much as I wanted to say, "getting my heart ripped out through my nose," I smiled as politely as I could. "You mentioned not having a proper Thanksgiving dinner, so I thought I'd bring you one." My eyes darted toward Jason before settling back on her. I shoved both plates toward her. "Guess I misheard you."

Her whole body tensed as she took them, her eyes never leaving my face.

"Anyway, I came back early to rewrite my paper. I hope I didn't misunderstand anything you said in that." I stepped back from the door, shoving my hands into my pockets. "See ya around, Mallory. Nice to meet you, Jason."

He nodded, glancing between me and Mallory. I backed away until I hit the sidewalk then turned and strolled across the street to my truck. My body shook with barely controllable anger. Not just at Mallory, but at myself. I'd misread the entire situation. If I'd been at the plate, I would've struck out looking. Hell, I just had. I never got a chance to swing my bat.

Chapter Seventeen

I drove around town, passing all the usual haunts: Deluca's Bakery, O'Malley's, The 9er Diner, and UnShelved. At least until my gas light came on. As soon as I got into the truck, I'd turned off my phone. There wasn't anybody I wanted to talk to anyway. The silence echoed in my ears. I filled up and headed back to school. The closer I got to campus, the more I wanted to turn around and get on the highway. Going home with my tail between my legs was not going to fix this. Mom would've been happy, at least. I pulled into the parking lot behind my dorm. After I got out, a black Jeep Wrangler at the other end of the lot caught my eye. My pulse ricocheted through my chest, but there was no way it was Mallory's. She had company. Jason fucking Carter. Unbelievable.

The building was mostly dark. A few windows were lit on the top floor where the foreign kids lived. I swiped my key to get inside and wished there was somewhere else I could go. O'Malley's was an option, but I really didn't feel like seeing that waitress. Or anybody else, for that matter. Even thinking about O'Malley's reminded me of Mallory. I stared at the dirty gray tile of the hall, wondering how I'd misread every single sign. Replaying everything we did, everything we said, as I stalked toward my room, I came up with nothing other than her distance. And I got it. Mallory pulled back because she was scared. But she should've told me about Carter.

It was too much to deal with. I needed a hot shower and a nap. Then maybe a bottle of tequila. When I glanced down the hall, someone was in front of my room. Mallory sat on the floor with her knees to her chest. She leaned her head back against my door and watched as I walked toward her.

I stopped, staring down into her eyes. "What're you doing here?"

Tears glistened on her cheeks. Despite what I'd just learned, I wanted to wipe them away. I bent my knees, a sharp crack snapping in the wrong way as I brought myself to her level. The pain seared through my thigh, but I kept my face blank. Mallory didn't need to know. Besides, it was getting better, and this rarely happened anymore.

She still hadn't answered my question.

Sighing, I ran my face over my hand. Fuck it. I was going all out anyway. Might as well take a swing away like a full count in the bottom of the ninth. "You lied to me."

"I—"

"You told me you didn't date baseball players, much less anyone else. And who's at your house? The reigning World Series MVP. All this time I waited, thinking I had a chance." I stood too fast and had to lean against the wall before I fell. The hallway swayed. My heartbeat raced like it was on its way to a Triple Crown. I didn't need all of this shit. On top of that, my damned knee cracked hard. It had been fine for the last few weeks. Sure I had an occasional snap that almost brought me to the floor, but it wasn't bad. The pain brought me back to reality. I'd take some meds, and it'd be fine. It had to be fine.

My hand shook as I stuck my key in the lock over her

head. I needed answers from Mallory. I deserved them. My fingers hovered over it, while I debated about what I wanted to really say to her. Nothing short of the truth would do. "Why'd you do this? You knew I was falling for you. You had to know. But you strung me along? I thought… Damn it, I thought I was being patient because you needed to work to let me in. I never believed you'd lie about this."

"Do you mean it?" Her soft voice echoed down the quiet hall.

I glanced down, the tears flowing faster along her cheeks. As much as I wanted that anger to surge through me like lightning, I was so tired of her games. "I've meant everything I've ever said to you."

She stood and took one of my hands in hers. They felt so tiny around my fingers. I stared into her eyes, trying like hell to figure out what in the world she was thinking and failing as usual. With one hand still holding mine, she reached up with her other one, running her fingers along my temple, down my cheek, over my lips. The light moan escaped without my permission.

"Jason's not…" She sighed and continued tracing my face with her fingers. I couldn't move. "I'm not with him, Aaron."

I leaned against her soft touch, wishing it meant as much to her as it did to me. The warmth of her fingers disappeared, and she let go of my hand as she stepped away.

"He's just an old family friend," she said as she continued to back down the hallway. "Okay?"

My head nodded before I realized what I was doing. Was it okay? It had to be. If it was okay, that meant there was hope. Even if it was a small sliver, it was there. I reached for it and held it to my chest.

Mallory stopped a few feet away, her brows furrowed. Her chest heaved, and she took a small step back toward me. Then another. I stood frozen by my door, not willing to move and scare her away. When she was close enough I could smell her soft vanilla scent, she raised onto her tiptoes and pressed her lips against mine. Before I could react, she broke away. With a small smile, she turned and escaped out the door. The cold air rushed down the hall, smacking me in the face, waking me from the obvious dream.

I unlocked my room and went inside. The first thing I reached for were the pain meds. The second, the needle. I filled the syringe and plunged it deep into my thigh. I needed to get better, faster. I needed to do this for Mallory. For baseball. I needed to become the next Jason Carter, and I needed to do it fast.

I stared at the remainder of the steroids. Seth had warned me to quit by Thanksgiving or I'd risk testing positive. Then I wouldn't have baseball. That wasn't acceptable. God, what was I thinking? I couldn't lose everything. NCAA regs were harsh, but Westland's were worse. The school had a zero-tolerance policy. One positive test and I was done. And it wasn't going to happen. I tossed the PEDs into the trash and cleaned out my mini fridge before taking the bag out to the dumpster. The vials thunked against the metal. I was officially done.

Except for one vial and a handful of pills. Only for an emergency. Just in case I needed it.

I collapsed on the bed, exhausted from driving two hours only to get on a roller coaster of Mallory Fine. It was nearing four when I woke and turned on my phone. Chelsea had sent ten text messages. Each more panicked than the first. I hit her number, a sense of dread souring my stomach. It didn't even get a full ring before she picked it up.

"There you are!" she shrieked.

"What's wrong?" My voice filled with the cold fear leaking into my veins.

"What makes you think anything is wrong?" She hit an octave I never thought possible in a human. Dogs in

Cincinnati could've heard her.

"Chelsea," I warned.

"Mom and Dad—"

I tightened my grip around the phone. "Are they okay?"

"Yes, will you just let me finish?" She sighed into the speaker with an exaggerated breath. "Just shut up and listen, because you're not going to like this one bit."

"Get on with it, Chels, before I get back in my truck and drive home." My teeth ground against one another.

"I overheard Mom and Dad in the kitchen. You *could* say I was eavesdropping—"

"I could, huh?" I raised an eyebrow even though she couldn't see me.

"Okay, I *was* eavesdropping, but this wasn't what I expected. They were supposed to be discussing my fate, not you." Her frustration fed through the phone.

"Me? Why were they talking about me?"

"Probably because you took off today, the day after Thanksgiving, Mom's favorite holiday."

"Yeah, yeah, yeah. I get that much. But I didn't do anything?" I hadn't intended on it sounding like a question. Hell if I knew what I did to upstage Chelsea's move to New York.

"Mom started in on him about you. Dad told her to mind her own business. She snapped at him that you were heading down the wrong path, blah-blah-blah."

Anger tinted my throat. "Really? You throw in a blah-blah-blah there?"

"That's not what's important. Listen, you know how Mom and Dad started dating in high school, right?"

"Yeah," I croaked. It had been drilled into my head for as long as I could remember.

"Apparently, they broke up for a while in college. Dad supposedly cheated on her or something." Chelsea's voice cracked on every other word. This news dug at her as much as it did me. "They really didn't get into detail, but it was implied that Dad wouldn't have ruined his baseball career if he'd never split with Mom. Anyway, this whole mythical perfect parent thing just blew up in smoke. Mom's freaking out that you're acting just like Dad. Dad's pissed because she's bringing up something that happened over twenty years ago. It was epic, Aaron."

"Wait, so you're telling me that Mom and Dad haven't been together since high school? Why in the fuck would they lie to us about that?"

"Think about it. Has Dad ever claimed that? Nope, it's always been Mom." She paused to let it sink in. And sink it did, like a boulder in quicksand. "The only reason I'm telling you is because Mom's determined you're ruining your life. She'll probably do an intervention at Christmas."

"I highly doubt that."

She inhaled sharply. "Is Mallory there?"

"No, she's not." God, how I wished it otherwise.

"Oh, I guess it didn't go well?" Her voice dipped to normal levels.

"I honestly don't know." I pictured Mallory walking away from me, but those few minutes before, when she touched my cheek, held my hand, kissed me, were almost perfect. *Hope.* "But it'll be fine. I think."

"I'm sorry. If you need to talk, you know…" Chelsea sighed loudly into the phone as if this whole conversation was a terrible burden she was finally rid of. "Anyway, I wanted to warn you about Mom. She's hell-bent on making you miserable."

"Thanks for the heads-up, sis."

"I'd expect you to do the same."

"Anytime. Talk to you later," I hung up just as someone knocked on the door. Kicking my duffel out of the way, I got up and strode across the small room to yank open the door. Seth stood in front of me, smiling like a cat that finally caught his mouse. "What're you doing here?"

"Eight-hour drive to hang out in a trailer? No thanks. I'd rather stay here and have a frozen dinner." He stepped into the room and closed the door. "You done?"

"Yeah, I'm done." *Except for an emergency stash. Just in case.*

"Good. Can't have you testing out." Seth tossed a large white bottle toward me. It rattled in the air, but I caught it with ease. "Some supplements, man. It'll help."

I glanced down at the bottle labeled "B-Complex." "You giving them to me?"

Seth shrugged. "Figured if we were going to win this year, we needed our center fielder."

A ball of worry unraveled in my gut. Mandatory drug screening would start soon. It was always random, and there were thirty other guys who might get called first. According to Seth, everything should be out of my system by then. "Nothing's gonna test if I drop, right?"

"Like I said before, no worries as long as you've stopped. You cleared to play yet?" Seth leaned against the doorframe.

"Not yet. Doc cleared me to take some swings after Thanksgiving. May hit the cages this weekend as long as I get this paper done." I chucked the bottle onto my bed.

Seth opened the door as his phone rang. "Cool. I'd get tired of watching tapes all the time while the rest of the team worked out." He pulled his phone out of his jeans and stared at the screen. A smile slipped over his face as he glanced down the hall. "Gotta go, man. See ya."

I nodded and closed the door behind him. The white bottle sat in the middle of my navy-blue comforter. When I took over center field, he had done whatever he could to make my life miserable. Shaving cream in my cleats wasn't that big of a deal. Peroxide in my shampoo, harmless fun. Childish pranks, nothing more. The more games we won with me in center, the less he did what he could to annoy me. He'd backed off after I hit four hundred. We became good friends.

The one thing Seth wouldn't do was sabotage the team or our chances at winning nationals. Winning was more important. Seth was like the rest of us; he didn't care where he played as long as he played. Moving toward the bed, I grabbed the bottle and put it in the closet. Nothing to worry about.

My phone vibrated against my leg. Reaching into my pocket, I dug it out and tugged it free.

Mallory's name popped on the screen.

Come over for dinner tomorrow night?

My smile was instant. I tapped in my answer.

Tell me when and I'll be there.

Six?

See you then.

I sat in front of the computer and booted it up. If I was going to play this spring, I needed to pass this stupid class. The burden weighed me down, but thoughts of dinner at Mallory's kept me going. It was time to scholar up.

Chapter Eighteen

The letters blurred on the screen, blending into one another until I couldn't tell where one word ended and the next began. Heat surged through my veins, sending my heart on a high-speed chase in my chest. It echoed in my ears, vibrated down my legs. The room started spinning.

What the hell was going on?

I tried to push myself to my feet, but my left arm gave out. My heart sped up until I couldn't recognize one beat from the next.

This wasn't right. Nothing was. Pressure built in my body as if I were underwater.

Then it stopped.

The rapid-fire pulse in my chest seized. Electricity shot down my arm.

The beat returned, not as fast, but not like normal. Who knows how fast their heart beats? I was aware of it after running or working out, but this was a whole other ballgame.

I managed to get to my feet and stumbled out into the hall. Seth just happened to be strolling by as my legs gave out.

"Whoa, man, what's wrong?" Real concern laced his voice.

"Hospital." It sounded foreign on my tongue and barely audible.

"Shit, yeah, let's go."

Seth held me up as we ran to his car. Hell, he pulled me. My feet recognized my brain's commands ten seconds behind. The racing in my chest sped back to hyperdrive, then skipped again as I collapsed in the passenger seat of Seth's Chevy.

"Fuck me." I yelled as loud as my hoarse voice would allow. "Hurry, Seth, I'm…"

It skipped again. I screamed as darkness filled my vision.

The steady beat of a heart monitor woke me. I had no idea how long I was out. The last thing I remembered was fire in my veins. Seth must've made it to the hospital on time. I thought I was dying. I'd actually hoped at one point that I would die just to stop the pain.

"Ah, you're awake."

I sat up enough to see a young doctor stroll into the room. His white lab coat hung past his knees, and round frames perched on his nub of a nose. He adjusted them, glaring at me through the thick lenses.

"You want to tell me what happened?" He stopped beside the bed, crossing his arms. It might've been an attempt at intimidation, but it failed.

"I don't know. You're the doc. You tell me." Glass cut through my throat.

He shook his head and reached for the flimsy plastic cup on a tray table. "Drink this."

The water was lukewarm on my tongue and ice cold on my swollen throat.

"So you've never been diagnosed with heart arrhythmia?"

I shook my head. Stars collided in my vision. This was worse than a hangover. My skull felt underwater.

He crossed his arms again. "You taking anything?"

Here it was, my chance to confess. I could tell him about the steroids, the HGH. Did I want that? It wasn't cheating, since the season hadn't started yet. It wasn't cheating, since I only needed the PEDs to heal. It wasn't cheating.

"You've got elevated levels of testosterone in your blood." He tapped a folder against his leg.

"Prednisone," I said, pointing to my knee.

He shook his head. "That doesn't affect the testosterone levels. Try again."

I opened my mouth, then closed it. What could I say? If I admitted it, he'd tell Coach Hummel or worse—the athletic director. Then I would be done.

"Look." The doc let his arms fall and sighed. "I can't prove you're taking steroids, but you and I both know you're on something. The only thing I can prove is that you've got a heart arrhythmia and high testosterone. You need to see a cardiologist. This isn't an isolated incident. It will happen again. And whatever you're taking will only make it worse."

"I'm not taking anything," I whispered. The lie tasted like sour milk.

The doctor shook his head. "Bullshit." He stared at the chart in his hand. "The nurse will be in to get all your information. Do you have insurance?"

I nodded. My parents had great insurance.

"What's your name?"

The reality sunk in slowly. He had no idea who I was. There was no way to report me to the school. No way to get me kicked off the team. I could sneak out of here without worrying about getting busted. I closed my eyes and lied through my teeth. "Trent Mitchell."

"Okay, Trent. I'm going to keep you overnight for observation. I'll have the nurse bring a list of cardiologists to check out. I recommend scheduling an appointment as soon as possible." He jotted something in the chart. "And stop taking whatever you're taking. It's probably what caused this attack in the first place."

He spun on his heel and left the room. I had to get out of here. Now.

It took some maneuvering, but I managed to find my clothes and get dressed. As soon as I could, I took off the monitors and slipped out the door as the buzzer sounded. Thankfully, my room was toward the front of the hall, and my escape happened right at a shift change. I blended into a crowd leaving the hospital and disappeared before they could catch me.

My dad's face, filled with disappointment, flashed in my mind.

God, what had I done?

Saturday night, I sat in my truck before going to dinner. I'd taken the HGH in the morning out of habit. The realization of what I'd done soured my stomach. I should've purged then and there, but I didn't. The ER doc said I had a heart arrhythmia. A Google search this afternoon put my mind at ease. It's not always serious, but I needed to stop this shit. Clean out my system then talk to coach about the condition.

I'd gone to the showers at the end of the hall and dumped the remaining three pills into the toilet. The vial had weighed in my hand like lead. It was harder than I'd expected. When I threw the other vials and pills away, I'd felt free, but that was only because I'd kept a small stash. Swallowing hard, I'd tipped the vial over and poured the liquid over the pills.

The door to the restroom opened, and I'd slammed the lever, flushing them into the sewer. The only way I could get more would be Seth. That was a rabbit hole I wasn't going down again.

I clutched my chest, more aware of my heartbeat than ever. It was steady, normal. I'd have to see a doctor about it. As soon as the PEDs were out of my system.

This time I was done with them for good.

The hot shower cleared my head. I spent more time on my hair than my little sister, and that was saying a lot. Then I went to my closet and felt like a schmuck. Nothing seemed right. I finally decided on a blue button-down and jeans. Casual, but not too casual. At least I didn't try on "outfits" like Chelsea. I just stared until I picked out a shirt. Probably would've taken the same length of time.

I drove to Mallory's faster than the law allowed. It was stupid, really. Nothing had been resolved between us, but it seemed like things were moving in the right direction. The memory of her brief kiss set my pulse into a dance that had nothing to do with any fucking arrhythmia. Unfortunately, Jason Carter answered the door after I knocked.

"Those for me?" he asked, pointing to the bouquet of daisies I'd brought for Mallory.

"Bend over and you can have them." I gritted my teeth through the smile. Mallory told me he was just a friend, but something about him set me on edge. Maybe it was the money. Or the fact that he could give Mallory everything she ever dreamed of *with* the money.

Carter laughed and slapped me on the shoulder, pulling me through the door. He was bigger in person than on TV, not that I was a slouch, but the guy had about twenty-five pounds of muscle on me. At least we were the same height.

"I like him, Rat," he said as Mallory stood in the small kitchen with her hands on her hips. Mickey wove between her feet. Carter turned back to me. "Heard you play ball. What position?"

"If you heard that much, I'm sure you know I'm in center." I shrugged his hand off my shoulder and strode up to Mallory.

Her smile could power the stars. "For me?"

"No, they're for Carter. I knew he'd probably be here." I loosened my grip, hoping I hadn't crushed the stems. They wouldn't stand right in a vase, and I'd look cheap. Lose-lose for me.

Carter's hand fell back on my shoulder, yanking me away from Mallory. "You got that right. I'll *always* be here."

"Stop it, Cutter," Mallory snapped. I'd seen that expression before. She was ready to break him in half. And I had a feeling that it was a pretty common occurrence with these two. She turned her gaze to me, and I swear I shrunk three inches beneath it. "You, too, Aaron."

"What'd I do?" I felt like a teenager called out for throwing a spitball in Chemistry. Okay, I had thrown the spitball, but that wasn't the point.

"Play nice." Her eyes darted to Jason. "Both of you."

Carter moved toward her and kissed her cheek. "Anything for you, Rat."

I clenched my fists, my jaw, hell even my ass puckered at the way he put his lips on her skin. I had to take my mind off it, so I focused on the second most annoying thing. "What's with the nicknames?"

Carter picked up the cat and held him like a football. Mickey purred as Jason scratched under his chin. "Oh, we've known each other forever. Mallory used to rat me out when I did something wrong."

"And I had a lisp when I was younger, so Carter sounded more like Cutter." Something altered in Mallory's voice. The sweet story made her sad. "Anyway, it just sort of stuck."

We stood in silence, eyeing one another. I didn't like how

Carter looked at Mallory one bit. Shifting to my left, I noticed the light glint off something behind the jackass. I glanced around him and nearly jizzed on myself.

In two steps, I stood in front of the World Series MVP trophy. It shone in the dim light of the kitchen; the large silver band spiraled toward the sky on small silver pillars. The black base was thicker than I imagined. Fingerprints marred the plaque that inscribed the honor.

"You can touch it," Carter said with a hint of amusement in his voice. He set Mickey on the couch. "I don't mind."

It dawned on me Carter wasn't just some guy after Mallory, and regardless of what she said, he had the hots for her, but he was a pro. I lifted the trophy like it was the Holy Grail. It was heavier than expected, which, for some dumbass reason, made me laugh.

That was the tension breaker. Mallory came up beside me and touched my arm. Heat surged along my skin through my chest. My breath got lost somewhere between the inhale and exhale.

She grinned, and a twinkle ricocheted in her eyes. I'd give anything to see her light up like that again. "I knew you'd like holding the trophy."

So that was the real reason she invited Carter over. The relief must have shown on my face. Jason took the trophy from my hands and placed it back on the table, rubbing the silver plaque with the hem of his T-shirt. He smiled, shaking his head as if he still couldn't believe that it was his. Turning to face us, he smiled. "Come on, let's talk baseball. Mallory says you've got what it takes. Is she bullshitting me?"

I followed him into the living room, sitting at the opposite end of the couch. Mallory brought a chair in from her small kitchen and sat near my end. Mickey jumped onto Jason's lap, curling into a ball and purring contentedly. At least he was happy. I couldn't stop staring at Mallory. She'd seen me play?

That was the only explanation for it. But when? Did she go to one game or more? And why would she lie about something like that?

"Mallory never misses a game, Betts." Carter answered my unasked questions. I glanced over as he dropped his arm over the back of the couch. He sneered as he lifted his eyebrows. "Didn't she tell you that?"

"Stop it, Jason," Mallory said.

I couldn't look at her for some reason. My feet were much more interesting; besides, I didn't want to see her expression. "You go to every game?"

"No, not every game." Mallory spoke like she was walking on glass.

"I don't get it. What's the problem?" Carter asked.

Mallory's feet edged closer to mine. "Right now, you are, Jason." She nudged my foot. "Are you okay?"

I shrugged. This was stupid. It shouldn't bother me that she'd seen me play. Hell, I should be thrilled she'd told Jason Carter that I had enough skill to make the big leagues. But, knowing what she'd said and how she'd reacted before, it felt like another betrayal. I'd walked around her feelings this entire time, while she couldn't be honest with me. I knew Mallory had held a lot of things back from me, but something as simple as going to a fucking baseball game?

Mallory's hand found mine, and she squeezed. As much as I loved her touch, I pulled away.

"Anyway," Carter said, dragging the word out like a knife to cut the tension. "Maybe we could hit the cages over the winter. I'd like to see this sweet swing you've got."

I turned toward him and forced a smile. "That'd be great."

For the next few hours, Jason and I went back and forth about the game. Mallory would interject with a few well-thought comments, but my hurt feelings wouldn't dissipate so easily, and I ignored her. I was being an ass and I knew it, but why would she lie about fucking baseball? It was almost midnight when Jason left. Any rivalry I felt was long gone once we started talking. Turned out he had a girl back in St. Louis he was pretty serious about. He just let the media continue to believe he was hung up on someone in Madison. We set up a time to hit the cages for later in the week. I had to admit, it would be pretty cool to swing with a pro.

Mallory closed the door and leaned against it, resting her head on the oak.

"I don't understand why you're mad at me," she said.

It took more strength than I thought I had not to scoop her into my arms so she'd feel better. "I don't understand why you lied to me."

"What're you…" She closed her eyes when she realized what I meant. The night I asked her to watch game one of the NLCS she'd said, "I don't watch baseball" loud and clear. "I… Aaron, I…"

Either she didn't know what to say or she didn't know how to say it. Maybe it was time she understood how patient I'd been. She already knew I loved her. Maybe she needed to know how long I've felt that way. I sat back on the couch and stared at the floor. "The first time I saw you in the library, I had a hard time paying attention because I was mesmerized by how smart and beautiful you are. You were very clear about your feelings for baseball players and the game in general. I thought if I gave you time, and if you got to know me, that might change. I figured I'd get to know you, too."

Mallory moved toward the other end of the couch. I watched her socked feet shuffle across the hardwood floor. She didn't say anything as the cushion gave to her slight weight.

"I never hid anything from you, Mallory, but you've kept almost everything from me." I swallowed the knot clogging my throat.

"I know."

"Do you?" I finally looked up to meet her gaze. Her eyes were dry, her expression like stone. I'd seen that look before and, after last night, I never thought I'd see it from her again. She came to me so I would know she wasn't with Jason. If she didn't have even one iota of feeling for me, she wouldn't have bothered. "Don't."

"Don't what?" she asked.

"Don't shut down on me because I'm not happy about something. Don't shut me out." I watched her stiffen. The rage had died inside me before Jason left, but the hurt hadn't faded. Knowing Mallory's skittish behavior, I kept my voice calm. It was a struggle, but I somehow managed. "You once said that you were trying to protect me. I don't think that's true. You're trying to prevent yourself from getting hurt again. I don't know who hurt you or why, but I'm not them. I'm not going anywhere."

"You're not leaving?" Uncertainty tainted her soft voice.

Shaking my head, I said, "Not unless you want me to. And I hope you don't want me to."

Mallory's stone facade crumbled like the walls of Jericho. She leaped across the couch, landing in my arms. God, I loved being her comfort.

"I know that you need time, love. I get that, but please don't lie to me." The image of my parents popped into my head. All these years, how much of that was a lie? And what about yesterday? Lying by omission was just as bad, wasn't it? "That's all I ask."

Mallory nodded against my shirt and said, "Mom and Dad are gone. Grandma left me. Jason left. Amie left. And D—" She paused and added, "Everyone I love leaves me."

"I'm not going anywhere." I kissed the top of her head, wishing she'd tell me more and knowing she told me a lot. "This is where I want to be. Right here with you."

We stayed like that for a while, neither one talking. I rocked her in my arms until she shoved me away.

"I'm sorry. I shouldn't…" She put a pillow's distance between us. "I'm not…"

I lifted my hand to brush away a wayward curl but let it fall to my knee when I saw the panic in her eyes. "I get it." My mouth crooked in a half smile. "I'm a patient man."

Her shoulders didn't relax, and she didn't smile. It wasn't giving me the warm and fuzzies.

"What?" I asked. No reason to hold back now. I'd laid it all on the line for this girl. It was up to her. She'd made strides, but something stopped her every single time we came close to this amazing thing we could have. Maybe I was fooling myself, but I didn't believe that.

"What if…" She closed her eyes. When they opened, her emotions flowed like swirls of light in her irises. "What if I'm never ready for anything more than what we have now?"

That may have been the question she asked, but it wasn't the one she meant. If I'd learned anything from Chuck over the last few years, it was to read between the lines. "And what if you are? Do you really want to give up before trying?"

She shook her head.

"Like I said, love, I'm a patient man." My voice remained steady as my swing, but my nerves shattered inside. She was going to close herself off again.

"I don't let many people in. You know that already," she finally said. Her eyes were directed to the rug, and she shifted from her left foot to her right, pausing before shifting back. "Nobody knows as much about me as you, and that scares me."

"Carter knows you." I tried to keep the jealousy out of my voice but failed miserably. Mallory shook her head, and I knew in my heart there wasn't anything but friendship between them. It didn't stop the ugly green monster from rearing its head and baring its fangs.

"He knows about me. But he doesn't know the little things, like you do."

"Like how you don't blurt out an answer because you need to think about all the angles." She nodded and I continued. "Like how you hum under your breath when you're reading or how your handwriting changes based on your mood. Like how you suck in your lower lip when you're concentrating."

Mallory swallowed and raised her head. "Just because he's known me my whole life doesn't mean he knows who I am anymore. He's been gone for a long time." She closed her eyes and kept them closed as she let the words out. "Jason was my brother's best friend. I…I had a brother. He died when my parents were killed."

I stood and walked toward her. Mallory was as tense as a lion on the verge of pouncing. I held out my hand. She had to make this choice. She had to decide if she wanted my arms around her. I couldn't do it for her. It took longer than I expected, but she reached for me and slid her hand in mine.

I didn't say anything. There wasn't anything *to* say. My family was far from perfect, especially with the recent revelations, but we stuck together. Knowing Mallory had to go through losing hers when she was only fourteen, knowing she'd finally opened the door and let me in, knowing she was willing, it healed me. It healed us.

"If I could make it better…but I can't," I said. It seemed like a stupid thing to say, but it needed to be said. "If I could…"

She tried to smile, but it fell the minute it hit her face. "Jason was there. So was Amie. They were the only ones who stuck by me."

"How so?" Squeezing her fingers, I lifted my other hand to wipe the tears from her cheeks.

"I lost everything. The house was sold for restitution. The cars, the furniture. Everything was gone." She leaned against my palm as her voice hitched on her words. "Grandma took me in. I had nowhere else to go." Her voice dropped to a breath. "And I'm terrified it will happen again. It's easier to be alone. Nobody can hurt me when I'm alone."

Restitution? I thought the accident wasn't their fault? My heart broke for her. I couldn't change her past as much as I wanted to, but I could promise her a future. I opened my mouth to do just that when she continued.

"You…God, Aaron, losing you would…. I can't stand…" She let go of my hand and rubbed her face, muffling her words. Pursing her lips, she stood and began pacing the living room. "I know I've pushed you away. I know how frustrating it must be, and I'm sorry. There's so much…darkness behind me. I don't want to talk about it. I don't want to remember it, because sometimes that's all I do. I lie in bed at night and relive getting the news. Then the reality of what happened. It's been seven years since this all started, but it feels like yesterday."

She backed away from me until her shoulders hit the door. I didn't follow her.

"I can't go through that again."

Nodding, I crossed my arms. "Okay. I get that."

"You do?"

"Yeah, I understand why you're scared." I dropped my arms and stood, walking over to her. She pressed herself against the door, but there wasn't anywhere for her to go. No escape. "But you're not living. You're surviving. You're getting through each day in one barely held together piece. Then you relive everything that happened as if you're still fourteen."

"You don't—"

"Know everything. Yeah, I get that, too." I pressed my forehead to hers. My hands found her hips and pulled her against me. We fit so well together, so perfectly. I needed to remind her of how that felt. The time for words was over. I wrapped my arms around her and kissed her gently.

She melted against me. That's when I knew it would be okay. Everything was going to be perfect.

I pulled away from her. "I don't want bits of you. I want all of you, darkness included."

"You know how I…" Her voice hitched and she inhaled deeply before continuing. Her fingers curled around the locket she hadn't taken off since I'd met her. "My brother… His name was Danny."

I squeezed her against me but kept my mouth shut. A little bubble of joy filled my chest. Not that her family had died, but because she wasn't holding back. Everything she'd hidden was going to get laid out in front of me. Finally, Mallory trusted me. It was a fragile gift.

"Dad coached Danny's high school baseball team. They loved it more than anything. Every chance they got, they'd go to a game somewhere. They were on their way back from a baseball game in Iowa City. Dad was stopped on a two-lane road to make a left when a tractor-trailer rear-ended the car. They spun into the other lane and were hit by a truck." With each word her voice grew softer. "Baseball always came first."

"I am so sorry." I kissed her forehead and waited patiently for her to continue. The floodgates had opened. And I knew there was no way that was all there was to the story. Baseball had always been first. No wonder she hated it.

"Mom and Dad… They said they died on impact. Danny died on the way to the hospital." She turned her face into my chest, and I could feel the tears sliding from her cheeks onto my shirt. "They were organ donors, so the doctors ran some standard tests. Danny had unusually high levels of testosterone. Grandma found needles in his room. They weren't really hidden, either. Just in a drawer by his bed."

Panic welled in my chest, but I fought to keep my breathing even. She could never find out. Never. Thank God,

I'd stopped taking that shit. *She'd never forgive me.*

"It didn't take long before other members of the team came forward about using. Dad had been drugging some of the guys for years. Cutter and a handful of others hadn't taken anything, but they knew what was going on."

I searched my memory, but nothing came to mind about a Coach Fine drugging his players. Then it hit me over the head like a sledgehammer. "Your last name isn't Fine, is it?"

Mallory shook her head. "It's Verbach."

The story made the national news. Coach Henry Verbach provided HGH and anabolic steroids to his team, drugging them into state champions. His only son had been ranked as the best player in the state of Iowa. He was supposed to go in the first round of the draft, but the accident happened. That's when the truth came out. The other players came forward. Including Jason Carter.

The second sledgehammer shattered my chest. Carter's tattoo 23V32. "Game seven. You were upset. Was that because—?"

She nodded. "Their numbers. Dad was 23. Danny 32. Jason thought he honored them with that, but he shouldn't have done it. They didn't deserve it."

I wrapped both arms around Mallory. How could anybody do that to their kid? I didn't realize the story was going to get worse.

"It started Danny's freshman year when he just missed the top fifty Iowa players list. Dad started him on supplements, and it went from there." Mallory put her hand on my chest and slid it up to my neck. "He was a great player. He didn't need to do any of it to get drafted. I…don't understand why he did it. And I'll never get the chance to ask him."

My eyes shut tight, wanting desperately to not hear this and knowing I had to.

"Did I ever tell you how jealous I am of you and Chelsea?"

Mallory lifted her head and met my gaze. "You guys are best friends and love each other. With Danny, it felt like every day of my life was a competition. Dad did everything for him, but he… I don't think he ever came to a softball game. Mom tried, but more often than not she'd end up going to watch Danny."

I tried to keep the fear out of my eyes.

Mallory's sad smile broke my heart even more. "Now do you understand why I have issues with baseball?"

Reluctantly, I nodded. What her father did, he did for the love of the game. He did it for baseball. Just like I did. God, she could never find out. It would destroy her. Had I known, I never would've touched the stuff. I shouldn't have to begin with, but I did. I couldn't change that. The only thing I could do was keep this one little secret from her.

After months of trying to get her to share her secrets, I had one of my own. One I could never, ever share.

Chapter Nineteen

I spent most of Sunday morning finishing up the stupid history assignment and thinking about anything other than the steroids and what it would mean if Mallory found out. At least the paper gave me something to focus on. By two in the afternoon, it was a solid B paper in any other class. That meant it'd net me a low C in Monroe's. I stood to stretch my muscles, my knee cracking as I bent the stiffness out of it. It felt like the bones were grinding against one another. While it wasn't painful, it wasn't exactly pleasant, either. I opened the drawer for ibuprofen and the supplements Seth had given me, popping two of each.

Grabbing my phone from my desk, I texted Mallory.

Paper's done. Do you want me to email it to you?

Less than a minute later, my phone vibrated.

No. Let's go over it together. I'm working until six. Come over around six-thirty? We can order Chinese.

Me: *A girl after my own heart.*

Mallory: *If all it takes is Moo Goo Gai Pan, you're pretty easy.*

Me: *Kung Pao Chicken.*

Mallory: *LOL. I'll order that, too.*

See you then.

My smile grew as I thumbed in each letter. It would've been easier to email it to her, but she wanted me to come over. Maybe things weren't as circular as I thought.

I stared at my disaster of a room. It wasn't just a mess, it was a disorganized mess. That wasn't going to cut it anymore. For the next hour, I cleaned and put everything in its place. Even things that never really had a place found a place. The energy surging through me was an adrenaline high. I had to keep moving. Glancing at the clock, I knew hardly anybody else was back on campus yet. Well, except the freshmen, and they didn't count.

Heading to the gym was my best option. I'd just have to take it slow on my legs. My workouts were closely monitored. I had to take it easy, rebuild strength in my knee. I wasn't even supposed to run on the treadmill until after the first of the year. Not that I'd followed that directive. I put on my Westland baseball T-shirt and cutoff sweats, grabbed my bag, and headed out the door.

The weight room and gym weren't far from my dorm, so I didn't think twice about wearing workout clothes. The cold November air bit at my bare skin but didn't really penetrate. I didn't feel anything but the need to move. The treadmills called my name. I dropped my bag and climbed onto the machine, setting it at a casual walk. But it wasn't enough. Before I'd gone a half a mile, I turned up the speed until I jogged. My knee groaned under the pressure, but it didn't break. I felt strong again, stronger than I had in a long time. I turned it faster, then faster still until I sprinted on the conveyor. Three miles felt like one.

Then my knee buckled.

It was like a lightning strike that started in my knee and shot up my thigh into my groin and down my leg until my toes cramped into a curled position. I caught the handrail before I fell and things were worse, yanking the key from the panel. Easing myself off the conveyor, I hobbled to the nearest seated machine, thankful for the safety shutoffs and for engaging it. Normally I didn't bother.

My heartbeat found a new home in my knee. It beat just beneath the patella, shooting pain through my thigh and calf in a rhythm. Fucking hell. Why did I push it? My teeth churned against one another. The more I tried to not think about it, the more it hurt. The more it ballooned. It didn't help that each breath made my chest tighten. My vision blurred as the room swayed.

"Fuck!" I screamed as loud as I could. There was no way I'd play this spring. Not unless some miracle happened. I fell back on the bench and stared at the holes in the ceiling.

I stayed like that until the throbbing subsided and my vision returned to normal. I should've gone to the ER, but I didn't want to face the doc I'd skipped out on. The shitty fluorescent lights bounced off the barbell above my head. That's what I needed. Take my mind off the knee by lifting. I glanced at the weights on the end. Two fifties, and maybe a twenty-five I couldn't see on the end. Nothing more than a hundred fifty. I could do that with one hand.

Sliding up the bench, my knee stretched, shooting another round of hell in every direction of my leg. I reached up and gripped the barbell, lifting it easily. Thank God, I'd kept the upper body workout going after my injury. I did five reps, rested, then did ten, rinse, repeat, until I had lifted fifty reps in a row. My arms felt like cooked spaghetti, but my knee wasn't throbbing like a drum line anymore. The surge of excessive energy was long gone, and a hint of exhaustion sizzled in my bones. The clock on my phone read four thirty. Just the right amount of time to head back to the dorm, shower, and nap before going to Mallory's.

I knocked on the door at six forty. I must've hit snooze on my alarm and overslept by twenty minutes. My knee had swollen up into a volleyball. An ice pack for ten minutes helped. I hated wearing the damn brace but didn't have a whole lot of other options. The amount of ibuprofen coursing through my blood would knock out a lesser man. I tugged on my shorts, wishing I could've worn jeans, but they didn't fit over the brace.

Mallory opened the door, her eyes widening as soon as they fell on my knee. "What happened?"

I shrugged like it wasn't the big deal it was. "Pushed it too hard. Coach's gonna kick my butt."

She stepped out of the door and let me in. I hobbled into the house, noting nothing romantic had been set up. Part of me had hoped, not that I could do anything at the moment anyway. I half fell, half sat on her couch, stretching my leg out along the length of the sofa. Mickey jumped onto the arm behind my head and rubbed against me. I scratched him under his chin, his purr ricocheting in my ear. It was the first time he'd let me near him. Guess he decided I wasn't that bad after all.

She pushed her books out of the way and sat on the edge of the coffee table. Her eyes glanced toward the brace before settling back on my face. "How?"

Suddenly, I didn't want to tell her. Anger boiled inside me with that simple question. I didn't understand why, but I didn't want her to know what a failure I was. "It doesn't matter. Can you drop it?"

She moved back as if I'd slapped her.

I closed my eyes and let my head fall back against the arm, sending Mickey onto the floor. "I'm sorry. You didn't…" I wanted to say she didn't deserve it, but didn't she? I don't tell her one little thing and I'm the bad guy. How I hurt my knee was insignificant to the shit she held back from me. She had no reason to stare at me like that.

"No, it's okay. If you…" Her voice hitched and I opened my eyes. She tried to smile, but it didn't last even a second. Why did I do that to her?

"I ran on the treadmill," I blurted out. The anger drained from me. I hated making her unhappy. I hated how much it pissed me off that I was the cause of her misery. I hated myself for caving. There were so many things I hated at the moment, I couldn't remember anything I didn't despise on epic levels.

Coming here was a mistake.

"Oh. I thought you weren't supposed to run until after Christmas." She stood and moved toward the kitchen.

"Yeah, well, I did, and it screwed up my knee." The smell of tomato sauce, garlic, and oregano filled my nose. My stomach rumbled like a lion warning the others to stay the fuck away. "What happened to the Chinese?"

She didn't say anything, but I heard her in the kitchen banging some pots around. Her voice was tighter than I'd ever heard it. "They closed early today. Did you bring the paper?"

"Shit. I forgot." I forced myself to my feet and moved around the couch toward the kitchen. Mallory stood at the stove, stirring the sauce. The steam swirled in the air until it reached her face. She inhaled, and I remembered why I was really here. For her. Anything for her. I hobbled toward her, wrapping my arms around her waist and burying my nose in her hair. "I'm sorry. I don't know why I snapped at you. This injury's been a curse and a blessing. Sometimes I don't know which is worse."

She stopped stirring but wouldn't look at me. "A blessing?"

"Yeah, a blessing because I met you." I pressed a kiss onto her neck. Her entire body stiffened under my touch. I let go, giving her the room I knew she needed. But it was fucking hard.

"I feel more like your curse," Mallory said. She pulled the spaghetti off the stove and turned to the sink to drain the water. "I thought…I thought it would be nice to make dinner instead. I hope that's okay?"

"It's perfect." My temper waited in the wings, ready to flare again. I couldn't give it a reason to. So what if she changed her mind for dinner? Spaghetti was one of my favorites, anyway.

We ate in silence. I kept replaying my attitude problem. She hadn't done anything to set me off, yet I was so pissed. It bothered me how many secrets she had, yeah, but she shared so much lately. And I had to hide this stupid thing I did. There was no way I could've predicted how much doping would affect Mallory. Who was I pissed at more: myself or her?

Mallory took my plate, and I stretched out on the couch again. I had no clue what to say to break the tension between us, a tension I'd caused. When she came back to the living room, she sat on the couch and put an ice pack over my knee.

"For the swelling," she said.

"Thank you." I wanted to pull her toward me, hold her until she knew I was sorry for being such a dick. I didn't.

Mallory adjusted the ice pack until she was satisfied and moved away from me, careful not to touch my leg. "Are you sure you're okay?"

"I don't know." I reached out and took her hand. "I…I've done nothing but dream of playing pro ball since I can remember. It's just hard to think that's slipping away. I want to be back to my old self."

Mallory squeezed my fingers. "You will be. But you have to give it time. Jason hurt his knee in high school and missed his sophomore year." She scooted closer to me. "He reinjured it by pushing too hard. If he had followed doctor's orders, he might have played later that season. Instead he had to wait until the next year. Be patient, and you'll get better."

If I had to hear another word about Jason Carter, my head was going to explode. If he was so fucking perfect, why didn't she just move in with him? Anger surged through me again. It wasn't rational. I knew that she didn't want anything more than friendship with Carter. I knew she was letting me in. I knew there was more between us, but I couldn't stop. I wanted to burn the fucking world.

"I should go." I stood and limped toward the door. Over my shoulder, I added, "I'll see you later."

"Aaron, wait," Mallory said as I pulled open the door.

The cold air didn't cool me off. My skin burned. My hands shook as I waited for her.

"Will you just come back in?" Mallory said. "Something's bothering you and…I just wish you'd tell me what's going on."

I barked out a laugh. "Guess you know how it feels now."

"Okay," she said, crossing her arms and shivering. "I deserve that. Just come back in. Please."

I stared at her beautiful face for a moment and saw how much I'd hurt her. It tore at me. I reached for her, but she stepped back out of my reach. I walked into the house, hanging my jacket on the coatrack.

She followed me to the couch, sitting on the opposite end. Mickey leaped onto the middle cushion. I put my foot on the coffee table and reached for the cat. Just as Mallory did the same. My hand covered hers. I squeezed it gently.

"I'm sorry." We continued to pet the cat together. "I've

been busting my ass on the paper, and I needed to burn off this surge of energy, so I went to the gym to lift. I guess I've been sitting on my ass too long. I got on the treadmill to walk, then pushed too far. Damn it." I rubbed my temples. "I'm pissed at myself for being a dumbass. I shouldn't have taken it out on you. You didn't deserve it."

"If…" She inhaled and exhaled slowly. "If we're going to be in a relationship, we both have to talk." She turned toward me, lifting Mickey out of the way and onto the back of the couch. He meowed and swatted at my head before jumping down. "I know I'm the worst at it, but I'm trying here. Please don't shut me out now."

This time when I reached for her she met me halfway. "We're in a relationship?"

Mallory slapped my chest, but a small smile curved across her face.

"I just wanted to hear you say it again."

She didn't. She kissed me instead.

Chapter Twenty

School kicked into high gear after the break. Mallory canceled our sessions for the week. She had a couple of freshmen on the verge of nervous breakdowns, so that killed the weekend, too. We ate lunch together when our schedules allowed it, but there weren't enough lunches or moments.

Sunday evening, we ate at the student union. Mallory video chatted with her grandmother about Aunt Chrissy, who had taken a turn for the worse over the holiday. Grandma wouldn't be home for Christmas, and it was too late for Mallory to find an affordable flight to Arizona.

"You okay?" I asked as I nibbled on a salad. It was a preemptive strike against my diet. I'd let myself eat too many greasy burgers and fries without enough exercise to stop any weight gain. Not that it was much, but it needed to come off.

Mallory shrugged and stabbed at her own lettuce. "It's not a big deal. We haven't spent Christmas together since she went to Arizona when I first started at Westland."

"Come home with me." The words shot out of my mouth without any thought, but I didn't regret them. It was perfect.

"You're not serious." Mallory stared at me, her fork halfway between her plate and her mouth.

"Yeah," I said, setting my fork down and taking her hand. "Why not? It's perfect. You can meet my parents, my sister. We can spend the holiday together."

"I don't know, Aaron." Mallory pulled her hand from underneath mine. "Can I think about it?"

Talk about an ego deflater, but I didn't balk. "Sure. No problem."

Mallory closed her eyes. "I'm sorry. I'm not trying to push you away again. I promise, but I just…this is a huge step."

It was. I should've realized that, but I didn't. So I did what I did best when it came to Mallory, I changed the subject. "Oh, I can't make it to the library tomorrow afternoon. Carter wants to hit the cages."

"No problem." Her alarm buzzed on her cell. Our brief lunch was up. Mallory grabbed her bag and kissed my cheek. "I'll call you later."

Monday morning, Coach called me into the locker room along with ten other guys. We stood in line to pee in a cup. Random drug testing had begun. For a moment, I almost panicked. Almost. It had been well over a week since I took anything. I was safe. No way I'd fail.

Seth came out of the stall. He raised an eyebrow at me as I took a cup.

"Relax," I whispered.

Seth nodded once as he passed by. Nothing to worry about.

Jason showed up on campus discreetly hidden under a Westland cap and sweatshirt. I met him at the parking lot of the training center. Anybody who glanced at him probably thought he was just another grad student. Until he showed up at the indoor cages. Everyone knew who he was then. Fortunately, I'd asked Coach to close the cages for exactly that reason.

"Hey, Carter, great series!" Rosenthal sidled up to him with three balls.

I shoved him out of the way. "Beat it, rookie." Jason glanced at him, and I smiled. "He's the reason I'm on the DL."

Carter shook his head and signed balls while fielding questions for ten minutes before Coach finally freed us from the masses. I had to admit being in his limelight wasn't a bad thing. Rosenthal weaseled his way back in, and I didn't kick him out. Jason Carter was everyone's hero these days. The rookie interrogated me on how I knew Carter and why I'd never shared that particular secret. I shrugged it off, but Jason told him we had a mutual friend. Neither one of us mentioned Mallory. Chuck and Seth stared at me with deadpan expressions. I knew what they were thinking, they'd get me drunk enough I'd tell them how I met the pro. I made a mental note not to drink with them anytime soon.

"All right, stud, show me this swing I've heard so much about." Carter leaned against the protective fence with a smirk.

"Stud, huh? Guess my reputation precedes me." I tugged on my batting gloves before stepping into the cages. My knee was wrapped tight under the brace. I had popped enough aspirin to kill a normal human. They only dulled the pain. I mentally thanked Seth for the supplements. I'd taken two after lunch, and it was like power surging through me. Even though I knew it was psychosomatic, it felt good to be strong again. Supplements can't make you feel like Superman. I double-checked the label to see what was in them. There was more B-12 than the body needed, but that was it.

"You better not have a reputation outside the field." Carter's voice darkened, and I turned before starting the machine. "Mallory means a lot to me, Betts."

I nodded but didn't respond. My gut tightened, and

anger raged through me like a volcano ready to blow. He had no reason to say that. Mallory wasn't his sister. She wasn't anything other than an old family friend. I reached out and turned the key, setting the speed at seventy-five to warm up. Hitting balls, that's what I needed to ease the fury swirling inside me.

My grip tightened around the bat as I took my stance.

"Relax, Aaron. You're too tense," Carter said behind me.

That arrogant asshole. Just because he played pro ball didn't mean he knew my stance.

The first ball lobbed in toward me, and I swung off-balance, fouling it back. The constant dull throb in my knee picked up the tempo. All that did was make me angrier. I'd barely gotten myself reset when the next ball flew toward the painted-on plate. I kept my head down and made solid contact.

"Nice," Carter said, following up with a whistle.

I gritted my teeth. To hell with his approval. My swing felt natural and smooth, except for the sharp pain growing in my knee. After ten swings, the throbbing was too much. I did my best to keep it off my face as I pushed open the door and exited the cage. At least my anger had disappeared.

"Mallory's right. You've got skill." Carter glanced down at my brace, then back up to my face. "Knee still bugging you?"

"Little. Tweaked it last Friday." I crossed my arms and dug my fingers into my ribs. Tweaked my ass. The fucker hurt worse than it did after the surgery.

"Just don't do some anything stupid." Carter didn't say anything else about my knee after he stepped into the cages. He took ten swings, letting his arms extend and his hips rotate in a smooth motion. I watched his form, studying the little details. His right foot pivoted on the heel only a fraction. He led with his hips, letting them decide where the ball was going. I hated to admit it, but Carter's technique was damn near perfect.

Bastard.

"She likes you, Betts," he said as he swung over a ball, sending it bouncing along the concrete floor. "Mallory keeps herself closed off from the world, but she's let you in."

I smiled. "A little bit, anyway."

He reached over to the machine and turned it off. "More than anybody else I've met. And I haven't met that many."

"You live in St. Louis. How many could you meet?" I pulled off my batting gloves. There wasn't a reason to leave them on. My swings were done.

"Yeah, maybe, but I'm home over the winters. I've met her ex-boyfriends. Not to mention Amie. That girl is... Let's just say she's Mallory's opposite." Jason left the cage and stared at where I'd dropped my gloves. "Mallory prefers to spend her time alone. For some dumbass reason, she doesn't mind you."

I huffed a laugh.

He leaned against his bat and stared at me. "How much do you know about her?"

Probably less than you. I kept that retort to myself, but it deflated me. "She told me about her parents, about her brother."

His eyes closed, and he rubbed his hand over the tattoo on his forearm. "Shit."

"What?"

"You know Faust?" He scratched his chin as he waited for my answer. I didn't have one. "Okay, not an English lit type of guy, I'm guessing."

"Yeah, not so much." My knee throbbed a lonely beat, and I had to sit on the bench nearby. "What's that got to do with Mallory?"

Carter sat beside me and stared off into space. "Mallory's the victim of a Faustian situation."

I tried to figure out what exactly he meant, but it didn't

make a lick of sense. "That tells me nothing, Jason."

He laughed and slapped my shoulder. "Her dad sold out his entire family to make Danny the best. He sold his soul to the devil, so to speak. When the devil came calling, he took more than Coach V. And Mallory's left to deal with it." He waited until I met his gaze. "Just do me a favor, Betts. Don't think her weak. Mallory's the strongest person I've ever known."

I didn't have a response, so I nodded. Of course Mallory was strong. She was a fucking mountain.

"And don't hurt her." He squeezed my shoulder. "She's not a risk-taker, but she's taking one by letting you in. If you do something stupid to screw this up, it could hurt her more than you realize."

Too fucking late. I faked a chuckle. "Seriously? I'm bound to do something stupid. I'm a guy."

"True. Anna's quick to point out my faults whenever possible. Says it keeps my ego in check." Carter grinned when he mentioned his girlfriend's name.

"I won't do anything to hurt her intentionally." I let the sincerity seep into each word. Doping wasn't intended to hurt her. Just heal me. Guilt sat in my stomach. "Believe me on that."

Jason nodded and rolled his shoulders. "Okay." He nodded again. "Okay. Enough of this sissy bonding bullshit. Let's hit some more balls. You up for it?"

I wasn't, but the competitor in me wouldn't let this go without a tiny fight. Even if it was one I would lose. "Yeah."

Carter took the cage first, and I watched as he trashed the balls. Mallory said I had a sweet swing, but it was nowhere near where this guy hit. I could learn from him. Maybe a scout would give me a second glance despite my knee. The roar of the crowd, standing at home plate for my first pro at-bat, the fit of the uniform.

Maybe this dream could become reality.

I smiled, and didn't stop until I fell asleep later that night.

Chapter Twenty-One

Finals made it hard to do anything but study. During the history final, Dr. Monroe slipped me a note requesting my presence in his office later in the afternoon. Finishing the test was damn near impossible, but I did it with time to spare. Instead of handing it in right away and bolting, my usual MO, I took Mallory's advice and reviewed a few of the harder questions. My mind refused to remember when Nixon resigned, and I doubted it was 1963.

I handed in my test, getting the stink eye from the good prof, and strolled out of the room knowing I had a passing grade on the final, even if it was a barely passing grade. My paper was another story. I pulled my phone out of my pocket and texted Mallory.

Monroe wants to see me.

She didn't respond, so I decided the best thing to do was get a late lunch and pretend the appointment didn't exist. The student union was empty except for a few people huddled over their books and laptops at individual tables. I had a Business Ethics final the next day, then my semester was over.

I sat at the usual spot with a plate full of fries and a burger so greasy it soaked the bun. A celebratory piece of perfection. Mixing the ketchup and mayo on my plate with an extra long fry, I lost my thoughts in the red and white swirls turning pink.

Regardless of whether or not I passed history, the semester was over. It was a huge relief.

"Where's your girlfriend?" Trish's voice rubbed against me like a cheese grater.

I shook my head and kept swirling the fry in the ketchup/mayo mix. Maybe if I ignored her long enough, she'd go away. Trish and I had shared so much, but I didn't know this girl sitting across from me. Her makeup was too heavy, her clothes too tight, and her eyes too dull. The Trish I knew barely wore makeup, dressed conservatively, and her eyes were bright lights on a dark night.

"Look, I know things are…tense between us, but I was hoping we could ride back home together." She drummed her nails against the table, each beat making my food less appetizing. "Daddy would appreciate not having to drive to get me."

"What's wrong with your car?" I slapped my hands together to get the salt off my fingertips.

Trish slumped in her seat, looking more worn down than I'd ever seen her. "Stupid thing's in the shop again. You'd think after all the recalls I'd have a completely new car by now."

A small chuckle escaped. Her father bought her a brand-new car when we left for college. It was a first model year, so it had a ton of recalls over the last three years.

"So, what do you say? Can I hitch a ride?" Her fake charming smile wasn't going to work on me, but her father was a good man.

"Maybe."

"Need the girlfriend's permission first?" She pinched her

nose. "Sorry."

"S'kay. But, yeah, out of respect for Mallory's feelings, I should clear it with her." I grabbed my tray and headed toward the trash. Half of the burger had gone cold, and my appetite had disappeared along with the heat. I shoved the tray into the trash, shaking the wasted food free.

"You're kidding, right?" Her shock made me smile.

"Nope." I set the tray on top of the trashcan. Mallory entered the student union just then. I waved her over with a smile.

"I'm sorry. I... That was uncalled for." Trish's gazed darted to Mallory. "Dad would appreciate it if you'd help him out."

Mallory stopped beside me and I put my arm over her shoulder. "Yeah, okay. As long as Mallory's cool with it, I'll take you home."

Trish turned her wide eyes toward Mallory. My girlfriend glanced at me, confusion covering her face.

"Yeah, sure. I guess," Mallory said, her gaze steady on me. "He's going that way anyway."

"Thank you," Trish said. She squeezed Mallory's arm. "I really appreciate it. And so will Dad."

Mallory waited until Trish was long out of earshot before rounding on me. "What was that?"

"What? I wasn't going to say yes unless you were okay with it," I said.

Mallory shook her head. "That wasn't fair. You never should've put me in that position. You're old enough to make your own decisions. It was...whatever. It's done." She glanced at her watch. "Don't you have to get to Monroe's office?"

I grabbed her wrist and checked the time. It was ten till. "Shit. Yes. And I'm sorry. I thought... I didn't want to piss you off by saying yes to her, but I did it anyway." I kissed Mallory's forehead. "I *am* sorry."

Mallory nodded, but a haunted look filled her eyes. I'd

have to make this one up to her big time.

I knocked on Dr. Monroe's door at four sharp. The man hated it when people were tardy for class; I could only imagine how pissed he'd be if someone he'd summoned was late.

"Enter," he ordered.

I pushed the door open and stepped into an office the size of a walk-in closet and filled from floor to ceiling with books. Some were old and others had shiny new covers. Monroe sat behind his desk with his head down and a pencil in his hand. He scribbled something onto the blue book flattened on his coffee-stained calendar. Even from the door, I could see all the red ink splashed like blood over that single page. I prayed it wasn't mine.

"Sit." He pointed to the lone empty chair in front of his desk. The one beside it was filled with dusty volumes of worn leather books.

I eased into the hard wooden seat, and my mind shifted from the problem before me to Mallory. She'd love this office with all the historical texts and the musty smell of old books. For a moment, I could imagine her sitting across from me.

Dr. Monroe looked up from his grading and glared. He tilted his head to the left, then to the right. "Mr. Betts, I must admit your paper was impressive." He reached down behind the desk and lifted a leather messenger bag onto his lap. I waited while he dug around and found my now crumpled paper. He set it on his desk, smoothing out the pages. "Now, when I first read this, I concluded someone else must have written it for you." I opened my mouth to protest, but he held his finger to shut me up. "In fact, I'd held onto the notion until you turned in your final. Surprise is not quite the right word, but it will have to do in this case." He slid the test back to me and dropped my paper on top.

I reached for them, half afraid of what I'd find. In the upper left side of the paper was a scratched out *F*, beside it was an *A*. I shuffled the final to the top and opened the bluebook to find a *B*. My grin made my cheeks ache.

"Based on the style of your test, you wrote that paper, Mr. Betts. While I'm not 100 percent certain it deserved the *A*, your work ethic shows a clear academic progression. Hiring Miss Fine as a tutor was probably one of your wisest decisions." Dr. Monroe slapped the worn vinyl arms of his chair as he leaned back. The squeak sent a shudder down my spine. "History is to be learned from as well as to learn. It is not common knowledge on this campus, but I believe this is something you should know."

I felt a long story coming on and extended my legs in front of me. The tightness in my muscles welcomed the stretch.

"When I was your age, I played triple-A baseball."

"Seriously?" The question shot from my mouth like an aboriginal dart.

"Yes, quite seriously. About a week before Labor Day, I got the call." His eyes glazed over as he went back to that time. "Being there was a dream come true. The lights of Fulton County Stadium were never brighter. I stayed with the team for three days, never making it out of the bullpen, before I was sent back to the minors."

"Wow. I never…" Even the idea that this man played pro ball struck me as incredible. Looking at him now, I could see only the snooty old professor.

Dr. Monroe smiled, something else I never expected. "Most people wouldn't guess. I blew out my elbow before the season was over and that ended my career." Monroe sat up and leaned forward, resting his elbows on the desk. "My point is you already know your body is fragile, Aaron. At any moment, your baseball career could end. Just be prepared for the moment it does, and you'll be fine."

"Do you think…do you think I can make it out of the minors? Can I get to the Show?"

"Yes." He smiled even brighter. "I've never missed a game, and you're better than you realize. You have doubts?"

I shrugged. "Yeah. I mean a lot of guys toil away for decades in AAA. The chance to play in the Majors is slim. I'd do anything to get there."

"Sounds logical." Monroe nodded. "But sometimes life requires us to be illogical. You've got the skills. You just need the same determination you used to get the grade you earned. But you must be prepared if you don't make it. And you're right. The percentage of guys who do against guys who don't…" Monroe tapped the table. "Now, if you don't mind, I've got more finals to grade. Good luck, Mr. Betts."

"Thank you, sir."

I hurried out of his tiny office and closed the door quietly behind me. The fresh scent of disinfectant washed away the musty books from Monroe's world. I replayed the conversation in my mind as I left the building and headed back toward the dorms. It was almost four thirty when my stomach growled. The too-greasy burger had stolen my appetite, but it was back tenfold. As soon as I got to my room, I grabbed a protein bar from my desk and a bottle of water from the fridge. My phone vibrated in my pocket as I finished the last chug of water.

What did Monroe want?

I read the text after fishing my phone out.

You're fired.

I smiled as I hit send, knowing she'd take it the wrong way.

What? Don't tell me you failed.

How about I tell you over dinner?

Sure. What time do you want to come over?

I almost typed "now" but thought better of it. I didn't want to celebrate passing my hardest class at Mallory's house.

I'll pick you up in thirty. We'll go out.

It took her several minutes to respond, but when she did, I wasn't sure what was going on.

Like a real date?

I smiled.

We've never actually had a real date, so yeah.

At least tell me where we're going so I know how to dress.

The best place for a romantic meal to celebrate our success was Peking Palace. But she might prefer something low-key like O'Malley's.

Wear whatever you want to define our plans. Then I'll pick a place.

We were celebrating in style tonight.

Chapter Twenty-Two

My knuckles barely touched her door before she pulled it open. Most of Mallory's hair was pinned back with wisps of curls escaping her hair tie and framing her angelic face. A light pink gloss covered her lips, making me want to spend the evening worshipping them. My mouth fell open. When I glanced down at her clothes, my heart sunk. She had on a pink sweater I'd seen before and jeans. Definitely not celebrating in style.

I, on the other hand, was wearing a black shirt with varying sized white and gray pinstripes Chelsea bought me before school started. I didn't think I'd ever have a reason to wear it, so I stuck it in the back of my closet until tonight. My black cowboy boots shined after a good scrub that almost made me late.

"Ready?" I asked, trying not to let my disappointment show. It shouldn't bother me, but Mallory and I had never had a real date. Classes, her jobs, my training, finals, and other shit kept getting in our way.

"Where're we going?" Mallory locked her door and

pulled her black peacoat tighter around her waist.

"O'Malley's. Is that okay?"

She waited until we were in the truck before answering. I fired up the engine, the heater kicking it into full gear. Mallory rubbed her hands together in front of the vent.

"O'Malley's sounds fine," she said.

If it wasn't for the cold air, I would've thought she'd answered through gritted teeth. Besides, what did she expect? I'd told her to dress to define the night. Obviously she just wanted to hang out. We'd have to put off our first official date until later. That didn't sit well in my stomach.

We didn't talk on our way toward O'Malley's, but I was fine with that. One of the things I loved about Mallory was her silence. She didn't need to fill up the quiet with unnecessary noise. It was nice. Peaceful. Until I started to feel the tension roll off her. By the time I'd parked, I felt like it was pushing me out the door.

"What?" I asked, not bothering to shut off the engine.

She turned toward me, her jaw clenched so tight she could crack walnuts.

My hands slid off the steering wheel, and my skull slapped against the headrest. "God, Mallory, if you don't tell me what I did wrong this time, I'm going to develop a complex."

"Why does it feel like you're mad at me?" Her words were sharp, and I honestly didn't know how to answer.

I opted for the truth. It hadn't failed me yet. "You know how I feel about you." I sighed and laid all my cards on the table. "I wanted us to celebrate tonight as a couple. On a real date. It feels more like we're just hanging out."

"Is that what you think I want? To just hang out?" Her sweet voice set my body into attention.

I turned my head, not expecting her to be so close. "I don't know what you want, love. I only know what I can give you."

She rested her head beside mine. "What's that?"

"Everything."

Mallory reached forward and pressed her hand against my face. "I kinda thought we were celebrating something."

"We are." I covered her hand with mine and pulled her palm to my lips. "We can go somewhere else."

Mallory watched our hands. "Why did you think I just wanted to hang out?"

"I told you to dress to define our plans."

She pulled her hand from mine. "And?"

I missed her touch already. "You wore that sweater last Wednesday, and you wear those jeans almost every day." I reached out and let one of her loose curls slide through my fingers. "You look gorgeous as always, but I figured you'd…" How could I finish that sentence?

"One, you didn't give me a lot of time to change, Aaron." Mallory pressed her knee against my thigh. "And two, I'm impressed you remember this sweater."

My fingers trailed along her jaw. We never broke eye contact as I slipped my hand behind her neck and tugged her toward me. Our lips met, and the fire that consumed me could melt the polar icecaps. I wanted to devour her, but that wasn't what Mallory needed. She set the pace, and the kiss ended much too soon. My fingers massaged her neck, and I wanted to bring us back together so much that each muscle in my body fought against my brain. Every kiss with her left me wanting more.

"Do you want to go somewhere else?" I whispered. *Please say yes.*

"No, here's fine." She leaned away from me and smiled. A light blush covered her cheeks and matched her sweater. God, she was the most beautiful creature on the planet. "Let's get inside so you can tell me why I'm fired."

I laughed and opened my door. The cold air wasn't enough to tame the blaze she set off in me, but I'd suffer. Mallory opened the truck door before I could get around and do it for her.

"Let me treat you like a lady." I reached down and linked her arm through mine. She squeezed in to my side.

When we got to the front door, she let me hold it open for her. The place was more packed than a usual Tuesday night. The student population at Westland celebrated finals like Mardi Gras in the French Quarter. Barry and Chuck sat with Candy and Hailey near the front windows.

"Betts, get your ass over here," Chuck screamed above the din.

I shook my head, but Mallory pulled me toward them.

She glanced up at me and shrugged. "We're not going to get a table anytime soon."

I stopped and she spun into me. "Not much of a first date, though."

"Let's say this is a pre-first-date date." She raised her eyebrows, a grin curving her lips. "We can call a do-over, too, if you want."

I wrapped my arms around her waist and lifted her off the floor until we were eye to eye. "I want you to be happy, Mallory. If you want to leave, we leave. If you want to be tortured and abused by Barry and Chuck, well…don't say I didn't warn you."

Mallory smiled and slapped my shoulder. I set her down and took her hand, weaving us through the crowd toward their table. Chuck raised his glass when we joined them and swallowed half of his beer in one gulp. Barry did the same, then both of them started laughing. I knew this routine. Whenever any of the guys on the team showed up with a girl they'd been after, everyone else did the "seal the deal" salute. I used to think it was stupid, but I appreciated the gesture. They knew how much I wanted Mallory and were happy I'd finally gotten more out of her than a tutoring session. We fell into a casual conversation, but it didn't take long before things turned a bit awkward.

"Is this Mallory?" a voice whispered in my ear.

I glanced over my shoulder, but the world dropped out from beneath my feet. The waitress grinned with wicked glee. I turned toward Chuck and Barry, but they didn't seem to realize the shit was hitting the fan.

"Hey, Mallory," the waitress said. "I'm Cat."

Mallory's eyebrows scrunched together when she glanced at me. She addressed Cat. "How did you know my name?"

Cat sharpened her claws. "You can say I heard Aaron scream it a few times." She jutted out her hip and put her hand on the table. "Okay, more than a few. Anyway, what can I get you?"

Mallory glanced between us several times, her embarrassment clear on her face. "Nothing. Thank you."

I reached for her, but she pulled away. The table had gone quiet. I glanced at Chuck who shook his head. Yep, I was royally screwed.

"Cat, can you call me a cab, though? I really need to get out of here." Mallory slid off the stool and pulled her coat on as she shouldered her way to the front door.

"You're a right bitch, Cat," I said before I went after Mallory. She stood outside the door, fighting back the tears. "Mallory?"

"Leave me alone, Aaron." She turned her back on me.

Anger filled my chest. This was bullshit. Punishing me for something I'd done months ago. Okay, it was pretty fucking stupid on my part, but I didn't deserve this shit. Not now. Not after waiting for her, being patient for her, letting her set the pace. And where did that get me? I finally get her to open up and she shuts me down when she learns I'm not a fucking virgin.

"If that's what you want, Mallory, fine." I stepped up

behind her, close enough she would know I was there and far enough away to not make her feel threatened. "But you're not being fair about this."

"*I'm* not being fair about this?" She turned to face me, inadvertently closing the distance between us. "Did you not hear what she said? You slept with her and called her by *my name*."

"Not true." I almost slapped myself in the face for the lie. "Yeah, I screwed Cat. When I was single. After I'd been rejected by the most perfect girl in the world." I moved a half step closer until our chests were almost touching. "But I never called her by your name."

She sucked the corner of her bottom lip into her mouth and dropped her gaze to my chest. I counted the heartbeats between us, waiting for her to throw me a bone. Or anything.

"I'm not perfect, Aaron." She lifted her eyes to meet mine.

"Neither am I, and I'm tired of pretending to be just to get you to like me." I ran my hand through my hair and stepped away from her. "Every time we move forward, something slaps us back. Maybe the universe is telling us something, huh? Maybe being with you wasn't supposed to happen." I shook my head at how absurd that sounded and laughed. "I sound like a fucking poet."

"Maybe we should take a break? From us?"

"You can't take a break from something that never really existed." It was like I'd stabbed her with a bowie knife when I'd turned it on myself. "Come on. I'll take you home."

A cab pulled up and honked. Mallory shook her head; the pain in her eyes was more than I could bear. She moved toward the cab, and I moved toward her. Before she could get the door open, I pulled her against me and kissed her like I'd wanted to in the truck. No more sweet pecks or chaste brushes of the lips. No more stolen kisses between classes. I kissed her like I'd never see her again, and honestly, I didn't think I would after the disaster inside O'Malley's. But she kissed me back. The hope built in my chest. This thing between us was right.

When we finally broke apart, the cab was gone.

"I'm no saint, Mallory," I whispered. "But I'll fucking burn the world to make this right between us."

"What about the universe?" Her breath froze in the air.

"Like I'm one to listen to the universe." I pressed my forehead to hers. "I call do-over."

"Do-over works for me." She sighed against my lips. "But let's go somewhere else, okay?"

"Deal."

I took her to The 9er Diner on the other side of town, away from the college and away from O'Malley's. We sat in a booth, ordered burgers and milkshakes, and celebrated my triumph in Monroe's class. We planned for the Christmas break, and Mallory agreed to come home with me. Talk about an early Christmas present. We talked like we'd known each other our entire lives. Even though there were still walls that needed to come down.

It was almost one when I dropped her off at her house. We stood in front of her door, kissing like teenagers until I had to leave. I still had one more final to deal with before I packed up my room for a few weeks.

I drove back to my dorm happier than I'd ever been, but a nagging voice in the back of my head reminded me that this thing with Mallory was as delicate as a spider web. If she ever found out, it wouldn't just break. It would disappear as if it never existed.

Chapter Twenty-Three

Mallory withdrew by the time I left on Wednesday afternoon. We'd barely seen each other since the near disaster at O'Malley's. Whether she was withdrawing from me because of regret or if there was something else going on in her head, I didn't know. It would only be a few days until I came back to Madison and picked her up, but it felt like an eternity.

To make matters worse, I drove Trish home. Two hours in the car with her was enough to make me want to drive off a cliff. If only we had cliffs in Iowa.

Trish turned off the radio ten minutes after we hit the highway.

"Never touch a man's radio," I said, reaching to turn it back to a normal, block-Trish's-voice-out level.

"Please, just let me…" Trish growled in frustration. I almost smiled. She'd always make that noise whenever she didn't know what to say. "Dammit, Aaron."

"Why is it always 'dammit, Aaron' with you? Jesus, Trish, in the years we were together, everything was always my fault. Hell, you even blamed me for the breakup. Take some responsibility for a fucking change." *See? I have grown some ginormous balls.* As much as I wanted to verbalize that thought, I kept my mouth shut. No point in poking a sleeping bear.

Trish huffed and crossed her arms. Her heated breath fogged the passenger window. I turned up the radio and let Hank drown out the sound of her irritation.

It took one song before she turned it off. "I'm sorry, okay?"

That almost sent me off the road.

"I'm sorry for blaming you for everything. I'm sorry for treating you like shit. I'm sorry for calling you boring—"

"Are you sorry for cheating on me?" I glanced at her out of the corner of my eye. Her mouth slacked open. "Don't try to deny it. Chelsea saw you."

She slapped her mouth shut and faced the window again. "I'm sorry for that, too."

I didn't turn on the radio again, half expecting her to start the conversation over. It took until I pulled into her driveway for her to say what was really on her mind.

"I do love you, Aaron." She squeezed the handle of the door, but she didn't open it. "I wish I could take back everything that's happened between us over the last few months."

I turned to face her and hated seeing her hurting, but she caused it. And, as much as I wanted to hate Trish, I didn't have it in me anymore. My father raised me to be a gentleman, and I hadn't been much of one lately. "Look, Trish, I'm not going to lie and say it didn't tear me up, but you were right." She started to interrupt, and I held up my hand. "We weren't working anymore. I just didn't see it, and you did."

"Does she make you happy?" Tears slid down her cheeks as she tried to smile.

I took her hand and squeezed. "Over the moon."

"I'm glad. You deserve to be happy."

"So do you." I touched her shoulder and squeezed. "Don't live your life by what your parents want for you."

We stared at each other, years passing between us. Trish leaned over and kissed my cheek. "Good-bye, Aaron."

She hopped out of the truck and gathered her bags from the bed before I could open my door to help. Not once did she look back toward me. Not even when she closed the door behind her.

When I parked my truck in our circular drive twenty minutes later, my phone vibrated in my pocket. The light snow gathered on the grass, glistening as the sun peeked through the clouds. I loved Christmas. I pulled the phone out and stared at the message.

You should be home by now. I'm sorry. Mallory's words were a comfort and a torture. She shouldn't be sorry for anything.

I just got here. Haven't even gotten out of the truck yet. Why are you sorry?

The phone danced in my hand, and I swiped to answer before it could actually ring.

"Hey," I whispered to keep the nerves out of my voice. Mallory sniffled on the other end, and I sat up. "Talk to me."

Silence filled the line, but I didn't let that deter my patience. A loud rap on the driver's side window scared the bejeesus out of me. I glanced up to see my little sister blowing air onto the window and drawing smiley faces in the fog. This was getting to be a bad habit of hers. At least her hair wasn't blue. I shook my head and pointed at the phone while I waited for Mallory to say something, anything.

"You still there?"

"Christmas is…and it…I'm nervous." She sniffle-laughed louder. "I'm sorry. I didn't want you to think…I… This is hard."

When I realized she wasn't going to keep going, I said as gently as possible, "It's okay. I know you're going through things. Just talk to me when you can, okay?"

"Okay." She sniffled then let out a long sigh. "You need to get inside. I'm sure your sister's waiting for you."

Something about the way she said "sister" made me cringe. I opted to ignore it. Mallory's relationship with her brother had been tough before he died. "Well, Chelsea is dancing around in front of my truck at the moment. She looks like a monkey on speed."

Mallory laughed.

"Can I call you later?"

"Yeah, I'd like that."

We hung up, and I opened my door. Before my foot hit the gravel, Chelsea had her arms wrapped around my neck. I hugged her back and set her on her feet.

"Was that her?" Chelsea grinned like a dog that had stolen a steak off the grill.

I tweaked her nose. "None of your business, little girl. Where're the parents?"

"Mom's knee-deep in piecrust, and Dad's delivering a new tractor to the Fergusons as a surprise." Chelsea snorted as we started toward the house. "Old man Ferg will probably have a heart attack when he sees it. He's been driving that Deutch Allis for longer than we've been alive."

It always struck me how much Chelsea knew about the business. Far more than I ever had, and here I was planning on taking it over once my playing days were done. Maybe I was the wrong Betts for the job. We climbed onto the porch, and I stopped before opening the door.

"Chels, can I ask you a question without a sarcastic response?" I dropped my hand from the doorknob and turned to face her. "Do you think I'm cut out to run the business?"

Her eyes widened so much she took a step back. "Why

wouldn't you be?"

I shrugged.

"Seriously, Aaron. Where'd this come from?"

"I don't know. Really. It just sort of popped into my head." I sat on the swing, the cold wood quickly chilling my ass. Chelsea sat beside me.

"You've always known you're going to take over when Dad retires. What changed?" She pushed against the railing, setting the swing in motion.

My breath froze in front of me. I loved winter. The chill in the air, a fire in the hearth, and a peace in our existence. My thoughts flicked to Mallory, but this really started before I met her. It started when Trish dumped me. "Me, I guess. I mean, when Trish and I broke up, I started questioning everything."

"Ah," she said with knowledge I clearly didn't possess.

"Ah what?"

"You know Dad doesn't expect you to take over the minute your baseball career is over, right?" Chelsea pushed off the railing again to keep the swing moving steady.

"Yeah, I guess."

"What do *you* want?"

A small laugh escaped my lips, and I shrugged again. "I wish I knew."

Chelsea draped her arm over my shoulder. She didn't say another word, just kept us swinging.

"Thought you were giving Trish a ride home." Flour dotted my mother's face and arms. I leaned in and kissed the one clean spot on her cheek. "Why didn't you bring her on by?"

"Mom, Trish and I are over. Just because I let her sit in my truck for two hours doesn't mean we're going to make up, get engaged, and start planning our lives together."

Mom actually snorted. "Sow your oats, Aaron. That's what you Betts men do, but you'll end up with Trish. Mark my words, that's the girl for you, for this family. Not some city trash you feel the need to play with."

"You don't even know her," I said, stunned by Mom's hateful words.

"I don't need to know her. I know her type. She finds a way to get in between a happy couple and tears them apart—"

"Mom, listen to yourself. I've *told* you Trish broke up with me. The night before I blew out my knee playing soccer, she told me it was over. It wasn't until after I had knee surgery that I met Mallory. *After*, Mom." My anger rose in my throat, and I swallowed to push it back down. "And she didn't even let me kiss her until a few weeks ago. Does that sound like the kind of girl you described? No, because Mallory's nothing like that. And you better be nice to her when she gets here."

Mom didn't say anything for a long time. She stayed quiet as her fingers curled into the dough. "If that's how you feel—"

"That's how it is."

"I wish I knew what got into you," she muttered. "I just want you to be happy."

"I'm not Dad. Trish and I...we aren't you guys. I know you want me to be happy. And, right now, I'm happier than I've ever been in my life. Stop trying to run our lives, Mom. Chelsea and I know what we want. And I'm sorry if it's not what you want for us, but our dreams are our own." I thought I'd go in for the kill shot. "And I'll drive Chelsea to New York if that's what it takes to get her there. Just so you know."

"Leave your sister out of this." Mom spun around and pointed at me. "She's not going to New York. She can go to Westland like you, or Iowa State, but not New York."

I shook my head and walked out of the kitchen. Dragging Chelsea into it was dirty play on my part. Dad had already told her he would send the check to secure her spot. Mom didn't know yet, but it wasn't my place to bring it up. I went up to my room, feeling for the first time in my life that I didn't belong in this house anymore.

I was lost. Every day, I'd look around the farm or even the shop and not recognize anything. Nothing had changed. The trees hadn't changed. The fields were plowed under for winter. The counter and garage hadn't moved. In all of my twenty-one years, everything was the same as always. But it felt wrong.

Chelsea snuck into my room on the night before Christmas Eve with two sodas and a bowl of popcorn with M&M's already mixed in. Our aunt had been pregnant with our little cousin when I was ten and Chels was six, and she craved microwave popcorn with M&M's. It sounded disgusting, but it wasn't. Chelsea and I made it a tradition. Whenever one of us was down in the dumps, the other would bring in a bowl of the concoction and we'd talk it out. We had one rule: no lies, no matter if the truth might hurt the other person.

"Spill," Chelsea ordered. She tucked her legs under my comforter and set the dish between us.

"Everything's different." I dug into the bowl and shoved a handful of the mix into my mouth. The butter, salt, and chocolate tasted like a piece of heaven. I finished chewing and swallowed half the bottle of soda before going on. "I don't know, sis. I just feel off for some reason."

"Is it because of this girl?"

I wanted to get pissed, but it would break the rules. "No. I mean, she's got a lot to do with some things, but not this." I took another handful and slowly popped a piece at a time. "I know you hated Trish—"

"Oh, yeah."

"—but I knew what was expected of me. I had a plan. Get drafted, go pro, marriage, family, World Series ring, retire, take over the business. I guess when she dumped me—"

"Thank God."

"—everything started to unravel." I glanced at her, but she wasn't looking my way. Chelsea stared at the map of the world on my wall. "Then I met Mallory, and she turned my life upside down and sideways."

A smile filled my sister's face, and she pointed at the poster. "Remember when I'd get scared during the bad storms and hide in here with you? You used to tell me all the places we were going to go on that map."

"Yeah, I remember. Why?" Those were some of my best memories. Chelsea and I would fight like any other brother and sister, but we were always there for each other when it mattered.

"Why can't we?" She turned, an excitement lighting her face. "Who says we have to stay in Iowa? Aaron, you're free from that image you've created about your future. That's what's changed. You don't have that anchor anymore. Now you can have the life you want and not the one that's been expected of you for so long. Let go of the fake dream and embrace the real one."

I started to shake my head, then I realized she might be right. Maybe the reason everything felt different wasn't because I was different but my image of the future was. I closed my eyes and pictured the future I'd daydreamed about for months. Me and Mallory on a beach. Me and Mallory at an art museum. In Paris. In London. Getting married. Mallory in the stands with our kids watching me rob a homer. Mallory grading papers in our dining room while I play with the kids. Me coaching a team somewhere. None of it included Betts Family Farm and Implement. It didn't necessarily include Iowa. We could go anywhere.

Everything I really wanted included Mallory. Those words filled my mind. I knew I liked her. I knew I wanted to get to know everything about her. Fuck if I knew that I had already fallen in love with her. Admitting it to myself was like opening Al Capone's safe. It left me empty. I'd held on to hope that she would love me back, that she would be the first to admit it and then I could allow myself to feel this way. But it was too late. I couldn't stop it now that I'd said it in my head.

I loved her.

"What?" Chelsea cocked her head to the side.

"What?"

The smile that grew across her face was knowing and full of laughter. "I think you just said Mallory."

"Yeah, I bet I did." My cheeks warmed. Damn, when was the last time I blushed like a schoolgirl?

Chelsea shoved my arm. "I can't wait to meet her."

"She's terrified of you." I threw a kernel at her head.

"Me? I'm the best in the Midwest." She tossed a popcorn kernel back at me, smacking me square in the forehead. "But I'll run interference with Mom. I do kinda owe you after you told her you'd drive me to New York."

"You heard that, huh?"

"Yep. And that's why you're the best brother I could ever have."

Chelsea left me with nothing but unpopped kernels and a realization. She'd given me the best Christmas present in the world.

Chapter Twenty-Four

I parked in front of Mallory's house at eight in the morning. That was when it hit me this might not be a good idea. I'd left at five, stopping for an extended breakfast outside of town. Mom always got up at six alongside Dad who would feed the animals before leaving for work. This morning would be different, but not by much. Instead of heading for work, Dad would be doing whatever it took to stay out of Mom's way. I smiled to myself. Normally, I'd be hiding with him in the basement. With both sets of grandparents set to arrive today, Mom was always hell-bent to make sure her spotless house was also sparkling.

This year would be different.

I stared at the front door, hope deflating in my chest. Finals, along with her job at the bookstore and my packing for break, had kept us apart since the near disaster at O'Malley's. We exchanged text messages, but Mallory's schedule at the bookstore went full time the minute the semester ended. Add Christmas into the mix and she was damn near impossible to reach. Fortunately, the bookstore closed Christmas Eve and reopened after New Year's. Steeling my nerves, I climbed out of the truck and strode up to her door. I wasn't this nervous in the bottom of the fourth inning during last year's championship game when we were already down by six runs and the bases were loaded with two outs. That moment had felt like a turning point before I hit the slam. That was easier than knocking on Mallory's door.

It took a few minutes before she answered wearing flannel bottoms and a tank. Her hands warmed around a steaming coffee mug. I wanted to throw her against the wall and kiss her in a way she'd never want anyone else to kiss her ever again.

"Hey," I said.

"Aaron? What're you doing here so early?" A breeze skirted around me and lifted her wild hair. She shivered and stepped away from the open door, motioning me inside. Mickey strolled up to us, swatting my leg with his tail before heading into the living room and curling up in his bed by the heat vent.

"I…" My mind froze when I noticed her living room. No Christmas decorations. No tree. Nothing but the wreath on the front door to even indicate a holiday. I stared at her, a new idea smacking the back of my head. "Don't you celebrate Christmas?"

Mallory shrugged and shuffled into the kitchen in a pair of bunny slippers. If it wasn't for the sad atmosphere, I would've found them endearing. She kept her back to me, but her shoulders sagged.

"Mallory?" I hurried into the kitchen, reaching for her. My hands fell to my sides before I touched her. Fuck it. I wrapped my arms around her shoulders and pulled her against me.

Mallory turned and buried her face in my shoulder. "Not really. I…"

I kissed the top of her head. A crack showed in her steely

resolve.

"Christmas is hard." Her raw voice tore at me. "After… So, I…just don't." She exhaled sharply. "Mom loved Christmas. She'd go all out on decorations and the tree. We'd have so many cookies, we'd give them to our neighbors."

There wasn't anything I could say. I wanted to kick myself for not thinking this out. Here I had expected Mallory to be happily sitting alone in her living room, waiting for me to take her home. It hadn't occurred to me that she would be miserable. That she didn't celebrate Christmas at all.

Mallory pushed away from me. "I'm sorry. I… You never answered my question. What're you doing here so early?"

I kissed her forehead. "I thought we…I just thought we could spend some quiet time together before we left. We've seen each other for five minutes in the last few days."

Her mouth froze in an "oh."

"I didn't think…you might not want to spend Christmas with me. That you weren't much of a holiday person." My chin hit my chest. "I didn't want you to be alone on Christmas. I wanted you to be with me. So, if this is too weird…"

I felt her before she touched me. Her hands slid up my chest and moved around my neck. My body melted as her lips brushed over mine. I tightened my arms around her waist, pulling her as close to me as I could. The chaste kiss turned hungry. She opened her mouth, her tongue darting into mine. I pulled away, letting my arm loosen around her waist. She stared at me, wide-eyed with need. She took my hand again and walked toward the stairs in the back of the house, pulling me up each step to the loft bedroom.

My gaze traveled around the small room. It was simple with a queen bed, a dresser, and more books than I could count stacked along the walls. My thumb caressed the palm of her hand. Finally, she turned around to face me. She stared into my eyes; no words were necessary to convey her determination. Her hand fell from mine. As much as I wanted to reach out and take it again, I didn't. Mallory was in control of what happened next. I wasn't going to push her into doing something she didn't want.

I waited, my gaze traveling her body. She closed the distance between us. Her hands slid up my chest, under my jacket. Slowly, she pushed the leather from my shoulders until it fell to the floor. Her hands retraced their steps, stopping at the first button on my shirt. One by one, her fingers opened a button. My breathing was out of control. It was taking a supreme amount of resistance to not grab her.

My shirt was opened, exposing my chest. She ran a finger from the center all the way down to my waistband. I let my head fall back. Ecstasy was an understatement. She slid my shirt off in the same manner as the jacket. Then her touch left me.

I glanced down at her, waiting for the next move. She stared up at me before reaching again. She pulled my head toward hers. I kissed her as if she might break under the pressure. My hands found her hips, my thumbs dug under her shirt, touching the softest skin God ever created. She moaned into my mouth. Slowly, my hands traveled higher, lifting the delicate cotton off her skin. She shivered beneath my touch.

Passion overtook me. I needed Mallory like I needed air. Screw patience. I pulled her shirt over her head, our lips breaking contact only long enough for the shirt to pass between us. The feel of her skin against mine, the scent of her excitement. My hands moved back to her hips, and I lifted her toward me. She responded by wrapping her legs around my waist. Turning, I pressed her against the wall. My lips moved down her neck, tasting every inch of her. Her moans grew louder as I kissed the skin above her breast. With one hand on her perfect ass, I reached her bra, tugging the cup down to free her, taking her into my mouth.

"Aaron," she breathed. Her nails dug into the skin of my shoulder.

"You're so soft," I whispered. My fingers glided over her skin, around her back, and unhooked her simple white bra. My mouth grazed across her chest, taking her other breast into my mouth. God, she tasted good. "So beautiful."

Her legs tightened around me. She grabbed my face, bringing our lips crashing back together. Using her shoulders, she pushed us off the wall. I took two steps back, my knees buckling as soon as they hit the bed. We fell back onto the mattress. Mallory straddled me, dragging her lips away from mine and down my chest.

Nothing had ever felt like this. Nothing had felt this right.

Her kisses were torturous, slow. She moved down my body, exploring each inch of it. Her fingers found the zipper of my jeans. My dick was pressed so hard against it that I thought I would explode the minute her skin hit mine. She lowered the zipper and unhooked the button. Her hand yanked my boxer briefs down as if she could no longer wait to see me completely.

Then I was in her mouth.

Her tongue circled me as she took me farther inside.

"Mallory," I moaned. "Oh God, Mallory, please."

She raked her teeth along my shaft, making me shudder.

I couldn't take it anymore. Reaching for her, I pulled her toward me by the shoulders, flipping her onto her back. Two could play the torture game. I took her hands, pushing them above her head and grasping them with my fingers. Leaning away from her, I stared into her eyes. The heat, the desire that I saw reflected my own.

But I had to tell her something before we went further. "I love you, Mallory. More than I've ever loved anyone in my life."

I leaned down, kissing her before she could respond.

With my free hand, I skimmed over her skin until I found the elastic waist of her flannel pants. My fingers slid underneath, slowly, waiting for her to tell me to stop. She didn't. I pushed her panties to the side, my fingers exploring her until slipping one inside. She was so wet, so soft, so ready for me. God, I wanted to be inside her, to feel her skin against mine. She struggled against the hand that held her wrists. I let go. She dug her fingers into my hair, pulling me closer still.

Mallory moaned and shuddered. She tightened, and I wanted nothing more than her pleasure to explode around me. She moaned my name as she went over the edge. It was like having heaven open before me. When her body calmed, I slipped off her pants. Kneeling back on my heels, I memorized every freckle on her body.

She stared back for a moment before sitting up and tugging my jeans and boxers off my hips. With a smile, she pulled my wallet out of the back of my jeans and found the ever-present condom. Her hands slid over my dick. I could fuck a thousand women, and nothing would ever be as good as the feeling of this girl's hands around my cock. She tore the foil open with her teeth and rolled the rubber over me.

I bent down to kiss her. Our lips met, and I worshiped them. She pulled me down on top of her, lifting her hips and wrapping her legs around my waist. I slipped into her and stilled when she gasped. This was so right. So perfect.

Kissing her gently, I pressed myself farther into her. "I love you, Mallory Fine."

"I love you, too, Aaron Betts." She groaned. "I have for a long time."

Need controlled me, and I showed her how much I loved her, slowly filling her and savoring every touch of our skin. Mallory moved with me, meeting each thrust with an intensity that drove me closer to release. Her gaze held mine with so much emotion that I needed to claim her completely, to make her scream my name. My pace sped up as she tightened around me until she broke and moaned "I love you." I gritted my teeth, riding out her orgasm until I couldn't control my own. I almost blacked out from the pleasure. Mallory sighed as I collapsed on top of her, inhaling the sweet smell of vanilla mixed with her sweat and sex. It was almost enough to make me hard again.

Rolling to my side, I pulled her against me. "Wow."

She laughed into my chest. "I'd say wow is an understatement."

She was right. It was more than sex.

I kissed the top of her hair, digging my hand into the locks like I'd imagined so many times. "I meant what I said, Mallory."

"I know."

I couldn't stop the yawn that left my mouth.

"Did I wear you out?" Mallory asked. I could almost feel the heat of her blush.

"I would say that's an understatement." I chuckled.

Her hand slid over my chest in a slow caress. "Thank you. For showing up early for me."

"Always."

Mallory leaned over me. "Are you sure you want this? For me to meet your parents and all the baggage that comes with it?"

I pressed back into her pillow to get a better look at her face. "I want you with me."

A smile spread across her face. "Okay."

I kissed her nose. "But not yet, right?"

Mallory laughed, a carefree laugh that was so rare for her. It warmed my heart. I flipped her onto her back, letting her feel why we didn't need to go anywhere immediately. I'd never get enough of this woman.

Chapter Twenty-Five

We got showered together and dressed slowly. Mallory clasped her silver locket around her neck. She rarely took it off.

"Where did you get this?" I asked, lifting it to my lips.

Mallory smiled, but darkness crossed her face. "It was my mother's."

"Speaking of mothers, mine has called every ten minutes since nine." As if on cue, my phone buzzed in my pocket. I pulled it out with a devious grin and showed Mallory. She tensed beside me, but she didn't push me away. We were definitely making progress in that regard. "And I'm going to tell her we're on our way home." I swiped the screen. "Hey, Mom."

"Thank God. Aaron, where are you? I thought you'd be back by now." The tremors in her voice turned into guilt in my stomach.

"We're getting ready to leave, actually." I stopped, squeezing Mallory against me.

"Stop by the store and get more milk. Your father forgot it." Mom sighed, letting her disappointment fill her breath.

"What took you so long? You said you'd be back by now."

I stared at Mallory as I answered. "Mallory's sink was clogged." *And we needed to take a shower.*

"Mal—" Her voice hitched, rising an octave. "Just get home."

"Relax, Mom." I sighed like she did, just to get my point across. "We'll see you in a few hours."

I ended the call before she could argue any further. We grabbed Mallory's bag and pushed the door open. The cold air blasted against my cheeks. It was going to snow sooner rather than later, and I hoped we'd make it back before it started. We ran to the truck, climbing inside before the dropping temps could freeze us completely.

"Your mother's going to hate me," Mallory said as her teeth chattered over the roar of the heater.

"Probably." I paused, not really wanting to admit what she didn't want to hear. But we didn't lie to each other.

"Great."

I reached out and turned her chin until she faced me. "Don't worry. She's not the one you need to impress."

Mallory raised her eyebrows. "Oh?"

"Nope. My little sister's the real judge, jury, and executioner." I smiled. "She doesn't hold back her opinion very often."

"Then I will be on my best behavior." Mallory put her hands on her lap and sat as if she had a stick up her butt. But the grin fighting for freedom on her face was anything but ladylike.

"And, as for the sleeping arrangements, my room is right next to Chelsea's. Nobody will know the difference."

Mallory's laugh filled the cab. "You're crazy. Now get on the road before I change my mind."

I leaned across the bench seat and kissed her. "Don't ever change your mind about me, love."

The snow started as I turned down the road to our house. Mallory tensed beside me. Once my tires hit gravel, she knew we were almost there. I reached across the seat and squeezed her hand. She turned with a smile, warming the cab more than the heater.

The house loomed into view. Mallory's sharp intake of breath after we crested the small hill surprised me. I knew our house was big, but she stared at it like it was a Hollywood mansion. The two-story white farmhouse with a wraparound porch was nowhere near a mansion, but I could see why she might think it was. The front door opened, and Chelsea bounced down, twirling in the snow.

"White Christmas," she shouted, adding a "woohoo" for emphasis.

The truck had barely come to a stop when Chelsea opened Mallory's door and yanked her down with a hug.

"Oh my God, I'm so happy to meet you," Chelsea squealed.

Mallory smiled, but the tension in her neck signaled her discomfort.

"Back off, Chels." I strode around the front of the truck and wrapped my arm around Mallory's shoulders. "I don't need you scaring her off. Let her see your freak flag later."

"Suck it, Aaron." Chelsea stared at me with a glint of mischief in her eyes. I didn't back down. Our gazes locked in intense competition. Under my arm, Mallory's tension turned her to stone. Chelsea cracked first, laughter erupting from her mouth before she smiled.

"You lose." I punched her arm gently and reached into the cab for Mallory's bag, tossing it toward my sister. "Your punishment is to take this to your room."

Chelsea cocked her hip with Mallory's bag over her

shoulder. "Sure you don't want to? The firing squad's loading their rifles."

I grimaced at her choice of phrasing. "I can handle Mom."

"Oh, it's not just Mom. Grandma Jean and Grandma Eddie are sharpening their bayonets." Chelsea shook her head and turned her gaze to Mallory. "Sorry, but they're going to bring out the big guns for you. Just a fair warning. Dad, on the other hand, has Grandpa Len and Grandpa Vincent half sloshed already. So there's that."

Chelsea turned on her heel and strode into the house. The screen door slammed behind her, almost hitting her in the ass. I squeezed Mallory closer.

"You ready for this?"

She shook her head and stared at the front door. "Maybe this wasn't such a great idea."

"Look at me," I whispered. She turned toward me and I put my hands on each side of her face so she couldn't look away. "It doesn't matter what they think. Just remember that."

"Okay," she whispered.

I lost myself in her eyes for a moment and bent to kiss her. Before my lips brushed against hers, a loud, embarrassing voice screeched through the cold December air.

"Pumpkin boy, get your sorry ass inside and stop letting that poor girl freeze to her death." Grandma Jean stood on the porch with a shawl draped over her shoulders. Her gray hair curled in tight cues around her head, and her reading glasses hung from the chain. Despite her grandmotherly appearance, Grandma Jean could probably still whip my ass and not break a sweat. "Get on."

"Here we go," I whispered to Mallory from the corner of my mouth. "If I can survive Monroe's class, you can definitely survive this."

Mallory snorted, but she didn't say anything else. Grandma Jean held the door open for us, smacking my butt as I passed her. The old lady was crazy, and I loved it. Mallory stopped inside the door. The foyer was small, but it opened quickly to the large living room. She stepped slowly forward, her head lifting to the exposed beams on the ceiling before moving toward the large fireplace on the far wall. As usual, Dad had gone too big on the Christmas tree, and it took up half the back wall near the dining room.

"It's beautiful," she said.

Grandma Jean skirted around us and sauntered toward the kitchen. Mallory matched her pace, pausing only at the wall of family photos. She glanced over her shoulder and pointed to one of Chelsea and me covered in paint. We were eight and twelve and decided to paint a mural on the wall of the barn. It looked more like a two-year-old did it. We didn't care. Fortunately, neither did Dad. Mom was a whole other story. That was a great day.

When we stepped into the kitchen, all eyes turned toward us.

Grandma Eddie was the opposite of Grandma Jean. She wore tight shirts and short skirts as if she had never aged past twenty-nine. Her piercing green eyes took in every inch of Mallory before she huffed and went back to peeling potatoes. Mom stared longer before finally stepping forward as the silence in the room threatened to strangle us.

"Mom, this is Mallory." I let my arm drop from around her shoulders and reached for her hand, but Mallory was already moving forward.

"Hi, Mrs. Betts. Thank you so much for inviting me into your home." Mallory's voice was sugary sweet as she reached out her hand to take my mother's. Grandma Jean pushed my chin up, closing my mouth. "What can I do to help?"

"You ever peel a potato, girl?" Grandma Eddie pointed to the mass of unpeeled potatoes on the table.

"Of course," Mallory said. She moved around Grandma

Eddie and sat on the other side of the table, picking up a peeler and a potato. "We should have these done in no time."

I stared at her, knowing she was doing whatever it took for them to like her and a little pissed that she was choosing to hang with the old ladies instead of me. Mallory glanced up and winked. The mischievous look in her eye made me nervous.

"So, Grandma Eddie," Mallory said as if she'd known the old lady her whole life, "what was Aaron like as a boy?"

Oh shit. Both grandmas smiled and stared at Mallory with glee.

"Well, child, I have stories that will straighten that hair of yours."

Mallory raised her eyebrows, and with that look, she told me to get out. As I left the kitchen, I heard Grandma Jean mention my matador attempts with a very lazy bull. My face burned with embarrassment. I would never live that down.

Christmas Eve dinner went by in a rush of holiday cheer. I barely saw Mallory as she endeared herself to my family. The grandmas loved her in no time, and the grandpas were even more easily persuaded.

"Now, Ms. Fine, I hear you're quite knowledgeable about the game of baseball. Or is my boy just bullshitting me?" Dad shredded a roll as he spoke, not once bothering to look down at the table. I knew this game. He was challenging. I sat back and crossed my arms, anxious for the show to begin.

"I know a few things." Mallory swirled her gravy into her mashed potatoes.

"Watch this," I whispered to Chelsea. "Dad's going down."

Dad nodded and picked up another roll. "Okay, then. How tall is the Green Monster?"

I snorted and Mallory quickly elbowed my side. "The left field wall at Fenway Park is thirty-seven feet tall."

"Who won the first World Series in 1904?" Dad finally

glanced up from his pile of bread.

"The first World Series was held in 1903. There wasn't one in 1904." Mallory leaned forward and put her arms on the table. "And Boston won the nine game series."

He leaned in, pressing his hands on the table. I glanced at Mallory who matched his stance.

"Who was the shortest man ever to play a Major League game?" he asked.

Mallory grinned. "Eddie Gaedel. He was three-seven and wore number one-eighth for the St. Louis Browns. He walked on four consecutive balls and never set foot in the batter's box again."

Dad raised an eyebrow and leaned back. They kept going, but he couldn't stump her, and that stumped him. It was fun to watch.

Mom refused to warm up to Mallory. She was polite, but never really kind. Mallory sensed it. I could see the way she stared at my mother as if Mom was a puzzle Mallory could solve. But Mom was pushing me too far. Mallory was nothing but polite. My blood boiled and I started to stand, but Mallory put her hand on my thigh. I sat back in my seat, my leg bouncing in aggravation.

"The ham is great, Mrs. Betts. What type of rub did you use on it?" Mallory tilted her head and smiled at my mother.

"Pineapple."

The blunt answer would've been enough to stop most people. Not Mallory. She kept peppering Mom with questions about dinner. By the time the meal was over, Mom wouldn't even respond. That simply pissed me off more. Mom had been nothing but supportive of me my entire life. Why she would be such a bitch now was beyond me. I wanted to scream at her, to tell her to get her head out of her ass.

Mallory offered to help the grandmas with the dishes while Mom and I cleared the dining room table. I waited until nobody else was around before I said anything.

"Stop it, Mom," I said through clenched teeth, blocking the door to the kitchen. My arms were filled with plates covered in the remnants of turkey and ham.

Mom smiled and patted my shoulder like the good little boy I wasn't. "Stop what, dear?"

"Stop treating Mallory like a disease. She's great, and you need to give her a chance, because she's not going anywhere if I can help it." I shook my head. "I love her. You need to accept that."

"You say that now, but how do you know you really mean it?" Mom moved to go around me, but I blocked her path again.

"I know because when I look at her, I see someone I can spend the rest of my life with. I see someone I can grow old with. I see someone I'd give my own life for." I let my eyes hold hers, my anger dissipated, but my frustrations did not. How could she not get it? "Mom, I see in her the life you want me to have with someone else."

Mom reached up and touched my cheek, wiping away a tear I hadn't known had fallen. "My God, you really mean that."

I could only nod.

Mom inhaled deeply and stood straighter. "Then I'll try harder."

"Thank you."

I moved so she could head into the kitchen and turned to follow. Mallory stood in the door with her hands squeezing each other. I stared at her, not sure how much she heard or if I was really ready for her to hear any of that. Our relationship was so rocky that a simple teeter one way would send us over the precipice.

"Did you mean all that?" she asked.

"Every word," I replied, knowing that the wind was

blowing us one way when I didn't want it to move.

Mallory didn't say anything as she took half the plates from my arms and carried them into the kitchen. We worked side by side, scraping the food stuck to the dishes into the trash. Mom's precious china had to be hand-washed, and only she was allowed to do it. Mallory dried, and I put them back in their cabinet until next year. The grandmas loaded the dishwasher, and then sat and watched us do the rest. They bickered with each other, but the rest of us remained quiet. Mallory slipped out of the kitchen as I finished the plates.

"She heard you." Mom wiped down the sink. "You hadn't told her any of that, yet, had you?"

"Not in so many words." I tucked the towels under the handle of the oven.

"Why not?"

"It's complicated."

Mom laughed, and the grandmas joined in.

"It always is. Now go uncomplicate it," Grandma Jean said. "Before I whoop your ass until you do."

"How…?" The words bit against my tongue, wanting to be said, but I wasn't sure if it was something my mom needed to hear.

"How what, Pumpkin boy?" Grandma Jean asked. I raised my head to meet the intense stare of a woman wiser than I'd ever be. "How do you tell the girl? You already did."

I never let my gaze leave Grandma Jean's. "How can I feel so much for someone I don't really know?"

"What in the world are you talking about?" Grandma Eddie slapped her hand on the table. "You've spent enough time with the girl to fall for her; you can't tell me you don't know her."

Mom put her hand on my arm, but I never broke my stare-down with my favorite grandparent.

Grandma Jean stood and took my hands. "Love doesn't

mean knowing someone, Aaron. I've spent damn near forty-five years with Grandpa, and we're still getting to know each other. Every day, month, year, we grow. We change. You never really know someone, but you know how you feel about them. And loving someone means wanting to continue to learn and grow with each other." She squeezed my fingers and let go. "Now, go tell that girl what you need."

I chuckled. "She knows."

"Overhearing something and having it said to your face is different, Pumpkin boy." Grandma Jean turned me around by my shoulders and pushed me toward the door. "Go."

Shaking my head, I took off in the same direction Mallory disappeared to and ran straight into Chelsea. She slammed one hand on my chest and offered me my coat with the other.

"I don't know what you did to scare her, but she took off outside." Chelsea smacked my cheek much like Grandma Eddie would've if I'd let her. "Fix it. I like her."

"Me, too." I grabbed my coat and kissed Chelsea on the forehead. "Thanks, sis. Which way do you think she went?"

"If it were me, I'd head for the big barn. Lots of places to hide and warm enough to stay outside for a long time." Chelsea smiled. "Besides, I told her to go there so she could have some quiet time. I just didn't promise to keep it quiet."

I nodded, appreciating Chelsea's talent for twisting things to suit her own needs. Grandma Jean was right. Mallory needed to hear me say how much I needed her in my life. I'd told her I loved her more than once, but her trust was more fragile than a spider web in a tornado.

The wind burned my face as soon as I set foot outside. Snow swirled as it fell. Taking Chelsea's direction, I hurried toward the big barn south of the regular size garage. The barn held the combine and tractors for the farm. There was also an office with a couch, TV, and electric heater. When we were kids, Chelsea and I would "run away" from home just to hide out in Dad's barn office.

I opened the door and found Mallory admiring the combine. Her gloved fingers traced the airbrushed words "Betts Family Farm" on the side. Dad liked to show off.

"Your family's amazing," she said without glancing toward me.

I hesitated at the door. "They have their moments."

She laughed, but it had to be the saddest laugh I'd ever heard. The hesitation disappeared, and I strolled up to her.

"Mallory…"

"Don't." Tears clogged her throat before spilling from her eyes. "Please, Aaron, don't."

I shoved my hands into my pockets and tried to quell the anger growing inside me. This girl was everything I ever wanted, everything I needed. How could she keep pushing me away? Grandma Jean was right. I had to clear the air, and I had to do it before I lost my nerve.

"Stop pushing me away." I put my hands on her shoulders and turned her toward me. She tried to twist away, but I moved my hands to either side of her face and made her look me in the eye. "I've treaded lightly around you for so long, but I can't do it anymore. Everything you heard me tell my mother, everything I've held back from you… You need to hear it again. You need to see that it's very real." I pressed my forehead against hers and inhaled her soft vanilla scent. So pure, so simple, so Mallory. My fingers massaged her temple and slid down to her neck as I leaned back so she could see my face. "I can't imagine not having you in my life. I can't think of a scenario where we won't be together. Because that would destroy me. Even when I thought for a moment you might not care about me, I tried to figure out a way to forget these feelings. But I can't."

I stared at her, waiting for her to say anything. She closed her eyes but said nothing.

"Damn it, Mallory. Talk to me. Whatever it is, whatever makes you put up these walls, we can get past it."

"I don't…" Mallory pulled away from me. She pressed her palms down her chest as she took a big breath. "Your family is everything I wished mine was. Maybe…maybe you'd be better off with someone like Trish, someone who doesn't have all this baggage. I just…I don't fit. I'm the square peg here."

I pulled her back into my arms. "You don't need to try to fit in anywhere. They need to accept you. And they do already. You're worrying about nothing."

"Nothing?" Mallory smacked my chest. Anger radiated off her. "This is huge for me, and you know it. I just…I need time to process."

I raised my eyebrows. "Did you just smack me?"

"Not where I wanted to," Mallory said. Her anger cooled with a grin.

"You know, I can think of a way to help you process this situation." I pressed my lips against her neck. "The cab of the combine is bigger than you think."

Mallory's head fell back and a moan escaped her lips.

"There's a hayloft we can explore." I kissed along her jaw. "And Dad's office has a couch, too."

"Stop talking, Aaron," Mallory said before capturing my mouth with hers.

She stepped back toward the office, and I opened the door with my foot. The latch broke years ago. We fell onto the couch and I showed her how much she belonged with me.

Chapter Twenty-Six

Christmas morning came too soon. I didn't want to get out of bed. My entire body was exhausted from the barn exploits with Mallory. Then she snuck into my room after midnight and we slept in each other's arms until she snuck back out around five. I fell back to sleep, but Chelsea refused to let go of tradition and jumped on the mattress at six thirty. She started singing "Jingle Bells" as loudly and as off-key as she could, which took skill for someone with a great singing voice.

"Come on, Aaron," she whined as if she were still seven. "You know Mom won't let us open up the presents unless we're all downstairs."

"Go away." I threw my baseball-shaped pillow at her and buried my head under the comforter. Chelsea tugged the comforter off my upper body, and the cold immediately set in. "Damn it." I reached for warmth and protection, but Chelsea was having none of it.

She yanked it completely off me and threw it on the floor. "Get up or I'm going to tell Mom you didn't sleep alone."

"You wouldn't." I grabbed a sweatshirt off the floor and

sniffed it to make sure the smell wasn't overpowering. It was wearable at least.

"Wouldn't I?"

"Does Mom know she spawned pure evil?" I slid my feet into sheepskin slippers I'd had since my senior year in high school.

"Suck it, Aaron." Chelsea plopped beside me. It never ceased to amaze me how my little sister could get up an hour early on Christmas to make herself look perfect. It started her freshman year. When I called her out, she told me she wasn't going to look back on these moments and wonder why she looked like death.

"Yeah, suck it up, buttercup," a soft voice totally not my sister's said.

"Buttercup? That's not what you were calling me yesterday," I said with a wicked grin.

Chelsea slapped her hands on her knees and stood. "Well, this has been fun. And awkward. I'm leaning more toward awkward at the moment. Either way, I need to get out of here and do some damage control downstairs." She squeezed Mallory's shoulder as she pushed into the hallway. Before closing the door, Chelsea popped her head back into my room. "I can stall for about twenty minutes before Mom comes to get you."

Mallory sat beside me on the bed with a small box on her lap. Her hair cascaded down and hid her face. She lifted the box and put it in my hand. "I wanted to give this to you alone."

"You didn't have to get me anything," I said.

"Of course I did. That's what couples do." Mallory sucked in her lower lip. It cracked me up that she was nervous. After everything we've been through to get to this point, it seemed silly. "Open it."

I lifted the lid. Nestled on a piece of cotton was a keychain.

It was a simple strap with Westland Hawks #4 stamped into the brown leather. And there was a key attached. I lifted it on one finger. There weren't any words. Nothing I could even think about saying to describe the moment.

Mallory shrugged, her face turning the color of a rose. "I just thought we might see each other more if you could come and go as you please. I mean, I know that you have to live on campus, but that doesn't mean you have to sleep—"

I pulled her into my arms, kissing her until I'd pressed her back against the mattress. Mallory's fingers tugged at the bottom of my sweatshirt. I needed more than twenty minutes to show her how much this gift meant to me.

Mallory pushed me off her and stood. "As much as I'd like to continue this, your mom's going to be looking for us."

I stood and pulled Mallory against my chest. "Let her."

As soon as the words were out of my mouth, a sharp rap on the door preceded my mother's unhappy voice. "Aaron, we're waiting for you. *And* Mallory."

"We'll be down in a second, Mom." I smiled at my girl. "I've just got to get dressed."

Mallory's eyes widened, and a small giggle escaped.

The door opened with a loud crash. Mom stood in the threshold with the wrath of God on her face.

"Kidding, Mom." I didn't let go of Mallory, but it was clear clothes had not been shed. Mallory's flannel pajamas were firmly in place. My boxers weren't exactly hiding anything, but I wasn't buck naked, either. Besides, Mallory blocked most of Mom's view of my lower extremities. "We're just talking."

Mom reached into the room and grabbed Mallory's arm. "Honey, you finish getting dressed. I'll take your girlfriend downstairs so you won't screw around. Your grandpas are getting crabby, and your grandmas are starting to bicker. If we make them wait any longer for their biscuits and gravy, World War Three might very well start in our living room."

Mom tugged Mallory out the door before looking me up and down. "And put on some pants."

I grabbed some sweats and took off down the steps less than a minute later. No way I was leaving Mallory to the wolves. Of course, when I found her in the living room, both grandmas had attached themselves to her and were telling stories about my misadventures. I stood in the doorway of the family room for a moment and watched. Mallory belonged here. She had to see that. She glanced up and caught my gaze. The smile on her face was enough for me to believe she finally knew it, too. This would be her home. Not necessarily the house we stood in, but this family would be hers as much as mine.

"Sit down, boy. Let's get these presents opened so we can eat." Grandpa Len pointed to a spot on the floor in front of him, my usual present-opening position. "We ain't got all day."

"Yes, sir." I sat down as Mom brought me a cup of hot chocolate. It didn't matter that I would've had the same coffee as everyone else; Chelsea and I would always get hot chocolate on Christmas morning. But she also handed a mug to Mallory. I reached out and took the mug from Mallory's hand and sat it on the floor beside me.

"What're—?"

I didn't let her finish. Grabbing her hand, I yanked her off the couch and into my lap. "You belong with me," I whispered into her hair.

Mallory smiled. "Yeah, I think I do."

There wasn't a better Christmas present in the world.

We left two days after Christmas. Mallory had won over my family. She cried when my parents gave her *The Civil War* documentary by Ken Burns. I'd given her a leather-bound collection of *The Complete History of Ireland* that I knew she'd wanted and refused to buy for herself, but I waited until we were alone again to give her the earrings I'd bought after Thanksgiving. They weren't anything fancy with big diamonds, but they were simple and meaningful. The gold Celtic crosses belonged on her ears. She'd told me how much she loved reading about all things Irish, which I witnessed by the stack of books by her bed and couch, so the earrings seemed perfect. She hadn't taken them off since the moment she put them on.

And I hadn't left her house since we got back to Madison.

Chuck and the guys tried to lure me out for New Year's Eve, but I brushed them off. I wasn't wasting another minute without Mallory in my arms. Besides, I knew exactly how I wanted to ring in the New Year.

The clock read 11:55, five minutes until midnight. I pulled Mallory on top of me, careful to keep the blanket covering our naked bodies.

"You're insatiable." Her hair fell around her face, the ends tickling my chest.

"When it comes to you, yes." I brought her face to mine and kissed her like a man possessed. And I was. She'd bewitched me. It didn't matter how many times we'd had sex over the last week, I wanted more. Hell, I needed more. I needed her again, but I held back. That was how we were going to ring in the change of the calendar. Together, as one. God, I was turning into a lovesick schmuck.

My hands traced along her spine, barely touching her. She shivered and pressed her body closer. I loved how she fit against me. She slid away, and I took the moment to glance at the clock. Two minutes. Smiling, I stared at her and wiggled my eyebrows.

Mallory's eyes widened. "What're you—" She screamed when I flipped her onto her back. "Aaron…"

"Shhhh," I whispered, pinning her hands above her head and kissing my way to the Promised Land.

Her moans almost sent me over the edge, but I managed to control myself. Barely. Once I'd secured her satisfaction, I kissed my way back toward her mouth. My lips never left her as we made love. This was the way it was supposed to be. Every bit of me belonged to this woman, and she belonged to me. I knew it with every beat of my heart. This was what love was meant to be. Nothing in the world could take it away from us. Nothing.

Half an hour later, Mallory snuggled against me.

"Are you cold?" I asked, tugging the comforter over her bare shoulder.

She shook her head, and her entire body tensed.

Oh shit. "Talk to me, love."

She snuggled closer to me and sighed. "This next semester's going to be rough. And it's my last here."

I almost let out my own sigh of relief. "Yeah, I know. But it's not the end of the world."

"You'll be busy with baseball. I'll be student teaching, then…" She let it hang there, but it didn't take a PhD to know where she was going.

"And you'll graduate in May. I'll get drafted in June. Neither one of us knows where we'll be going." I pressed a kiss to her forehead. "Is that what you're getting at?"

She nodded.

"It won't be easy, but we'll be fine." She snuggled closer, and I tightened my grip. "We're going to be fine."

"I've been accepted to Iowa's grad program. And Northwestern. And Mizzou. And Arizona State." She lifted her head, resting her chin on my shoulder. "I don't know where I'm going to go."

"Where do you want to go?" My heart clenched. Not because she could go anywhere she wanted, but because she wanted to make this decision with me. As a couple.

"I wouldn't mind Arizona because Grandma's there. But Iowa's all I've ever known." A sad smile crossed her face. "I'd miss winter."

"Me, too." I pulled her on top of me. "We never know what the future's going to bring. We just have to roll with it. And if we're going to make it, we're going to hit a lot of waves."

Mallory kissed me, then laid her head on my chest. "There's going to be some pretty big waves."

She had no idea.

Chapter Twenty-Seven

Mallory's student teaching kept her too far away for too long. Thank God for the key she gave me. I spent most nights at her place. When she wasn't at her classes, she was at the bookstore or tutoring. I became the defacto cook on nights when I stayed over, and I made enough food that she'd have dinner when I wasn't there. It was our little bit of domestic bliss. And bliss it was.

Baseball season officially started in a few weeks. Conditioning and practice took up much of my time. It felt great to get back to the game again. My knee was almost good enough to play. And that weighed on me. It shouldn't have been, but the steroids helped me heal. That was the only reason I'd taken them. Not to *be* better, but to *get* better.

A week after classes kicked off, Coach Hummel called me into his office. Chuck slapped my shoulder and frowned.

"What?" I asked.

"Something's up, Betts." He nodded toward the closed door. "Did you see the athletic director go in about half an hour ago?"

"Yeah. So?" The hammer knocked inside my heart. But it wasn't possible. There was no way they'd found out. No way I tested dirty. I'd followed Seth's directions. I'd also done my own research. I stopped with plenty of time to get the 'roids out of my system.

"When was the last time you saw Ross down here?" Chuck shook his head. "Your nose better be clean."

I nodded and turned away from my friend. Coach Hummel's office was less than ten feet away, but I had suddenly developed tunnel vision. The door narrowed to the size of a pin and never seemed to get closer until I reached for it. Then it was a hundred feet tall.

Calm down, Aaron. It's nothing. Ross probably just wants to check on my knee. The lump forming in my throat said different, but I had no choice. I opened the door.

Coach Hummel leaned back in his chair with his Westland hat tipped back on his head, so all the lines on his forehead were visible. The bookcase behind him had scouting reports stacked by school and position. Not that anybody could tell. Hummel's organizational skills were the stuff of legend in the clubhouse.

He sat forward, waving me in with two fingers and pointing at the unoccupied chair in front of his desk.

"Have a seat, Betts. Dr. Ross and I have something to discuss with you," Hummel said in his soft commanding voice. During the season, he'd usually punctuate any sentence with a spit of sunflower seed shells.

Ross turned to his left. His sharp profile and thick neck screamed "football player," even for a guy in his late fifties. Dr. Ross also had the professor thing going. His dark hair discolored into white racing stripes above his ears. He turned toward Coach without saying a word, but his hands clenched the arms of his seat. In his past incarnation as a semipro noseguard, he would've snapped the cheap wood.

"What's up, Coach?" I did my best to keep the tremor from my voice.

Hummel raised his eyebrows. "Something you want to tell us, son?"

I glanced between the two men. Hummel's gaze never left my face, and Ross didn't even bother with so much as a glimpse at me. Knowing the coach was on my side for whatever was going down, I looked him square in the eye and lied. "No. Why?"

"Mr. Betts, you took a drug screen before winter break, did you not?" Ross's smooth timbre rolled through me until my toenails rattled.

I could only swallow and nod.

"The results came in this morning." Coach Hummel leaned forward and put both elbows on his already coffee-stained calendar. "You tested positive for elevated levels of testosterone."

The bottom didn't drop out. It disappeared. Everything I'd worked so hard for was gone. Everything. There was no way I could hide this from Mallory.

"There's an appeals process to go through." Coach's voice gurgled, sounding as if he was underwater.

"But it's unlikely to change the results." Ross finally faced me for the first time. His nostrils flared. "Clean out your locker, Betts. You're done."

"Now, wait a minute. He's got the right to appeal. It's possible they switched samples. Or they screwed up the results. Look how damned long it took the lab to get them over to us." Hummel leaned back in his chair again and took off his cap. He threw it on the desk. "Tell me this is just a mistake, Aaron."

I wanted to deny it. I needed to, but damned if I didn't want to come clean, too. After everything that Mallory had told me about her family, the guilt of what I'd done just to play baseball weighed me down like cement shoes. I kept sinking further and further into the depths of the river of 'roids. Still, I couldn't tell them the truth. I couldn't give up. If I said it was a mistake, then she would have to believe me. But it would be another lie on top of the biggest one of all. What choice did I have?

"It has to be, Coach. I was taking prednisone for my knee. Maybe that's what messed up the test." The words rolled off my tongue and out of my mouth with far too much ease.

"Prednisone doesn't cause a positive test, Betts," Ross snapped.

Hummel's shoulders fell as he visibly relaxed for the first time since I stepped into the room. "Good. That's what I thought." He shook his head and sighed. The doubt hovered in his eyes. I knew that look. It was the one thing he couldn't hide. Coach had faith in his players to tell him when we were injured or mentally unable to play. If we lied, he'd give us the same stare he gave me now. "Something like that could destroy the baseball program here."

"It still can." Ross sneered at me. He was a notorious hard-ass on all athletes, but his reputation was on the line. Any positive test reflected poorly on the entire athletic department. And prospective students could accept scholarships elsewhere instead of playing for Westland. "You're still suspended from any and all baseball activities until the appeal process is completed. If your appeal is denied, not only will you be unable to play baseball, but you'll be expelled from this university. Am I making myself clear enough?"

"Yes, sir." I had a few days to come up with a plan. On top of that, I had to keep my secret as quiet as possible. "What do we tell the guys?"

"I could give two shits what you tell the guys." Ross stood abruptly and strode to the door. He buttoned his Armani jacket. "Get a good lawyer for the appeal, Betts. You're going to need one."

Ross slammed the door hard enough to rattle the filing cabinets. I cringed, not at the noise but at the last slap.

"He's got a good point, son." Coach Hummel leaned forward in his chair again. He loved doing that. "If there is any chance that you failed, tell me now. Ross is gone. Tell me you didn't take anything."

I opened my mouth. Then closed it. There wasn't anything I could say to Coach without lying again. He didn't deserve that. Ross could suck my left testicle for all I cared, but Coach Hummel deserved more respect.

"Jesus, Aaron. How fucking stupid can you be?" He slammed his hands on the desk. In the time I'd known him, he'd never raised his voice to any of his players. Until now. "What in the hell did you take? And where in the fuck did you get it?"

"HGH mostly. But I stopped taking it before Thanksgiving. It shouldn't have…" My head dropped into my hands. God, I never wanted to admit to taking anything, and here I was spilling my guts. My chest heaved like a baby. "I swear to God, Coach, I only did it to heal faster, not to—"

"It doesn't fucking matter why. It only matters that you did it." His anger filled the air until it exploded, and everything on his desk flew off with one sweep of his arm. "Fuck. You've ruined this team. This school. Your fucking chances. Jesus H. Christ, get the fuck out of my office."

"Coach—"

"I ain't your coach anymore." Hummel sat in his chair and glared at me.

"What about the appeals process?" I grasped for anything to keep my head above water. But I was drowning in my own shit.

"There ain't going to be an appeals process, kid. I won't lie for you." His voice dropped to normal level, but with an added layer of exhaustion. "You made your bed." He rubbed his face again. "You've got two days until I tell Ross."

This couldn't be it. I couldn't be over. Everything I fought for, the very reason I took the damn injections, was baseball. "What about the draft? My future? You're going to ruin—"

"I ain't ruining shit, Betts." He shook his head. "You did this. All of it. Quit school. Just drop out, and this can all be swept under the rug. If you don't…"

He didn't need to finish. If I dropped out, he could keep the real reason quiet. If I stayed and fought, everyone would know what I had done. If I stayed and fought, I'd lose. I nodded and stood. After taking in every bit of his office, I moved toward the door.

"I…I just wanted to play."

"Yeah, greed will do that to you." He shook his head. "And if any scouts come sniffing around here asking questions, I ain't lying for you. Get out of here."

Greed. The word ate at me. Was that why I shot up? As I headed toward my locker, I tried to keep my face expressionless. Coach calling me into his office was weird enough, but if I let even one little hint of trouble show on my face, the guys would be all over me. Most of them just stared. I smirked and flexed my arms. They smiled and went back to whatever bullshit they were doing. I dropped my gaze to the tile floor with gray grout, knowing I'd fooled them.

A hand clamped hard on my shoulder, squeezing the fingerprints of my assailant into my skin. I didn't even have to look to know it was Chuck.

"What's going on?" He kept his voice low enough nobody could hear a bit of our conversation. Not that I planned on giving him a conversation.

I shrugged him off my shoulder. "Nothing."

The voices died down, and I chanced a glance around. The locker room emptied out. Rosenthal laughed, and I couldn't help but think all of this shit I'd stepped in started with him. If he hadn't fucking tripped me during that soccer game, I never would've torn my ACL. I never would've needed surgery. I never would've taken the steroids.

And I never would've met Mallory.

Just the thought of her crumbled my facade. I fell back into the door of my locker. The metal bit at my back, but it didn't hurt. Nothing could hurt as bad as the expression I imagined on Mallory's face when I told her the truth.

The hand clamped on my shoulder again. "What the fuck's going on, Betts? You're paler than a vampire in sunlight."

I almost laughed. Almost.

Chuck guided me to the nearest bench and pushed me down. "Spill."

The second to last person I wanted to tell the truth to was Chuck. I didn't have to tell him a damn thing, but I needed to. Mallory wasn't going to listen. Once I opened my mouth, she'd be gone. This was going to destroy her more than it would me. What was I losing? A baseball scholarship? Big fucking deal. Respect? Oh, yeah, that was gone. My degree? I'd get it somewhere else. A chance to go pro? There was a possibility I'd still get drafted, and I could always work to score a non-roster invite. But Mallory was going to lose something she'd only just gotten back. The ability to trust another person. I'd gotten her to trust me and I was going to rip it away.

My head fell in my hands, and I fucking started crying.

"Whoa," Chuck said beside me.

"Whoa is a fucking understatement," I said after I managed to grow my balls back. The bottom of my shirt became a snot rag, which was gross but necessary. "I screwed everything up, man."

"Come on. It can't be that bad." The concern in Chuck's voice was nice, but there was an underlying quiver. Like he knew it was indeed that bad.

"Bad enough that I'm leaving." I gulped the guilt welling inside my throat and glanced at my friend. We met during our first team meeting freshman year. Chuck challenged me to a hitting contest. He lost, but not by much. I was going to miss him.

"What do you mean, you're leaving? You're quitting school?" He flexed his jaw as if trying to work out a particularly hard calculus problem. "You better start explaining yourself, Aaron, because this shit ain't funny."

"No, it's not." I paused, dropping my head to my chest and breathing deeply to build courage, but it didn't work. My fingers wrung together, twisting and turning until the dry skin burned. Finally, I told myself this was a trial run for when I tell Mallory. *Just rip the Band-Aid off.* "I took something I shouldn't have. If I drop out, Coach said he'll sweep it under the rug. If I stay, Ross'll let it ruin the team."

Chuck didn't say anything. The tension rolled off him, building to the point I almost had to get up. He beat me to it, though. His rapid stance shook the bench. I couldn't face him. How could I? Chuck loved the team more than he loved his girlfriend. We had been in this together.

A locker slammed, open or closed, I had no clue. My eyes stayed fixed on my hands. Grunts and the occasional sound of clothes rustling were the only indicators he hadn't left yet. A short silence ended when my duffel dropped at my feet, like a line in the sand with Chuck's cleats on the other side.

"Go." That one little word held a lifetime of disappointment.

I nodded, watching as his feet left my sight. The soft clack of the metal on cheap tile stopped.

"You know, Betts, everyone was right about you." He paused, and I hoped he was done. "Do you know how many times I defended you when people called you a selfish ass? Stupid me. They were right all along."

My head shot up, and I met his stare. "You don't—"

Any calm Chuck had disappeared. "I don't understand? You sit there and have the balls to pull that bullshit with me? Fuck you, Aaron." He rushed toward me, pointing his finger like I was a button that wouldn't work. "I don't give a rat's ass why you did it. And I don't need to understand. The fact is you were willing to fuck everyone else's lives up without giving a damn about the consequences."

Each vein in his neck popped against the angry tint of his skin. I'd never seen Chuck this pissed. His hands balled into fists, the veins growing blue under the thin skin of his arms. The anger exploded, and he pulled back his fist and crushed it against my jaw. The pain that shot into my eye and down my neck was nothing compared to the boulder sitting in my chest.

"Get out of here." Chuck clenched and unclenched his fist. "Get the fuck out of here before I do something worse."

I grabbed my duffel and stood. It took all my self-control not to rub my jaw as I stood toe-to-toe with my friend. "If I could change things, I would."

"Yeah, hindsight is twenty-twenty." Chuck crossed his arms, and I was fairly certain it was only to prevent himself from breaking my nose.

"I really didn't think…" The words wouldn't come. I couldn't explain exactly what I was thinking when I'd started taking the PEDs. It was irrelevant anyway. It was over.

"You didn't think about anybody but yourself." Chuck freed a hand and jammed it into my chest. "That's the fucking problem."

He turned and walked out the door toward the team. I took my last look at the clubhouse and glanced inside my own locker. My jerseys hung inside. The home white with Westland in cursive across the chest and the blue away with a golden hawk on the upper left were ready for a new season. They were the only things Chuck hadn't tossed into my bag. I traced my fingers over each blue letter of my name and along the gold stitching of the four. Then I left them behind as I headed out the door.

All evidence of my PED use had been pitched from my room, but the memory of taking the pills and the injections hung in the air. They had since Mallory confessed her past.

The guilt over what I'd done overwhelmed me. This wasn't supposed to happen. I dropped my duffel and sat on the bed, wishing I could cry again like the wuss I was. I knew better. Coach was right. Greed ruled every action I'd taken. No matter what I'd told myself, it wasn't about the game. It was about me being better than my father, doing what he'd failed at. It was about my plan, my goals. It was about me and nobody else. After about ten minutes of pity-party time, I stood and opened my trunk, throwing clothes inside. It took about two hours to pack up. There wasn't any careful touch in it. I tossed shit in without looking at what was in my hand.

I pulled out the last drawer of my desk and dumped the contents on the bed. A white bottle with B-12 on the label stood out on the mattress. I picked it up and shook it. There were still pills inside. I opened the bottle and tapped a few into my hand. The oblong pills looked like any other vitamin I'd ever taken. But there was something carved into them. I pulled it closer to my eyes.

Why hadn't I seen this before? That son-of-a-bitch.

The hall outside my room filled with the noise of my teammates. I pressed my ear to the door.

"Betts got sick?" someone asked.

"Yeah," the distinct timbre of Chuck's voice answered. To anyone else, it would've been Chuck being Chuck, but I heard the underlying tension vibrating that one word.

"Weird. He seemed fine before we hit the weights." It sounded like that fuckwad Rosenthal. I wanted to open my door and beat the living shit out of him.

"Yep."

I closed my eyes. It wasn't Rosenthal's fault. As much as I wanted to blame him, he didn't stick the needle in my thigh. He didn't hand me the pills.

But someone else had.

"Yo, Chuckie." Seth's voice rang in my ears like he stood just outside my door.

This time I didn't hold back. I threw the door open and charged him. My fist felt the satisfying crunch of his jaw. His gaze met mine, and he knew. That fucker knew. In my gut, it hit me harder than a bowling ball to the head. That son of a bitch sold me out. I pulled back to hit him again, but somebody grabbed my arm. It took two other guys to pull me off Seth.

"What the fu—"

"Shut up, Seth!" I shrugged the guys off and jammed my finger in his chest. "It's over."

Seth rubbed his jaw. The bruise started forming instantly. "I don't know what your problem is, Betts, but back the fuck off."

I laughed, my voice cracking on the jumbled sound. "The hell you don't." I stepped back and held out my arm. "Tell them."

He shook his head like he had no clue what I was talking about, but I saw the fear in his eyes. Fuck the baseball program. Fuck the school. It was then and there I decided the team needed to know. If it got out to everyone, it got out. I was done. And I was taking Seth down with me.

Closing my eyes, I cut open the vein. "Chuck's covering for me. For the rest of you." I glanced around at my teammates, guys who'd had my back when I hurt my knee, guys who'd helped me out while I recovered from my surgery.

"I didn't leave practice because I was sick. I left because I…" I swallowed hard. "I left because I failed a drug screen."

First came the pale white faces of disbelief, then the red rush of anger.

"For what?" Devin Miller pushed in by Chuck.

"PEDs."

Devin held my gaze while he let it sink in. "You cheated? I never thought—"

"I never thought I would, either. But it happened, and I'm gone." I held up a hand to stop them from screaming at me. Then I held up the other with the bottle. "But Seth's not. And he should be." I met his glare. "He's the one who sold me the PEDs." I threw the bottle at him. It bounced off his chest. Barry picked it up and stared at the label. "And when I stopped buying, he gave me those 'supplements' to help out."

The silence that descended equaled the sound of night in the middle of the field during winter. Not a peep from anyone or anything.

"Fuck you, Betts." Seth snarled. Rage contorted his face and elevated his voice so the entire floor heard him. He had tunnel vision: me against him. Like it had been all along. I was just too stupid to believe it. "You never were better than me, just fucking luckier. Coach Hummel made a huge mistake thinking you were the savior leading us to the championship. I sacrificed everything for this team. And you got all the glory."

"You're supposed to be our friend. Our teammate. What the hell?" Barry asked, slamming into the group surrounding Seth. "How many people did you poison, Seth? How many lives did you decide to fuck with?"

Seth's face fell, then the panic set in. He tried to push through the guys to get to his room, but they pushed him back. Chuck clasped my shoulder and stepped around me toward Seth.

I didn't stay. It wouldn't give me any satisfaction. It

wouldn't change the fact that I had to leave, that my college baseball career was over. Worse, it wouldn't change what I had to do next.

My door was still open. I reached inside and grabbed the keys off my dresser.

Chuck blocked Seth's door. Barry held Seth against the wall. A few of the other guys stood around with their arms crossed, looking every bit the intimidating nightclub bouncers they could become.

None of them noticed me or even glanced my way.

I turned toward the doors at the end of the hall and didn't look back.

Chapter Twenty-Eight

It took every ounce of willpower not to keep driving past her house as I got closer. But I had to do this. I had to tell her what I'd done. It had to be face-to-face. Anything else would be a coward's way out, and she deserved so much better than that. I pulled up behind her Jeep and parked the truck. The tears I'd expected earlier threatened to show themselves. On the way to her house, every scenario on her reaction flashed through my mind. Every single one ended the same way. Mallory would never forgive me. I knew that. I knew this was the end of us.

And I knew I'd never recover.

The short walk from the truck to her front door was longer than the walk from the locker room to Coach's office. Each step forward reverberated in my skull like a hammer breaking granite. When I reached the door, I pushed the ancient doorbell instead of using my key.

She opened the door a few moments later with a wet plate and dishtowel in her hand. In a flash, her expression went from irritation to surprised to sultry.

"Booty call?" she asked as she stepped back to let me in.

God, I wished it was. I shook my head as I walked past her into the living room.

"What's going on, Aaron?" Her hand rested on the back of my arm, and I stepped away from her. Her touch was enough to make me want to jump off a bridge.

We stood like that, me facing the living room and her somewhere behind me, for too long to count. Finally, I found my voice. "I fucked up."

"What do you mean?" Mallory's words were punctuated with confusion, fear, and disappointment.

I swallowed hard and tried to figure out the easiest way to tell her. The scenarios I'd imagined replayed in my mind as I kept searching for a way out of this mess. My heart crashed into my ribs.

"Aaron?" There was the desperation I'd hoped not to hear.

I closed my eyes and opened my mouth. "I… You have to understand one thing, Mallory. I didn't know anything about your family. Please remember that?"

"You're scaring me." She tensed, and I could see every single wall I'd torn down rebuild brick by brick around her. "Did you… Please tell me you didn't sleep with someone else."

My eyes flew open and I spun on my heel. "God, no. I'd never do that to you. I love you, Mallory."

"Then what?" Tears filled her eyes, but she wouldn't let them fall. I knew her better than that.

I reached out and ran my finger along her jaw. "I'm so sorry."

She stepped back from me, letting my hand linger in the empty air where she'd stood. "Tell me. Or I'm going to think the worst."

I dropped my hand and willed myself to look away from

her, but I couldn't. My gaze held hers. "And it wouldn't be bad enough."

Mallory stared at me. I knew she was trying to work out the problem and a potential solution. There wasn't one. I had to just tell her.

"I...last year while I was recovering, I took HGH." My breathing became quicker, my pulse raced. I ignored the tightening in my chest, waiting for her to say something. But she said nothing. She didn't even move. I closed my eyes and swallowed hard before opening them. "And steroids."

The plate fell from her hand, shattering around her bare feet.

"Get out." Her voice was too calm, too soft. The walls I'd watched her take down slowly, slammed back into place.

"Can I ju—" Desperation filled my throat, clogging it with everything I needed to say to her.

"Get out." Her tone stayed neutral as her gorgeous eyes turned to glass.

"Ple—"

"GET OUT!" Her scream rattled the windows. She stepped on the broken glass as she turned away from me.

"I didn't know," I whispered. She had to understand that. How could I have known this would hurt her so much? Hell, I didn't even think she'd give me a chance when I'd started taking the PEDs. My chest tightened again as my heartbeat played in my ears. I reached up and rubbed my left pec. "Please, Mallory. I didn't know."

"You didn't know?" Her voice was calmer than it should've been as she faced me. "That's your excuse? That you didn't *know*? You think that somehow makes this okay?" She breathed with barely controlled rage as her chest heaved like she'd run a marathon. "You're just like my father, my brother. Baseball's the only thing that will ever matter to you. Baseball above everyone else. Even yourself. Get out of my house, Aaron. Get out of my life."

She turned around, keeping her back to me, and pointed toward the front door. I glanced down at her feet where the blood pooled near her toes. She didn't shift her feet away from the broken plate, or even act like the cuts hurt. Maybe they didn't because my confession hurt her more.

"You're bleeding."

"I can take care of myself." Her head dropped to her chest. The coldness left her voice, and the agony radiated from her. "Just go. You can't...you can't fix this."

My feet wouldn't move. It became a standoff between what she wanted and what I wanted. She would win.

"Leave," she ordered. "We're done."

"I know." The reality of hearing it was much worse than imagining it. I shuffled over to the door and turned toward her. She shifted so I couldn't see her face. "If I could turn back time, I would. But I can't. I was only thinking about getting on the field. I let my team down. I let my coach down. Hell, I let myself down." I reached for the door, not really sure how to put what I knew I'd done to her into words. My fingers tingled and turned cold. I let my left arm fall and reached again with my right. "And you..." The tears I'd held broke free. I sobbed like a baby. "You're the last person I ever wanted to hurt. I was selfish and childish. And I never wanted to hurt you." I wiped my nose with the arm of my coat. "All I wanted was to protect you from everybody who ever hurt you. When you told me...when you told me about your family..." I banged my left fist against the door, hoping to wake up the numbing sensation. "I love you. If that's not enough to even consider giving me a chance to make it up to you, there's nothing I can do."

Her body lost its rigid stance, and her shoulders heaved with her own sobs.

I fell against the door. "I would do anything for you.

Anything. If you'll just give me a chance to try—"

"Please just go." She tiptoed around the rest of the glass and hobbled through the kitchen, turning into the bathroom. The click of the door echoed in the silence.

I couldn't move. Once I opened the door and stepped outside, that would be it. I didn't want this to be over. Mallory was the girl I was supposed to marry. She'd stolen my heart, and I'd never recover. And I knew she'd never forgive me. I understood why, but I didn't want to accept it. I waited, hoping she'd come out and talk.

Twenty minutes later, I hadn't moved, and neither had she.

What little hope I thought there was, I let go. I held the key in my hand, taking it off the keychain she had made for me, and dropped it in the bowl on the table. Turning the handle, I whispered, "I'm so sorry," and walked out her door for the last time.

Chapter Twenty-Nine

When I got back to the dorm, campus police crowded the hall. I shouldered through them to my room, opening the door to the mess inside. Not a mess, exactly, but my packed belongings. It was my life that was the real mess. There wasn't any reason to hang around anymore. Even though the team knew, my test results would be all over campus by morning, especially after Seth's arrest. At least, I assumed they arrested him.

I turned at a knock on the doorframe. Chuck still looked pissed, but he came to see me. That had to mean something.

"Need some help?" he asked.

Or maybe he just wanted me off campus. I nodded. The numbness had crept up my fingers into my elbow. I doubted I could carry much with how weak it felt. Together we loaded my truck in silence. Once the last bag was stashed, Chuck turned to leave.

"Wait." I practically begged. Chuck stopped and faced me. "I know I don't deserve to ask, but can you do me a favor?"

He cocked an eyebrow but didn't say no.

"Will you keep an eye on Mallory? She's going to need

a friend."

Chuck squinted at me, trying to find an angle. "She dumped you?"

"I fucked up, man, but more so with her than anyone." I ran my hand over my face to try to gain some form of composure. It didn't work. "You remember that high school coach who died in a car crash with his kid? The steroid scandal?"

"Yeah, Verbach. He was drugging his..." Chuck's eyes widened. "Oh, fuck."

I snorted. That was an understatement. "Just watch out for her. She didn't deserve this."

Chuck nodded and stared over my shoulder. "Why'd you bust Seth?" He dropped his gaze to mine. "You could've just left and let sleeping dogs lie."

"He gave me that bottle of B-12, but there weren't any vitamins in it. I stopped doping well before the drug screen, Chuck. He set me up." I shoved my hands in my pockets and stared at the brick of my dorm. "Besides, who would Seth sell to next? Rosenthal? Murray? Or any of the other guys?" I leaned against the truck and shook my head. "I couldn't let somebody else fuck up their lives like I did. It's not worth it."

"No, it's not." Chuck leaned against the truck beside me. "They found his stash. He's busted for having illegal drugs on campus, but nobody else came forward about him dealing. You willing to testify against him when the time comes?"

"Yeah." I stood a little straighter. It was the least I could do to get the 'roids off the campus. Maybe something good could come from this. My heartbeat played my ribs like a xylophone. "Yeah, let Coach know, would you? And Ross?"

Chuck nodded. He pushed off the truck and stood in front of me, holding out his hand. "Good luck, Aaron."

I tried to lift my left hand. My arm wouldn't move. I stared at it as if that would make it work.

"You okay?"

Electricity shot down my arm, setting my skin on fire. I grabbed my arm and reached for Chuck.

I knew my heart stopped beating.

The monitor beeped steadily. I blinked my eyes, blinded by the fluorescent lights above me. The disinfectant hit my nose. I hated the smell of hospitals. I hated why I was here.

"Hello, Mr. Betts." The voice had that eerily familiar sound.

I glanced over and met the steady gaze of the same doc who treated me last time I was here. When Seth dropped me off and ran. When I snuck out without even telling them who I was. Shit. I closed my eyes, willing all of today to just fucking disappear.

"Had you stayed the last time, we could've prevented this."

"I should've." My voice was harsh and dry, like all I'd had to eat was gravel.

"Yes, but that's in the past. Let's get your future started." I glanced at him. There was a warm smile, the first I'd seen. "Your family's here. They want to see you."

I nodded and pushed the button raising my bed. "What happened?"

"Ventricular fibrillation leading to cardiac arrest." He crossed his hands at the wrists and rocked on his heels. "You'll be fine, but your heart needs to be taken better care of. We'll get you set up with a cardiologist."

I swallowed hard. Not even twenty-two and my heart wasn't working right. This was my fault. God, I'd screwed up my life so much. For no reason. No real fucking reason.

"What did you take, Aaron?" Doc's voice held an ounce of sympathy surrounded by the coldness of my reality.

"HGH and anabolic steroids." I sighed. "I only took them for a month or so, but the guy who got me the stash gave me a bottle of what I thought were B-12 supplements. I took those for another month. And took more than I should have."

"So, you're saying this isn't your fault?"

My head snapped toward him. "No, I'm not. I doped. I made the decision. He may have screwed me over with that bottle, but I started it. Either way, it's all my fault."

He nodded. "Good. At least you recognize that."

"Yeah, boy." Dad's voice filled the room.

I closed my eyes for a moment before facing him. The doctor slipped out of the room, past my father who stood alone at the door. Disappointment covered his face like deck paint.

"Why?" He still hadn't stepped into the room.

"To play."

"Why?"

"Because I didn't want to redshirt. Because I was greedy. Because I wanted to be on the field. Because I didn't care about anything but baseball." I paused and stared at him. "Because I didn't want to end up…like you."

Dad snorted. "I ain't got heart problems, boy. You do."

Tears welled in my eyes. In all my life, I'd never cried in front of my father. He was tough, manly. It wasn't something he'd tolerate. I blinked hard, willing them to stop. They didn't. Once they started, they wouldn't stop. I opened my eyes. Dad had moved into the room and stood at the foot of the bed. His hands pressed into the metal footboard. His fingers were whiter than fresh snow.

"We could've lost you, boy." His voice hitched, making my tears flow faster.

"You didn't. And you won't."

He moved around to the side and wrapped his arms around me. "No, we won't."

I don't know how long we sat like that before two more sets of arms joined us. Mom and Chelsea cried as I confessed again. Then we talked about what happened next. Basically, I was going home. Because of my participation in bringing down Seth, who, it turned out, had sold steroids since his freshman year to other athletes and to regular guys, the university would allow me to stay enrolled but online only. I could still finish my business degree on time. I just wasn't allowed to set foot on campus. Not even for graduation.

Mom and Dad stepped out to talk to the doctor about my release, leaving my little sister alone with me.

"Guess New York seems tame in comparison now?" I joked, trying to lighten the mood.

"This isn't funny." She sat on the edge of my bed. I couldn't remember the last time I'd seen Chelsea without makeup or her hair perfectly styled. She was a mess.

"I know." I couldn't look at her. My father's disappointment was enough. I didn't need to see it on my little sister. "Just don't fuck up your life like I have mine, sis. I've lost everything."

"Not everything. You've still got us."

I huffed a laugh. "Yeah, and nothing else. I'll never play ball again. I'll never get that feeling of walking onto the field again. And I'll never see Mallory again."

Chelsea took my hand. "She was here."

God, what had I done to her?

"She told me everything. Aaron, there was no way you could've known about her family the way she kept it all bottled up. You're still an idiot, though."

I nodded, but the pressure building on my chest wouldn't let me speak.

"She loves you, you know?"

"But it's not enough." The words choked out of my throat.

"No, not this time. Can you blame her?"

"Blame's all on me, sis. All on me."

Mom and Dad came back in with a nurse. I closed my eyes, willing darkness to come. Willing the pain, the heartache, and the reality away.

Nothing like that would ever happen. I'd have to live with my decisions. And I'd live with them alone.

Chapter Thirty

Ten months later

I stepped inside Franklin High School with plenty of time. The traffic getting into Iowa City moved slower than a snail because of a tractor-trailer accident and holiday travelers. I'd planned the drive with an extra hour to spare just in case. I'd learned my lesson a month ago when I was scheduled to speak at a high school in Cedar Rapids, and construction on the interstate set me behind by half an hour. Since then, I planned extra drive time.

"Hi," I said to the woman behind the bulletproof glass. "I'm Aaron Betts. Coach Withers is expecting me."

She smiled and glanced at a paper on a clipboard. "Yes, here you are. Actually, it says Principal Boudreau wants to see you." She pushed a button, and the door to the office clicked open. "Come on in."

I sat in a chair not meant for an adult ass and waited for the principal. After my humiliating exit from college, I came up with a game plan. With the help of my father, I started contacting high school sports teams and summer programs throughout Iowa and offered to speak in front of them about my use of PEDs. They needed to understand the dangers of using, not just to their bodies but to their lives. I never brought up Mallory. It still hurt too damn much. Every night when I closed my eyes, I relived the moment when I told her what I'd done. It haunted me.

"Mr. Betts?" A woman in a sharp gray pantsuit stood before me with her hand extended. Her blond hair hung in loose waves around her shoulders. The warmth of her smile surprised me. When I shook her hand, she squeezed it tighter than most men I knew. "Coach Withers told me about you, but I'm afraid I've got other plans."

"Other plans?" I almost took a step back from this obviously crazy woman. What the hell else could she have in mind?

She smiled, and I was glad she wasn't my principal in high school. I wouldn't have gotten away with shit. "Please come into my office. I'll explain."

Forty minutes later, I sat onstage in the auditorium filled with student athletes who were more excited about Thanksgiving break than an assembly. Principal Boudreau decided I needed to speak to all the teams. Even the cheerleaders were in the room. She also wanted me to open up the floor for questions. That wasn't an issue. I'd done that at every school I'd visited since September. Most of the time, the kids didn't ask anything at all. Instead, I'd field questions from the coaching staff.

Sometimes I felt good when I left, like I got through to the athletes. Sometimes nobody cared about what I said.

Principal Boudreau gave a small introduction with some very detailed information about my exit from school. I shook it off. It wasn't a big secret. I'd given interviews and testified during Seth's hearing over the summer.

I smiled when I stood before the kids, taking the

microphone off the podium before I started. "Sorry, but I can't stand still," I said, earning a few laughs.

"As Principal Boudreau said, my name is Aaron Betts, and I tested positive for performance enhancing drugs my junior year of college. I was eligible for the draft and a top prospect. Now here I am," I began. The crowd quieted down after that, and I launched into my story, leaving Mallory as the only part I held back. Hell, I didn't even bring up how Seth sabotaged me. That didn't matter. All that mattered was that I used. "I'd hurt my knee during a soccer game, tearing my ACL and meniscus. The initial surgery was successful, but I didn't listen to my doctor. I pushed too far, too fast, and I wasn't healing as quickly as I thought I should. My recovery was hampered by my own stupidity. I wanted to play baseball. That was all I ever wanted. So I started using HGH and anabolic steroids to recover faster." Even as I neared the end, I knew I was getting through to the vast majority of the students. It felt good. It felt right. It felt like redemption was possible. "Using cost me my college career, my future, and my health. I've suffered some of the aftereffects of steroid abuse, even though I only used for a few short months. My face broke out, but that was on the outside. The worst was 'roid rage, I'd get uncontrollably angry. Nobody was safe. I was lucky. It never got beyond verbal abuse, but it was still abuse. That was when I was using. Now I still suffer."

I met the eyes of a student in the front row who hung on every word. He bounced his leg nervously, and I knew he was using. Maybe it wasn't steroids, but he was taking something. I held his gaze. "I have unreasonable panic attacks. My heart developed an arrhythmia. I went into cardiac arrest. And I lost *everything* that mattered to me."

His eyes widened, but he didn't break my stare. For the first time since I started this, I opened up completely so this kid could see what was at stake. It wasn't just the physical toll; it was the emotional toll they didn't get. I opened the vein and let it bleed. I told them about Mallory.

"After I suffered the knee injury, I had to hire a tutor to help me pass a class." I half smiled at the memory of seeing Mallory through video chat the first time. "She was smarter than anyone I'd ever met. And she didn't put up with my crap." A few people chuckled. "I'd fallen in love with her almost immediately, but she was resistant to my charms. It took me until Thanksgiving to finally get her to trust me. There wasn't anything I wouldn't do for her. Honestly, there isn't anything I wouldn't do for her now. If she walked back into my life and needed a kidney, I'd give it to her." I paused and took a deep breath before I went on. "But she never will. What I did was unforgivable, and she won't have anything to do with me. When I say I lost my future, I mean it in every sense of the word. I wanted to marry that girl. And I lost her."

A few of the girls in the front wiped their eyes. Heck, I had to wipe mine.

One raised her hand, and the Q&A began.

"Do you know where she is?" a girl with dark hair asked. She couldn't have been more than fifteen or sixteen.

"No. She told me to go, and I honored that. But there isn't a moment I don't think about her and wonder." Talking about Mallory hurt like hell, but this was a good thing.

"You said you stopped taking the PEDs before you tested positive. How'd that happen?" the boy in front asked.

"My dealer had supplied me with what I thought were B-12 supplements. They weren't. I didn't know I was still taking PEDs when I tested positive." I stared him directly in the eye. "But that doesn't excuse the fact that I start taking them in the first place. I could've let all the blame fall on the dealer. I could've tried to lie and save my college career. But that wouldn't have been right. I'd cheated. I needed to own up to that."

"Why was a doping scandal such a big deal for this girl?"

a cheerleader in full uniform asked. "I mean, it's not like you killed somebody."

I smiled. "No, I just almost killed myself. She had her reasons, and let me tell you, they were damn good ones."

Even when we began to run out of time, we kept going. The bell rang, and Principal Boudreau let us continue. Halfway through the next period the questions dried up, and the students were dismissed.

"That was amazing," Principal Boudreau said as the kids cleared out. "Really, Mr. Betts, you did a great job. We've had a lot of speakers, but few got through to the students like you did."

I smiled and glanced down to where the nervous kid had sat. His seat was empty, but I hoped he'd seek help for whatever he was using. A few of the coaches came up to thank me.

Principal Boudreau gushed some more, but I didn't hear her. Over her shoulder the most beautiful woman in the world stood at the edge of the stage. I reached for the podium to steady myself.

"Mr. Betts, are you okay?" Boudreau asked.

I nodded slowly, not taking my eyes off Mallory. Her hair was pulled back into an oversized ponytail, and she had glasses on, but every single thing about her stopped my heart in a good way. I knew she'd started teaching somewhere, thanks to Chuck, but he didn't know exactly where. Or he wouldn't tell me. The fact that he'd given me that much information was enough.

"Ah, Mr. Betts, this is Ms. Verbach. She's actually the person who told Coach Withers about you." Boudreau seemed to sense something going on. She glanced between me and Mallory. "But I think you might know each other already."

"You…you brought me here?"

She nodded and took another step closer.

"That…that was nice of you." I wanted to wrap my arms around her and pull her against me. She was here. In front of me. She was real. And she was talking to me.

"Why?" she asked.

"I needed to do something. This seemed like the right thing. I wondered after I left if I would've taken the drugs had someone been honest about what would happen. I don't mean the physical effects, either." My grip tightened on the edge of the podium as I tried to control the panic attack. "Not that the physical side doesn't suck."

Mallory nodded and took another step closer to me.

"Verbach?" I asked.

"It was time…" Her gaze never wavered from mine. "It was time to let go. To forgive them."

"Will you ever forgive me?" I asked. I'd wanted to ask her this for so long. Hell, I needed to hear her say no just so I could move on with my life. Not that I wanted to let her go. I held on to that brief month we had together like it was the Holy Grail.

"Maybe," she said.

My entire body froze. I wasn't expecting anything other than no. "Do you mean that?"

She nodded again.

"Mallory, I—"

"Wait, not here." She glanced around at the quiet coaches who were watching us out of the corners of their eyes. "Can we maybe have coffee after school?"

"Yeah, that would be nice." I offered my hand to her for a handshake. And just to feel her skin.

She slipped her fingers into mine.

"Then maybe…" I let the implication hang in the air. She knew what I wanted. Her. All I wanted was her back in my life.

A small smile crossed her lips. "Maybe."

Acknowledgments

A huge thank you to Heather Howland and Kari Olson for helping me bring this story to life. It really shines because of the amazing work they did. Mallory and Aaron are so much better because of y'all.

Thank you to Nancy Cantor, the best copy editor on the planet, who put in all my commas and deleted all the ones that didn't know where to go.

Thank you to Liz Pelletier for the beautiful cover.

Of course, I have to thank my parents for taking me to Opening Day in St. Louis and starting my love affair with baseball after watching Ozzie Smith flip at short. (Go, Cards!) And for taking me to Kauffman Stadium in Kansas City to watch the Royals. Thank you both for teaching me the rules, how to keep score, and for being at all my softball games.

I dedicated this book to my two older brothers, Dexter and Mark Murphy, and our neighbor Miles Cameron. Growing up, they let me play baseball with them in the front yard of our farmhouse in rural Missouri. Honestly, I think they just wanted me to chase the home run balls lost in the cornfields, but I loved every minute of it.

A special thank you to Alex Nader who made sure that I didn't make Aaron sound less than masculine.

Thank you, Julia Weber, for believing in me and working so hard on this book. I cannot say thank you enough for everything you've done for me.

Thank you for reading!

About the Author

Lynn Stevens flunked out of college writing her first novel. Yes, she still has it and no, you can't read it. Surprisingly, she graduated with honors at her third school. A former farm girl turned city slicker, Lynn lives in the Midwest where she drinks coffee she can't pronounce and sips tea when she's out of coffee. When she's out of both, just stay away.

Discover more New Adult titles from Entangled Embrace...

TALK BRITISH TO ME
a *Wherever You Go* novel by Robin Bielman

Mateo Gallagher isn't being cocky when he says he gets attention from millions of women. As the Dating Guy on morning radio, it's his job to give the single guy's perspective on love and dating, and with a faux British accent, nobody knows who he really is. That he's contracted to stay single is no problem—until he meets Teague Watters. She changes the rules of the game, and for the first time he wants more.

CONFESSIONS OF A FORMER PUCK BUNNY
a *Taking Shots* novel by Cindi Madsen

Confession #1: *I used to be a puck bunny.* But after a hockey player broke my heart, I gave up all things hockey. Unfortunately, if I want to graduate college, I'll need the help of Ryder "Ox" Maddox—my sexy, hockey-playing tutor. The closer we get, the harder it is to remember why I need to stay away. If I'm not careful, I'll fall for Ryder, and then I'll be totally pucked.

RUSH
a novel by Shae Ross

Priscilla Winslow has a mouth that spits fiery sarcasm faster than I can throw a touchdown. But I've wanted her ever since I saw her in that Bo Peep outfit on Halloween. Yep, I'm a sheep who will follow that little hottie anywhere. There's one problem…she hates me. Just because we ended up in jail and quite possibly ruined both our futures…

Made in United States
Cleveland, OH
08 June 2025

17577298R00164